PHILOSOPHY MADE SIMPLE

Philosophy Made Simple

A NOVEL

Robert Hellenga

LITTLE, BROWN AND COMPANY

NEW YORK   BOSTON

Little, Brown and Company
Time Warner Book Group
1271 Avenue of the Americas, New York, NY 10020
Visit our Web site at www.twbookmark.com

First Edition: March 2006

Parts of this novel originally appeared in somewhat different form in Black Warrior,
Columbia, Crazyhorse, and Mississippi Valley Review.

The author is grateful for permission to reprint the following:
"Sonnet XI" by Edna St. Vincent Millay is from Collected Poems, HarperCollins.
Copyright © 1931, 1958 by Edna St. Vincent Millay and Norma Millay Ellis. All rights reserved.
Reprinted by permission of Elizabeth Barnett, literary executor. The excerpt from "Long-legged Fly"
by W. B. Yeats is reprinted with the permission of Scribner, an imprint of Simon & Schuster Adult
Publishing Group, from The Collected Works of W. B. Yeats, Volume 1: The Poems, Revised,
edited by Richard J. Finneran. Copyright © 1940 by Georgie Yeats; copyright renewed © 1968
by Bertha Georgie Yeats, Michael Butler Yeats, and Anne Yeats. "Vicksburg Is My Home" is
by Hans Theessink. From Hard Road Blues — Blue Grove
(BG-6020). Copyright © 1994.

Library of Congress Cataloging-in-Publication Data
Hellenga, Robert.
  Philosophy made simple : a novel / Robert Hellenga. — 1st ed.
    p.   cm.
  ISBN 0-316-05826-2
  1. Fathers and daughters — Fiction.   2. Moving, Household — Fiction.   3. Avocado industry —Fiction.
4. Middle-aged men — Fiction.   5. Philosophers — Fiction.   6. Elephants — Fiction.   7. Widowers —
Fiction.   8. Weddings — Fiction.   9. Texas — Fiction.   I. Title.
PS3558.E4753P48   2006
813'.54 — dc22   2005010883

10 9 8 7 6 5 4 3 2 1

Q-MART

Designed by Iris Weinstein

Printed in the United States of America

FOR MY WIFE, VIRGINIA

PHILOSOPHY MADE SIMPLE

Allegory of the Cave

Rudy took up philosophy late in life. He wanted some answers, an explanation, or at least a chance to ponder the great mysteries, before it was too late — love and death, the meaning and purpose of human existence, moments of vision, the voice of God, the manifest indifference of the material universe to injustice and suffering, the insanity of war, the mysterious tug of beauty on the human heart. What did he know about these things? Not a lot. But something. He'd never had a college education. He'd turned down a basketball scholarship at Michigan State University in order to go to work for Harry Becker up in Chicago. But he hadn't peddled avocados for thirty years on the South Water Street Market without learning a thing or two about life, and Helen, his wife, had practiced all her lectures on him when she'd started teaching art history at Edgar Lee Masters, dropping her slides one at a time into the projector on the dining room table, the front end propped up on a couple of paperbacks so that it cast a slightly top-heavy image on the wall over the sideboard. So he knew a little bit about Beauty too. Beauty with a capital *B*: not just a pretty face or a picturesque landscape, not just a Greek Aphrodite or a Renaissance nude or a Turner sunset, but something that might shoot out of an old man's face or out of a side of beef, sharp as his carbon steel kitchen knives, sad as bent notes on his guitar, but joyful at the same time.

Rudy'd met Helen after a basketball game in Gary, Indiana, back in 1925. He'd played for a semipro team sponsored by the commission merchants on the market, the South Water Bluestreaks. Helen's uncle, who worked for the Leshinsky Potato Company, next to Becker's on the market, was one of the refs and had introduced them after the last game of the season, in which Rudy'd made the winning basket. A week later, Saturday night, they'd taken the trolley up to Rogers Park to see Lon Chaney in *The Phantom of the Opera* at the new Granada Theater, and afterward they'd walked down to the lake. By the time Rudy got home it was three o'clock in the morning, but he wasn't tired.

Helen had been dead for seven years now; Meg, their oldest, had a law degree and two kids and was planning to go back to work full-time; Molly, their middle daughter, was teaching social dancing at the Arabesque Dance Studio in Ann Arbor, Michigan, while she studied to get her real-estate license; Margot, the youngest — a book conservator at the Newberry Library on the near North Side — had just gone to Italy on the spur of the moment, right after the big flood in Florence.

What had happened? Where had it gone? Life? His life? What would happen to him now? Looking back, he wondered about the scholarship. Of course, if he'd accepted it, everything would have been different, wouldn't it? He'd never have met Helen; he and Helen would never have bought this old house, never have had three daughters; Helen would never have gone to Italy and met Bruno Bruni, and so on. On the other hand, maybe in a parallel universe he *had* accepted it. And maybe in a parallel universe Helen was still alive, living in Italy with Bruni. That's what his daughter's Indian boyfriend, Tejinder Kaal, nephew of the philosopher Siva Singh, seemed to be getting at in an article that Molly'd sent him. Rudy hadn't been able to make head nor tail of the article, which had been published in a journal called *Physical Review Letters*. Parallel universes. What a crock, he'd thought, but then Tejinder's picture had appeared in the science pages of *Time* and *Newsweek,* along with sketches of ghostly people from parallel universes superimposed on photos of a playground (*Newsweek*) and a cemetery (*Time*). Both *Time* and *Newsweek* cited one of Helen's favorite poems, "The Road Not Taken," by Robert Frost, because, according to Tejinder, there *were* no roads not taken.

Thanksgiving was the same as always — turkey, dressing (dry and moist), mashed potatoes, sweet potatoes, avocados stuffed with chutney, cranberry relish, apple pie — except that Margot was still in Florence, and Molly had stayed in Ann Arbor in order to be with Tejinder. Dan, Meg's husband, had taken the car to get gassed up for the trip back to Milwaukee. Meg had put the boys down for a nap and was helping him with the dishes. Rudy was washing and she was drying bowls and plastic containers and wooden spoons — all the stuff that didn't go in the dishwasher — and spreading them out on towels on the kitchen table.

She and Dan had just bought a house up in Milwaukee, and when she said, "Pop, uh, we've, uh, been kind of wondering," Rudy thought she was going to ask him for some money, which he didn't have enough of. But she said, "We've, uh, kind of been wondering about having Christmas in Milwaukee this year."

Rudy rinsed off his hands, dried them on a dish towel, and poured himself another cup of coffee from the pot on the stove. He wasn't sure who was included in the "we."

She started to talk a little faster. Now that Philip was in first grade and little Danny was starting nursery school, she said, she needed to get out of the house. She'd joined the newly formed National Organization for Women, she said, and she was going to start working for a firm of young lawyers in Shorewood — Berlin, Killion, and Wagner — and expected to be very busy getting her feet on the ground; she'd be lucky to get Christmas Day off. Molly was working hard too and would probably be staying in Ann Arbor anyway, Meg explained, so he knew they'd already talked it over. The train schedule was really impossible, and Molly had sold her car, and TJ had relatives in Detroit. But all he, Rudy, would have to do — and Margot, if she ever got back from Italy — was hop on a train in Union Station and he'd be in Milwaukee in about ninety minutes if he didn't feel like driving, or if the weather was bad.

Rudy's life — or maybe it was just Life — had always had a way of sneaking up on him, catching him by surprise. He'd think a chapter was about over, and then it would go on and on. Or he'd think he was in the middle of a chapter, and all of a sudden it would stop. It hadn't been so bad when he was young, because most of the chapters had been ahead of him; but at Rudy's age, six zero, there weren't so many chapters left. He hated to see a good one come to an end, which was what was happening.

"Well," he said, looking down into his empty coffee cup, "suit yourself, if that's what you really want." This was a phrase he'd used a lot when the girls were in their teens. One of them — usually Molly — would want to hitchhike out to California with her boyfriend, and he'd say: "Suit yourself, if that's what you really want."

And that's the way they left it, because just as Meg was about to say something that might have settled Christmas one way or another, Dan came in the back door, kicking snow off his boots, saying that the weather was looking bad and they ought to get going before it got dark.

After they'd gone Rudy sat down in the kitchen and started to work seriously on a bottle of pretty good Chianti that was still sitting on the table, imagining what Christmas would be like in Milwaukee, or here in Chicago with just him and the dogs, and maybe Margot, and by the time he got to the bottom of the bottle he'd pretty well convinced himself that he ought to sell the house and go down to Texas and buy Creaky Wilson's avocado grove. Creaky had died of a heart attack in September, just at the start of the season, and Maxine, Creaky's widow, had called to see if he was interested or knew anyone who might be interested. Rudy'd never raised avocados, but he'd raised peaches and apples with his dad, and he'd been handling Becker's avocado account for thirty years. Most avocados come from California — thick-skinned Fuertes and Hasses — but Rudy preferred the thin-skinned Texas Lula, pear-shaped with creamy sweet flesh. Well, he thought, swirling the last of the Chianti in the bottom of his glass, it would be a good way of making them — his three daughters — appreciate what it meant to come home for Christmas to the place you grew up in.

He went down to the basement and pulled out an old one-by-twelve board that had been lying on the floor behind the furnace ever since he'd taken down the bunk beds in Meg's old room — the board had been used to keep Meg from falling out of the top bunk — and cut off a two-foot length with a new saw. The saw — a present from the Texas Avocado Growers Association — was Japanese and cut on the upward pull rather than on the downward thrust, which confused him a little but didn't stop him.

He didn't bother to sand down the edges; he just opened a can of the paint he'd been meaning to use on the storm windows and painted:

FOR SALE

in big black letters. Underneath FOR SALE he painted:

by owner

When he was done he brought down an electric fan from the attic and turned it on and pointed it at the sign to make the paint dry quicker, and then he went upstairs and sat down in Helen's study, as he sometimes did when he was upset or lonely. It was a small room but it held a lot of books, on shelves he'd built himself. The curves at the top of each bay were modeled on the curves of a famous bridge in Italy. Helen had given him a photo and he'd made a jig to cut the curves. The door on the east opened into the hallway, the one on the west into their bedroom. On the north wall three mullioned windows with leaded glass opened onto the roof of the porte cochere. Helen and the girls had liked to sunbathe on the roof in the summer.

Helen had been raised by an aunt and uncle. The old post-office desk, with a sloping surface and a shelf at the back, had been her uncle's. It was big and solid. Rudy had had to take the jambs off the door to get it into the room. It was where she'd graded her papers and written her articles. She'd taught art history at Edgar Lee Masters, a small liberal arts college on the near North Side, not far from her aunt and uncle's two-story brick bungalow. Her specialty had been medieval and Renaissance art, but she'd liked modern art too, and the bay on the right of the desk was filled with books about modern artists. From where he was sitting Rudy could see that the artists' names on the spines were in alphabetical order: Bacon, Beckman, Braque, Chagall, Dali, de Kooning . . . Helen was always rearranging her books — alphabetical order, chronological order, by nationality, by period — just as she was always rearranging her life.

Rudy looked out the north window at the vacant lot next door. The house had been bought by a crazy contractor who'd knocked out so many of the supporting walls that the city condemned it and finally bulldozed the whole house and filled the basement with rubble. The contractor offered to give Rudy the lot, and he'd thought about it. He could have built a garage and put in a garden, but there were too many liens against the property and no way to untangle them.

Rudy sat down at the desk and picked up a large paperback, printed on cheap paper, that Molly had sent him from Ann Arbor. It was the fifteenth edition of a student handbook called *Philosophy Made Simple* and had been written by her boyfriend's uncle, the philosopher Siva Singh. From the copy on the back Rudy learned that Siva Singh had studied at Oxford and then at Yale, that his scholarly reputation rested on his magisterial *Schopenhauer and the Upanishads,* and that no one was better qualified to guide the reader on "a never-ending quest to explore the profound mysteries of human existence."

The wine was wearing off, and Rudy was depressed, hungry too, not for more turkey, but for . . . He wasn't sure what to call it: knowledge, wisdom, certainty? Some sense of what it all meant? *To explore the profound mysteries of human existence?* He was tired, and lonely, and the house was empty. He always felt like this after the girls left. It was a kind of seasickness. He needed some Dramamine. But you have to take Dramamine before you start to get seasick. He went downstairs to see what the dogs were up to — Brownie, a German shepherd, and Saskia, part

Lab, part retriever. Not much. They were getting old, arthritic, but they could still make it up the stairs at night to sleep at the foot of his bed. He liked to hear them breathing, liked their familiar smells.

He fixed himself a cup of coffee and went back upstairs to Helen's study and opened *Philosophy Made Simple.* "There are two kinds of people," he discovered: Platonists and Aristotelians. It didn't take him long to figure out that he was a Platonist. Him. He. Rudy Harrington. And in a funny way he knew that he'd known it all along, at least since his geometry class in seventh grade. The circles he'd drawn with his little compass had been imperfect shadows of a real circle, a Platonic circle, a circle that existed on another plane of reality. He'd known it all along: that the world of the senses is unstable, always changing, but that there's got to be something beyond it that stays the same, like the perfect forms: triangles and circles and squares, and ideas too, Beauty and Goodness and Love. He'd known it all along, but he'd suppressed it. Because he hadn't wanted to look foolish.

The chapter ended with a long discussion of a famous cave that Plato wrote about in his book *The Republic.* It was hard to figure out at first. Rudy got a piece of typing paper and tried to sketch the cave with his fountain pen, Helen's old green and black striped Pelikan with an inscription on the black cap: *una cosa di bellezza.* Rudy was sure it had been a present from Bruno Bruni, but he carried it with him at all times because even though the hand that once held it had long ago been reduced to ashes at the North Shore Crematorium, it seemed to him to contain — like a powerful totem — something of Helen's spirit.

He drew a cross section of a cave. Then he added some stick people facing the opening of the cave. Then he took another sheet of paper and drew another cave and this time he put the stick people facing the back of the cave. Behind the stick people, outside the entrance of the cave, he drew some jagged lines to represent the flames of a fire. Then he drew some more stick people, passing by outside between the entrance of the cave and the fire, which acted as a sort of projector. The stick people outside the entrance carried different objects that cast shadows on the back of the cave. Rudy crosshatched the shadows.

It was a rough sketch, but he thought it captured what Plato had in mind: the stick people in the cave can see only the shadows cast by the figures that pass by outside. These shadows represent the unstable world of appearances. *We are the stick people,* he thought. This is what *we* see. But there's another reality behind appearances. Real reality. Sometimes a person — one of the stick people — gets a glimpse of this reality. Maybe he manages to break out of the cave into the bright light of day, and then, just because he's a little disoriented, people think he's crazy. And if he goes back into the cave and tells the other stick people what he saw outside, *they* think he's crazy. Is that what had happened to Rudy many years ago in his seventh-grade geometry class, standing at the blackboard long after the other students had returned to their seats, trying to prove — with everyone staring at him — that if the bisectors of two angles of a triangle are equal in length, the triangle is isosceles? He could *see* it was true. It *had* to be true. It couldn't *not* be true. It had been true before he drew the triangle on the board, and it would be true after he erased it. It had always been true, and it always would be true. He could *see* this truth as clearly as he could see Miss Buck, his favorite teacher, sitting at her desk, looking over the top of her steel-rimmed glasses at a set of papers she was marking, making little ticks with her red pencil. He could *see* it was true, but he couldn't *prove* it was true, even though he'd memorized every axiom and every theorem in the book. And every corollary too. All he could do was stare at the imperfect triangle, Triangle ABC, that he'd drawn on the board with a piece of chalk.

Finally Miss Buck said, "You may take your seat now, Rudy."

❖

Reading *Philosophy Made Simple,* Rudy made another discovery that was perhaps equally important. He may have been a Platonist, but Helen, he realized, had been an Aristotelian. She'd attended DePaul University, "the little school under the El," which is a Catholic school, but there wasn't a religious bone in her body. She had no use for another world. Other worlds spelled trouble. The Roman Catholic Church, she maintained, was the most corrupt institution in the history of the world, and other religions weren't far behind: "Just look around: Catholic versus Protestant; Methodist versus Free Methodist; Christian versus Jew; Jew versus Muslim; Shiite versus Sunni; Sephardic versus Ashkenazi; Hindu versus Muslim; Hindu versus Sikh. And so on."

No, this world had been enough for Helen. She'd had no interest in another world beyond the realm of appearances. She would have dismissed Plato's ideal forms — the real reality behind the world of appearances — just as Aristotle, according to Siva Singh, had dismissed them, saying they had no more meaning than singing *la la la.* Then why did she love medieval and Renaissance paintings? all those saints and madonnas and crucifixions and resurrections and epiphanies . . . ? All of a sudden Rudy understood: it was because she insisted on looking *at* them, as if they were just *things,* whereas he tried to look *through* them. It was the same with music. Bach's *B Minor Mass* or "Mr. Jelly Roll Baker," it didn't matter. She listened to the notes; he listened *through* them. She heard melody and harmony and counterpoint; he heard something calling him from far, far away.

For Sale

From his office window in the back of the warehouse, Rudy could see in silhouette everything that passed by on the broad, sloping sidewalk in the front: forklifts, flat-trucks, two-wheelers, hydraulic dollies carrying pallets, skids, bushels, baskets, hampers, crates, lugs, sacks, bags, flats, potatoes and cucumbers, tomatoes and peppers, beans, nectarines, oranges, avocados, kiwis, coconuts, strawberries, apples, cantaloupes, mangoes. Sitting at his desk he wondered: are these just shadows cast upon a screen? Am I trapped in this cave, this office, unable to turn my head and look directly at the reality, at the thing itself? And he doodled a sketch of the cave on a yellow pad with Harry Becker & Son printed at the top till the phone rang — his own dedicated line — and he answered it: "Rudy here."

And then the pressure of the holidays pushed the cave out of his mind, and he didn't think about it again till Christmas Eve, when the beauty of this world hit him so hard it reminded him of the true beauty beyond, and his soul, like a bird, began to sprout wings.

❖

Meg and Dan had decided to come home for Christmas after all, and Molly was coming too, bringing Tejinder, now her fiancé, she told him on the phone. They were getting married in the summer, and Rudy could hear that her voice was full of love and joy. Everyone called him TJ, she said. He had a joint appointment in math and physics at the University of Michigan, and he'd signed up for lessons at the dance studio, and he'd really like to see an American Christmas. Instead of spending Christmas with an Indian auntie in Royal Oak, a suburb of Detroit, he was going to come with Molly to Chicago.

Rudy was relieved, like a man who's come through a serious traffic accident without a scratch. He vacuumed up the dog hair and brought down the boxes of Christmas decorations from the attic: the crèche that Helen had brought back from Italy, the snowman candles, like skaters, skating on a pond made out of a mirror. He bought a tree and put it up, but he didn't decorate it, because they never decorated the tree till Christmas Eve. He got out the old ornaments that the girls had made out of baker's clay when they were little: salt and flour and water rolled into a paste, cut with cookie cutters, baked in the oven, and then painted. And on the day before Christmas he bought two fresh capons instead of a turkey. It wasn't till he carried the capons down to the basement in the big roaster — to keep them cool but not frozen — that he remembered the FOR SALE sign, which was still propped up against the freezer. The electric fan was still blowing on it. His first impulse was to hide it, in case one of the girls came downstairs to get something out of the freezer. But then he decided it might be a good idea to put it up, just for one night, just to shake them up, make them think. Sometimes it takes a little jolt to make us appreciate what we've got, to keep us from taking it for granted. That's what he had in mind — a little jolt.

The ground was frozen too hard to drive a stake into, so he nailed the sign to the pillar of the porte cochere and turned the outside light on so you couldn't miss it as you drove up the driveway. Then he went inside and rolled out the dough for a sour-cream apple pie, which he always made in a springform pan so that it stood, straight-sided, about four inches high. He used eight big Granny Smith apples.

He hadn't heard from Margot since right after Thanksgiving, when he'd gotten a card saying she was staying in a convent. The card was up on the refrigerator, held by a magnet shaped like a ladybug. It was a picture of the Virgin Mary and an angel with big gold wings. He figured he'd come home from work one day and she'd be there — Margot, not the Virgin Mary — but she wasn't. Icelandic Airlines had flights to New York on Tuesdays and Thursdays, but it was Friday, and she hadn't come home. Rudy called Alitalia and TWA, which had direct flights from Rome to Chicago, but they wouldn't release the passenger lists, so he had no way of finding out if she was booked on any of the flights. By Christmas Eve he'd just about given up hope.

"How sharper than a serpent's tooth," Helen used to say, "it is to have a thankless child." She was joking, but there was some truth to it too. How much trouble was it to write a postcard? Or to pick up the telephone? What was she doing for money? Was she going to become a nun? Nothing would surprise him.

Rudy'd given considerable thought to where Tejinder — which means "the embodiment of power" in Hindi — ought to sleep and had finally decided on the floor of Helen's study. He lugged one of the extra mattresses down from the attic and made it up nicely with matching sheets and pillowcase and a Pendleton blanket. *He's probably used to sleeping on a mat on the floor anyway,* Rudy told himself. But Molly carried Tejinder's suitcase right up to her own small room, with its single bed. Rudy followed her.

"I've got a bed made up for him in the study," he said.

Molly plopped the suitcase down on the floor, sat on it, and looked around at the empty aquarium, the books, the portable Smith Corona on the desk, the beanbag chair.

"Wouldn't he be more comfortable in the study?" Rudy asked.

"He might be more comfortable," she said, "but he wouldn't have as much fun."

"Well," he said. "Suit yourself, if that's what you really want."

When he came downstairs, Meg and Dan and the boys were bustling in the front door carrying a portable television set. "Merry Christmas," they said. It took him a while to realize that the television set was his Christmas present.

Helen and Rudy had never had a TV. With Helen it had been a matter of principle. Rudy'd never cared much one way or the other, but he'd gotten used to not having one, and he got a kick out of telling people that he didn't have one. *"Whaaaat?"* they'd say. "You don't have a TV?" No one could believe him. He might as well have told them that they didn't have indoor plumbing. Babysitters had looked around the living room in desperation. Guests at Thanksgiving couldn't believe they were going to miss the football games.

"We just never got around to getting one," he'd say. Or, depending on his audience: "On account of the kids, you know. We'd rather they read books or played the piano."

And now Dan was hooking the thing up in the living room. He'd brought along the sort of antenna you set on top, with two spikes sticking up, and was turning it this way and that. The TV was making a loud staticky sound. Daniel, three, and Philip, five, were waiting impatiently.

"C'mon out here, you guys," Rudy shouted from the kitchen. "I've got some baker's clay here. You can make Christmas tree ornaments, like your mama used to. We'll bake them and then you can paint them."

But either they couldn't hear him or they preferred to watch the snowy screen.

One Christmas was much like the next at the Harrington house, just as in the Dylan Thomas story *A Child's Christmas in Wales,* and one of the things that was always the same was that one of the girls would give Rudy a copy of *A Child's Christmas in Wales* — a record in a red and white jacket with a little booklet with the text. There were half a dozen of them in the record cabinet. On the other side of the record was a poem called "Do Not Go Gentle into That Good Night," and sometimes Rudy wondered if maybe *that* was the real message they were sending him. He liked to think so.

For supper they ate pizzas, which Rudy had made, instead of the *spaghetti alle vongole* that Helen had always insisted on because that's what they eat on Christmas Eve in Florence. Helen had liked traditions, especially Italian ones.

After supper they left the dishes to soak in the sink while they put the lights on the tree and decorated it with strings of cranberries and popcorn and the old baker's-clay ornaments. They must have had three or four hundred of these ornaments in the attic, enough for several trees. Daniel and Philip had not forgotten about the TV, which could not be coaxed into working, much to Rudy's satisfaction. But without a TV the boys were restless, so

Rudy and TJ, who was an amateur magician, went back up to the attic and brought down a metal footlocker that held Rudy's dad's old magic tricks, many of them still packed in their original boxes. TJ entertained the boys with coins that materialized out of nowhere and silks that disappeared into nowhere, magic rings that passed through each other, ropes that mended themselves when cut in half, and Rudy fooled everyone, including TJ, with a trick he'd learned from his dad involving two hats and little wads of paper that he passed back and forth through the solid surface of the dining room table. Instead of calming the boys down, Rudy and TJ got them even more worked up, but TJ was able to reverse the process by demonstrating several yoga positions that the boys were eager to imitate: the Lotus, the Fish, the Bird, and finally the Dead Man's Posture, which, he said, was the most difficult of all. The boys lay quietly on their backs.

"Not even your toe must twitch," TJ warned. "Not even the tip of your finger must move."

Rudy helped them write a note to Santa. Dan wanted a G.I. Joe, and Philip wanted an Erector set so he could build a Ferris wheel, and a magic set, and an electric train, and it struck Rudy that his life would have been totally different if he and Helen had had three sons instead of three daughters. Maybe, in a parallel universe . . .

The boys sat on either side of him on the living room sofa while Rudy hunched over the coffee table and wrote out their lists with Helen's fountain pen. They left them in front of the fireplace along with a glass of milk and a plate of cookies. At first Rudy hadn't been as excited as he felt he ought to be at having grandchildren, but now it was a pleasure to read them the stories that his mother had read to him, and that he'd read to his daughters. They were a little young for *The Wind in the Willows,* but not for Winnie the Pooh.

The boys brushed their teeth at the little sink in Margot's room. Rudy located *The House at Pooh Corner* on the bookshelves, next to one of the Italian schoolbooks Margot had brought back from the year she'd spent in Italy with Helen, and read the story about Owl's house blowing down, and then the one about Pooh and Piglet taking a pile of sticks that turned out to be Eeyore's house. The boys fell asleep halfway through the second story, but he kept on reading till he got to the end. He put the book back on the shelf next to Margot's Italian geography book, *Il nuovo libro Garzanti della Geografia.*

When Rudy came downstairs, TJ was demonstrating his parallel universe thesis to Dan and the girls. They'd propped up Helen's old projector on the dining room table so that the beam of light was aimed at two tiny slits in a piece of tinfoil that had been fastened with a clothespin to a makeshift frame made out of a coat hanger.

"Like Plato's cave, Rudy, don't you think?" TJ said. Rudy, who had drawn a new sketch of Plato's cave while they were sitting at the kitchen table after supper, pulled up a chair and sat down.

"Right, Rudy?" TJ said. "We're in the cave, and this little beam of light on the wall is all we can see of the reality of the world. But what can we conclude from this little band of light? That's the question. Can we use our minds to explore the world outside the cave?"

Rudy was afraid he couldn't have concluded much himself.

"What you see," TJ explained, "is that the two slits have divided each color — each wavelength — into two waves. When the crests of these waves overlap, you see a band of light on the wall; when a crest and a trough come together, they cancel each other out. If this were a laser projector, we'd see just light and dark, but with white light we see a rainbow. The principle is the same, though. Each photon has a particular wavelength that will determine the angle at which it will have interference maxima, bright spots. The separation into different angles is what causes the rainbow effect."

Now this was something Rudy could almost understand. Or, if he couldn't understand it, at least he could imagine understanding it; but he couldn't follow the argument any further, couldn't understand how the pattern of light on the wall led to the theory of parallel universes.

What he really wanted to know was if these parallel universes were like Plato's forms or ideas, but he couldn't pin TJ down. TJ's ultimate truths were not geometrical, like Plato's; they were probability waves.

What he really wanted to know was if Helen might be living with Bruni in a parallel universe, and if it might be possible to visit her. But he didn't ask, because he didn't want to appear foolish.

Nobody said anything about the FOR SALE sign till it was almost bedtime and they were finishing off the last of a bottle of wine in front of the fire. The dogs were on the side porch, banging to get in. TJ and Dan were still at the dining room table.

"I see you've got the house up for sale," Meg said.

"Oh, that."

Molly got up to let the dogs in. Rudy suddenly realized that she'd quit smoking.

"Molly and I've been talking," Meg said. "We think it's a great idea. This place is too big for you. You must rattle around here all by yourself. You'd be better off in an apartment, or one of those new retirement condos. Dan and I heard them talking about one on the radio on the way down, Carleton Estates, something like that. You'd have everything you need right there. A pool, a sauna. You'd have your own kitchen if you want to cook, but there's a dining room too. The best of both worlds."

A pool? A sauna? What do I need with a pool and a sauna? "What about Margot?"

"She's twenty-nine years old," Molly said. "It's about time she got a place of her own. You're too protective. She's got to get out in the world."

"Where do you think she is? She sure as hell isn't upstairs in her room. And what about the dogs?"

"They're getting old, Papa. How much longer do you think they've got?" Molly ran her fingers through her hair. She was the beauty of the family. She had Helen's red hair and Helen's golden freckles. Repeated applications of freckle cream when she was a teenager had failed to dim their luster.

"Well, I dunno. They don't look so old to me."

"We could take the dogs, Pop," Meg said. "We've got plenty of room now. We were thinking of getting a dog anyway. It would be good for the boys."

"If you go back to work you'll be gone all day."

"You're gone all day too, Pop. We'll fence in the backyard. They'll be okay."

"This neighborhood could go downhill, Papa," Molly said, "but these old places are still trendy. It's good you're selling while you've got the chance. In three months I'll have my license. I'll take care of everything for you, the listing, showing, financing, closing, the works."

"You going to have a license to practice in Illinois?" Rudy asked.

"I'm planning to take the test for Michigan, Indiana, Illinois, Wisconsin, New York, and California. How about something like this: Victorian fantasy. Shingle style. Four bedrooms, study, two bathrooms. Parquet floors. Baccarat crystal chandelier. Leaded glass windows. Butler's pantry. Beautiful millwork. Fireplace. Modern kitchen, laundry room. Full basement. Excellent condition.

"How does that sound? You'll get a good price for this place, I promise you."

Rudy didn't know what to say. He was dumbfounded. "You might as well get on the phone and call the undertaker right now," he said. "Tell him to bring the hearse around to the back door. Or call the knacker, for cryin' out loud. I've lived in this house for over thirty years. You don't think I'm going to pack up and move out just like that, do you? After thirty years? Your mother and I paid eighteen thousand dollars for this house. Why, you couldn't build a house like this today for a quarter of a million dollars."

"Papa, that's not what we meant and you know it." Meg unfastened her hair and shook it loose. "What we meant is that we want you to do whatever you want to do, and that if you want to sell the house, it's okay with us. You don't have to worry about us, we'll go along with anything. *You're* the one who put it up for sale without saying anything to anybody."

"Suit yourself," Molly said, "if that's what you really want to do."

About an hour later the phone rang. Rudy was sitting at the kitchen table filling stockings and he grabbed it on the first ring. There was a click and the phone went dead, and he froze. The phone always clicked like that and then went dead on overseas calls. It would ring again in a little over a minute, and the overseas operator would be on the line. It was a special kind of click. He knew it was the same for good news as for bad news, but it made him uneasy anyway.

Spread out on the table before him were six large gray wool

hunting socks with red tops and six piles of stuff: oranges, apples, dried apricots and raisins (wrapped in saran wrap), chocolate kisses in foil, salted peanuts, ballpoint pens, mechanical pencils, little bars of scented soap for the girls, penknives for Dan and Tejinder, crayons and protractors for Daniel and Philip. He'd always filled stockings and he didn't see any point in stopping now. He opened one of the penknives and tested the blade. His pulse was speeding up, his chest was tight, his arm was going numb. He had to get hold of himself. The house was strangely silent except for the occasional clink of a metal dog collar and a strange pounding that might have been his heart. It was strong enough to rattle the copper saucepans hanging from a rack over the table.

The phone rang again. It was Margot, all right. At first he didn't pay any attention to what she was saying. He was listening for something else, like a mechanic listening to an engine idling.

"Is it really you, Papa? I had trouble getting through. Say something."

"How are you?"

"Oh, Papa, I'm so happy. I'm in love, really in love. Head over heels. Can you hear me all right? I don't want to say it too loud."

"Where are you?"

"At the post office."

"In the middle of the night?"

"It's nine o'clock in the morning here. What time is it there?"

"It's two o'clock in the morning."

"Is it Christmas yet?"

"It's still Christmas Eve. I'm filling the stockings. I gave yours to Molly's boyfriend. His name's Tejinder, but she calls him TJ. He's from India; his father's dead and his mother lives in Assam. She runs a tea garden."

When he knew she was all right he was tempted to scold her:

Why didn't you write? Why didn't you call? Why didn't you come home? You promised . . . But he was too overwhelmed, too happy.

"Well," he said. "That's wonderful. Who's the lucky guy?"

"He's an Italian."

"Married?"

"No, Papa. Well, yes, but he's getting a divorce. He's from the Abruzzi. He's the head restorer for the whole region of Tuscany. He's working on the frescoes in the Lodovici Chapel in the Badia. You remember the Badia? The monastery, where they had the foosball game in the cloister? It's still there."

Rudy'd gone to Florence back in 1953. Ike had moved into the White House in January; the Soviets had tested their first H-bomb; the Braves had moved to Milwaukee; Jonas Salk had developed a vaccine for polio; and Helen had started her affair with Bruno Bruni. He'd gone to Florence to bring her back home, but he'd come back alone. The foosball game he remembered, after all these years, but that was about all — the foosball game, and the big piazzas and the little coffee bars, and the trip to Venice, and how he felt sick to his stomach the whole time.

"It doesn't matter," she said. "And the Martini *Annunciation*. I sent you a postcard of it. Didn't you get it?"

"I got it; it's up on the refrigerator."

He tried to picture her in the post office. He couldn't remember anything about Florence. He'd been too upset to pay much attention to the city. But he imagined Margot in a booth, with her friend — her lover — standing outside, waiting, impatient, eager.

"What are your plans? I mean, are you coming home, or what?"

"We're going to the Abruzzi sometime in January to see Sandro's parents, and then to Rome."

"Have you written to your boss at the Newberry? He called here the other day. To tell you the truth, I don't think you've got a job anymore."

But she didn't hear him, and he didn't repeat himself. It might just be possible, he thought to himself. A mature man with a good job, a responsible position. But married?

He suddenly realized what was shaking the saucepans. It was the bed upstairs, in Molly's room. The Indian was humping his daughter. They were shaking the whole house with their lust. It gave him a hard-on, just the cruel fact of it. It made him ache for Helen the way he'd ached for her in Florence, and they hadn't made love once the whole time he was there.

"I didn't know you could get a divorce in Italy," he said.

"It's an annulment. It's the same thing. You'll see. Don't worry, Papa, I'm all right, I'm fine, I'll write to you, I really will. I have to go now."

"Take care of yourself."

"You take care of yourself too. I love you. Tell everyone I love them." That was all she said. But it was enough. He was sorry now that he'd tried to stop her from going, had refused to pay for her ticket. He could see now that she'd needed to get away, to reinvent herself. She was tired of being a mousy librarian. And now she was in love with a married man in Italy.

He finished filling the stockings and carried them into the living room, where he spread them out on the coffee table in front of the fireplace. He moved the TV into a dark corner in the dining room, ate the cookies the boys had left for Santa and wrote an answer to the note they'd left, which was what his father had done for him, and what he'd done for the girls.

Thanks for the milk and cookies. Be good.
— Santa

He filled the humidifier, turned down the thermostat, let the dogs out, turned off the tape deck, which had been left on, let the dogs back in, put the garbage container up on the kitchen table so the dogs wouldn't empty it. The house had started to shake again, the pots and pans to rattle. Rudy got a hammer out of his toolbox, pulled on his jacket, and went outside to take down the FOR SALE sign.

He still had a hard-on, a great lump of sensation swelling against his trousers. He'd almost forgotten how good it felt, and even though he didn't know what he could do about it, he was grateful. It was good to be alive. He felt like a young man, young and strong, the way he'd felt when he and Helen had moved into the house, which looked just the same now as it had then. They'd kept the red trim. Cardinal red. Rudy thought of the first Christmas they'd spent in this house, after his father's death, and of Mr. Ballard, the previous owner, whose downstate paving-brick business had fallen into the hands of the receivers, and who had driven off to California with his whole family in a broken-down Pierce-Arrow. And he thought of the French doll-house and the steamer trunks that the Ballards had left in the attic, and the letter that Ballard had sent him about a year later, telling him about the house: how Harald Kreutzberg, the famous German dancer, had been entertained there, and Cornelia Otis Skinner, and Matthew Arnold, and Aleka Rostislav, who was Princess Galitzine and whose husband's father was the brother of the last czar, and many other famous people. Rudy kept the letter in a fireproof box on the shelf on top of the big desk, along with Helen's will and her other papers and the girls' school records.

The sign had worked its way loose — he hadn't hammered the nails all the way in when he put it up — and he could have pulled it off with his hands. He didn't need the hammer. But instead of taking it down, he walked down the driveway to the street, to pick up the empty garbage cans that had been sitting there since that morning, and to have a look.

It was windy and the snow blew upward in spiraling flurries. The ornamental streetlights glowed like beacons marking a broad channel. Most of the big old houses on the street had long ago been broken up into five or six apartments — sometimes even more. Their owners didn't live there anymore, and the lawns didn't get cut as often as they should, and the houses got painted every ten or twelve years instead of every six or seven. Helen used to say that when she looked down the street at night from their master bedroom, she could imagine — if she squinted a little — that she was living in Paris, St. Germain or St. Rémy. To Rudy, who'd lived there longer than he'd ever lived anywhere else, it just looked like home.

The living room window, which was curved at the top, was divided into three panels, like one of Helen's Renaissance paintings, a triptych. The window was filled with little white lights that were doubled by the beveled edges of the glass; in the large center panel stood the Christmas tree, full of light and promise. The light under the porte cochere was on too, and the FOR SALE sign was clearly visible from the street. Rudy loved this house. *"Come on in, this old house,"* he used to sing to Helen; *"ain't nobody here but me."* But now it was time to move on, time to let go. He didn't know how he knew this, but he knew it. He knew it as surely as migratory birds know when it's time to leave everything behind them and head out who knows where, and no one has ever figured out how they find their way, but they do. It was as if he were sprouting wings, big golden wings, like those on the angel on Margot's postcard, wings that would carry him out of the past and into the future, wherever he needed to go.

The Second Coming

Rudy didn't say anything to the girls about his vision, because he was trying to understand it himself. After Christmas, after everyone had gone, he sat down in Helen's study and reread the first chapter of *Philosophy Made Simple*. He was trying to figure out what had happened to him on Christmas Eve. He was looking for a passage in which Uncle Siva — TJ's uncle Siva — quotes Socrates' comparison of the soul to a bird, and when he found it, he underlined it: <u>for a man who beholds the beauty of this world will sometimes be reminded of true beauty, and his wings will begin to grow and he will desire to spread his wings and fly upward, and because he gazes upward, like a bird, and cares nothing for the world below, he will be considered mad.</u>

Maybe that was it. He couldn't be sure, but in the second week of the new year he took some time off and flew down to Texas to look at Creaky Wilson's avocado grove. Avocados had been a luxury fruit when Rudy started working on South Water Street. They were high in calories and they had a reputation as an aphrodisiac, so middle-class housewives were afraid of them.

But they'd become popular in California, and the rest of the country had followed. Texas seemed to him an ideal place to raise avocados. Although Texas *consumed* a lot of avocados, it didn't *produce* many — probably fewer than a thousand acres were under cultivation in the Rio Grande Valley — but there was no reason that couldn't change. Creaky Wilson had always sent good fruit, the finest, and the only thing to worry about in Texas was frost. Besides, raising avocados is easy — relatively speaking, of course.

The dogs were banging at the door of the side porch when he left the house, but they'd have to wait for the neighbor's kid, who'd be staying with them, to get home from school. He grabbed the mail and shoved it in the outside pocket of Helen's old leather briefcase, along with his copy of *Philosophy Made Simple*. He left the car at Midway Airport and boarded a flight to Dallas and then a connecting flight to McAllen. On the flight to Dallas he kept *Philosophy Made Simple* on his lap while he read through the emergency landing card and the in-flight magazine and the catalog of stuff you could buy, and then he remembered the mail. There was nothing from Margot, but there was a letter from Edgar Lee Masters College, asking for money, which he stuffed in the flap on the back of the seat in front of him, and there was a large, formidable envelope bearing a stern warning:

This Cash Winner Notification may not be delivered by anyone except US Government employees.

A partial list of sweepstakes winners was enclosed. Rudy could see his own name displayed through a little window, but he stuffed the envelope, unopened, into the pocket of the seat in front of him, next to the letter from Edgar Lee Masters. The mail also included a trial issue of a senior citizens' magazine called

The Golden Age Digest, and finally, there was a letter from East Africa, from his nephew, one of the few remaining Harringtons, who had sold his house in Wheaton, Illinois, and become a missionary.

Rudy set the letter aside and glanced through *The Golden Age Digest* to see what his cohort was doing. They were, mostly, playing golf. Happy foursomes in fruity two-toned shoes with fringe on them, like the hair that hangs down over a sheep dog's face, waved from pea green links. The men wore cardigans and blue or white oxford shirts, the women bright-colored skirts and pale blouses with wide collars. The same folks were buying condominiums with little work islands in the kitchens, which were tiled for easy maintenance. The idea was that old age wasn't a downhill slide but the culmination of life, the peak.

Rudy stuffed the magazine into the seat flap, drank some airline coffee, and then opened *Philosophy Made Simple* and started to read the chapter on Aristotle. Happiness. Not Plato's Goodness or Beauty or Truth, but Happiness: something final and self-sufficient, the Supreme Good, the end at which all actions aim. But to achieve Happiness, one had to bring Reason to bear on one's Passions and Desires.

Rudy had to admit that Aristotle had a point. Would he be happy, he started to wonder, if he won the sweepstakes? He closed *Philosophy Made Simple* and retrieved the sweepstakes envelope from the flap and learned that he was in fact a "verified sweepstakes winner," though it wasn't clear just what he had won. He read through a lot of fine print. There were prizes in his category that ranged from two hundred fifty thousand dollars to one thousand dollars to "many thousands of substantially lesser cash prizes (as stated in the official sweepstakes rules)." He started to shove the brochure back into the seat pocket, but then his eye was caught by another stern notice: "Failure to claim prize will result in loss of your cash award. Company is not responsible for unclaimed cash awards." There was no entry fee or purchase necessary for Rudy to claim his award, but in fact they wanted him to buy some perfume — real perfume, not cologne or toilet water. Perfume that might cost a hundred dollars in fine stores in New York and Paris, but which he could buy for only five dollars: Chanel No. 5, Climat, Rapture, Miss Balmain. The perfumes came in different-shaped bottles, but it was hard to tell how big they were. One resembled a tomb or cut-glass mausoleum; another was squat and round and dark, like a sea creature that had been flattened out. One had a stopper shaped like a bird. One was hard to figure out: it looked like a fried egg that had been folded in half, with a yolk that was much darker and yolkier-looking than the pale yellows of the other perfumes. The name Alexandra Dali was written in script on the white part of the egg. Was Alexandra Dali Salvador Dali's wife? His daughter? His granddaughter? Rudy had no idea. But the egg looked like the sort of egg you might see in a Dali painting.

You didn't have to order any perfume to enter the sweepstakes or claim your prize, but they made it very difficult for you if you didn't. You'd have to cut out your randomly generated number from one place and paste it on a three-by-five card, and then you'd have to cut out other bits of information from other parts of the official form and paste them on different parts of the card. And you'd have to cut out the "NO" paragraph from the lower left-hand corner of the Grand Prize Claim Document and affix it to the card too. There wasn't enough room, and if you failed to arrange them in a certain way, you would be disqualified. You would also be disqualified if you used staples or cellophane tape. What the hell! Rudy stuck the ad in Helen's briefcase. He'd deal with it later. But two hundred fifty thousand dollars. A quarter of a million dollars. What would he do with it? He wasn't sure. He closed his eyes, tried to imagine. He could get close to the feeling he'd have right after he'd opened the letter telling him he'd won, how he'd hold himself together, not tell anyone but the dogs for a few days, just riding high, till he'd gotten used to the idea.

When he was a boy he used to have daydreams like the one he was having on the plane — waking fantasies, about success, about love, about how women would want to be possessed by him, how everyone would be forced to acknowledge how extraordinary he was. But he'd thought that when he got older, when he'd grown up, he wouldn't do that anymore. Now here he was, no better than a kid. It wouldn't have occurred to him in a million years that his dad or his mom might have had thoughts like that. He could see his dad, standing in the door of the empty packing shed, looking out at the empty trees. Three years in a row they lost the entire peach crop, before the Depression, before Rudy'd gone up to Chicago to work for Becker. What had his dad been thinking?

"Well," he'd say, "looks like you and me can eat the whole crop." And they'd wander up and down the rows, looking, and find maybe three or four peaches. But what was he thinking, imagining, dreaming? And his mom, her hands up to her elbows in soapy water, looking out the kitchen window. What was she looking at? The pump? The packing shed? Or something beyond? What was *her* heart's desire?

He put *Philosophy Made Simple* back in his briefcase and opened the letter from his nephew, Gary, in East Africa. Gary was the son of Rudy's older brother, Alfred, who'd been killed in action in World War I when Rudy was only ten. It was a belated Christmas card. "Dear Uncle Rudy," Gary wrote,

I meant to get this off in time for Christmas but didn't get around to it. Everything is chaotic, and in fact I've been down with a parasite called giardia, found in the water here, so now I drink bottled water only, which is a nuisance.

The country here is beautiful, the natives are friendly and speak French. Vivian and I spent six months learning Kikuyu at the Institute training school in Zurich, Switzerland, but it's a difficult language and we're still having trouble, and it's very expensive here.

The way things are going it seems to me the Lord Jesus Christ is coming very soon, in fact any minute. I fervently hope so. This is a very wicked world these days and I wonder at God's patience with humanity.

I hope you had a nice Christmas and will have a good year.

Lovingly,

Gary and Vivian

There was some literature from Gary and Vivian's employer, the Christian Bible Institute, an international organization dedicated to the task of translating the Bible into every single language in the world, including Kikuyu, and a request for support. He crumpled it up and then smoothed it out again so he could slip it in the flap with the airline magazine and the letter from Edgar Lee Masters.

What kind of Christmas message was that? "The Lord Jesus Christ is coming very soon, in fact any minute"? What got into people? People will believe anything. But these beliefs weren't like ordinary empirical knowledge. They couldn't be treated in the same way, because they weren't based on anything that could be examined or evaluated. But what about Plato? What about Aristotle? *What about me?*

◇

He didn't give another thought to Gary's letter till the next morning, when he woke up at three o'clock in the Starlight Motel on the border between Mission and McAllen. He had a hangover and couldn't get back to sleep. He'd drunk too much Lone Star beer and eaten too much chili at a diner on Highway 83. His head and his stomach were both churning, like electric motors that were running at different speeds, pulling against each other, and there was a neon sign that made a loud buzzing noise as it blinked on and off, on and off, outside his window. It made you realize why a lot of people preferred Howard Johnsons and Holiday Inns, where there were no surprises, no crumbling tiles in the bathrooms, no little boxes of roach powder in the closets. He lay there in the dark thinking, *What am I doing here? What on earth am I doing here?* It had seemed like a good idea back in Chicago, but it didn't seem so hot right now. A man his age ought to be thinking about retiring, not raising avocados.

He reached over and turned on the clock radio on the stand next to the bed. He turned the dial but didn't get anything except a lot of static. There was lots of space between stations down in Texas. He finally picked up a talk show way down one end of the dial, on the right. He started back the other way and then reversed. There was an urgency in the slow Texas voice on the talk show that spoke to his condition. Something was wrong, really wrong:

"What we're telling people to do," a woman's voice was saying, when he found the station again, "is to stay home with their families, to read their Bibles, and to pray. That's about all you *can* do at this point. Bob and I will be leaving the station at five a.m. to join *our* families. Until then, we're here to take your calls." She gave the number.

"Should we go down to the basement?" the next caller wanted to know.

"No, we think you should stay right in your living room. Going to the basement's not what will save you."

Rudy switched on the lamp and sat up in bed. Another missile crisis, or worse — only this time it would be LBJ climbing into the ring with Brezhnev. He'd seen something about it in the *McAllen Monitor* that had been lying open in the diner:

U Thant Predicts
WWIII if US Doesn't
Leave Vietnam

But he hadn't read past the header. *This could be it. My last night on earth. The missiles might be in the air already: Titans, Minuteman 1s, Soviet SS-8s. NASA headquarters in Houston would be a prime target. Mission Control.* He thought he heard a siren, but it was only the buzzing of the neon sign. That's when he thought of Gary's letter again: "The Lord Jesus Christ is coming very soon, in fact any minute . . . I wonder at God's patience with humanity." *Could this be IT? Christ himself pushing the button, all she wrote, end of story?*

Rudy was wide awake. He had to go to the bathroom, but he wanted to listen. It took him a while to figure out what the folks at the station were worried about: not a nuclear attack but the Second Coming.

Momentarily relieved, he slipped on the Italian silk robe that Helen had ordered for him from Marshall Field's shortly before her death, sat down on the edge of the bed, and continued to listen. It turned out that a former computer scientist, while working as a janitor at NASA, had secretly programmed the big computer — the one that was keeping Gemini 9 on course — to determine scientifically the date of the Second Coming, which was going to be tomorrow, at sunset in Jerusalem. Ten seventeen a.m. Texas time. He went outside and got a bottle of Dr Pepper from the pop machine.

Sitting at his kitchen table thumbing through the evening paper, Rudy would have laughed at this sort of stuff. But he was a thousand miles away from home and had three bowls of Texas chili from last night's supper still sloshing around in his stomach — nothing but shredded meat and jalapeño peppers, no beans, no tomato sauce — along with three or four bottles of Lone Star beer, and he'd been brought up as a Methodist, even though he hadn't been to church in twenty years, except for weddings and funerals and a few times after Helen's death, so it was pretty upsetting.

What was he supposed to do in the meantime? That's what callers wanted to know. They wanted instructions. Practical advice. Just the idea of it was unnerving. People shouldn't be allowed to broadcast such nonsense. Rudy was annoyed. But he didn't turn off the radio. He listened to a string of commercials and then the Bob and Helen Show came back on the air. Helen, Rudy's wife's name.

The next caller was a woman from Hidalgo named Marge, with a message for her husband: "Gene, please come home." She was on the edge of tears. "I'm sorry. If you can hear me, come back." Someone else wanted to know what Bible passages would be good to concentrate on. Helen suggested John 3:16–21, "For God so loved the world . . ." Bob voted for the parable of the vineyard, Matthew 21:28–41. And then a mother from Weslaco followed Marge's lead by trying to reach her daughter, who'd run off with a Mexican farmworker: "Debbie, this is your mom. Your dad and I been prayin' for you every minute of every day and every night. Won't you please call us right away, before it's too late. We love you so much." Sobbing. There was a call from somewhere in Mexico. Bob and Helen spoke to the man in Spanish. Rudy knew enough Spanish to know that they were talking about betrayal and infidelity, and then the man started to sob too — masculine, Mexican sobbing that was different from anything Rudy'd ever heard, but easy enough to understand.

He finished his Dr Pepper. The calls kept coming in — husbands and wives, moms and dads, children too, all reaching out with the same message — Come home, or if you're too far away, call us before it's too late. We want to talk to you once more before the end. We want to tell you we love you, we just want you to hear it one more time; we just want to hear your voice.

Who were these people? What were they doing up at three thirty in the morning? Then it hit him. They were people just like him, listening to the radio because they couldn't sleep, because they were lonely. Did they know something he didn't know?

He got to thinking: What if it *was* the world's last night? What would *he* do? If he called the station, who would be listening? His daughters? They were all too far away; and they wouldn't be listening anyway. Besides, if he wanted to call them, he'd call them at home. At least he could reach Meg and Molly at home. But what about Helen, his wife?

It was a foolish impulse, but he yielded to it like a man yielding to a sudden and irresistible temptation. He picked up the phone, dialed 9 and the number of the station. It rang four times and then someone answered — not Helen or Bob but an operator who was taking the calls. There were three people ahead of him, she said, could he hang on? She took his name and put him on hold and he started to hear music, a song he hadn't heard in years:

Dee-eee-ee-e-eep river,
my home lies o-o-ver Jor-do-uh-uhn.
Dee-eee-ee-e-eep river, Looord,
I want to cross over into campground.

It was a song the men's chorus used to sing at the campground in Berrien Springs, where he'd gone with his mom and his aunt Martha every summer when he was a kid. He was thinking about the campground — the wooden cabins, unpainted and sagging, and the white porcelain chamber pots, and the men's deep voices — when the operator told him he was about to go on the air, and then he was on the air and Bob was saying, "Hello? Rudy? Hello? Rudy, are you there?" And suddenly finding himself short of breath, he said, "I've got a message for my wife, Helen. Helen, this is Rudy. If you can hear me, please call me, I'm at the Starlight Motel in Mission, Texas, the number is" — he had to look closely at the phone to get the number. "I love you," he said. "Good-bye."

He hung up the phone immediately. He'd heard his own voice on the radio just a fraction of a second or so after he'd spoken the words, as if someone else in the room had been repeating the words right after him, and then Bob was thanking him and taking the next call.

He tied the belt of his robe around his waist and went out for another Dr Pepper, something to clear the cobwebs from his throat. He lay down on the bed and nursed the soda as he listened to the calls that kept coming in. He could hear the phones ringing in the studio, and a couple of times, just as he was drifting off to sleep, he woke up with a start, thinking that the phone beside the bed was ringing, that someone was trying to reach him. But when he picked up the receiver, all he got was a dial tone. By the time Bob and Helen signed off and went home to wait for the Second Coming with their families, Rudy was fast asleep.

Sunset in Jerusalem

Creaky's grove was halfway between Mission and Hidalgo, forty acres, twenty-nine and a half under cultivation. A man can raise a lot of avocados on twenty-nine and a half acres.

Rudy picked up the real estate agent at an office at the edge of town and they followed a farm-to-market road south till they came to a fork. The agent, whose name was Barney, indicated the right fork, pointing with his whole arm, his hand held flat, vertical, as if he were giving himself directions. Barney, whose car was in the shop, was too big for the little two-door Chevy Nova Rudy'd rented at the airport. His stomach rubbed against the dash, so that he had to spread out his knees and cross his feet over each other, and his head kept banging against the roof. He filled the silence with plans for golf courses, hospitals, retirement communities, condominiums — all the things Rudy was trying to get away from. "Highway 83's the longest main street in the US," Barney said. But what really bothered Rudy was that Barney seemed to have an instinctive understanding of what was driving Rudy himself: "It's a great thing to live on the land," Barney said.

"There's times of heartache and weariness, but there's times of great satisfaction too. Be your own man, your own boss, live your own life. See the sun come up in the morning, when everything's still. Listen to the birds. Go out into the grove at night, hear the trees grow, hear the fruit ripen. It's like you're part of nature, part of God's great plan of things." He spoke without turning toward Rudy, who was looking, in the rearview mirror, at the trail of dust they were leaving behind them.

Rudy had in fact felt some of these things, but he hadn't put them into words. The words made him uncomfortable. Made the whole thing seem sad and pathetic, like putting a panther in a dirty little cage. Pretty soon the poor thing gets dispirited and just lies there. Something like that had happened to Rudy. He was trying to recover the feeling that had led him to Texas in the first place, a feeling that he could only compare to the migratory bird business of Christmas Eve — spreading your wings, as if you *were* a bird preparing to take off and leave the world behind. His old life began to call out to him, to present itself to his imagination in warm, rich colors. Harry Becker had always treated him right. He'd miss the South Water Market with its big awnings, the fruit and vegetables piled up on the sloping sidewalks, the hum of the rollers, the chuffing of the big semis, the clatter of dice in Neumann's Market Bar. He'd miss his house too, the polished parquetry — scratched by the dogs but still beautiful — of the dining room floor, the porte cochere, the eyebrow windows, the balcony. And all the work he'd put into it: the new soil pipe, a downstairs bathroom, insulation, painting, the curved storm windows he'd framed himself for the bay window, and the bookcases he'd built in Helen's study; the Purington paving bricks in the patio, which Helen called a terrazzo, the grape arbor. *You'll never escape,* his old life seemed to say. *You're rooted in this house. It will shelter you and your children and your children's children.*

Love and work, that's what's here — your history, your past is embedded here. This is where you belong.

He was ready to turn around and head back when they came to a little trailer park — two rows of silver Airstreams, nestled together like cows in their stanchions.

"Winter Texans," Barney explained.

The park was protected by an army of yard ornaments: concrete statues of the Virgin Mary and St. Francis, birdbaths, big round reflecting balls supported on little pillars, rear-view cutouts of women bending over to tend their gardens and of old guys in straw hats taking a leak, pink flamingos, deer, a grotto sparkling with bits of colored glass. Just beyond the trailer park Rudy saw an elephant — not a concrete one but a real one — standing in front of a small pole barn and painting at an easel.

"Barney," he said. "Is that what I think it is?"

Barney nodded. "Norma Jean. Belongs to a Russian fellow. He brought it over from Mexico and taught it how to paint pictures."

Rudy said, "That's amazing, Barney. That's really astonishing."

Barney shrugged. "You can buy yourself a painting for twenty or thirty bucks. Depends on what size." He pointed to a stand by the side of the road, like a little vegetable stand. He looked at his watch. "Maybe on the way back. He sells postcards too, with a picture of Norma Jean painting. He used to take her over to the river market in Hidalgo on Saturdays and sell paintings there, but I don't know if he's still doing that."

Plato says that philosophy begins in wonder. Aristotle too. Had they ever seen an elephant painting?

The property was a small part of one of the old Spanish land grants, or *porciones,* a strip of land about three thousand feet wide that had once extended twelve miles inland from the river. The original *porciones,* which had been measured out on horseback by throwing a waxed rope, were narrow so that as many *rancheros* as possible could have access to the river. Creaky'd bought it from the Oblate Fathers, who'd raised cattle on it for a hundred and fifty years, and had laid out the grove himself.

Rudy had done business with Creaky for years and had talked to his wife, Maxine, dozens of times, before and after the accident that left Creaky a paraplegic, confined to the wheelchair that was still sitting in his study in the back of the house. An auto accident, ten years ago. A window in Creaky's study opened onto the upper grove. Maxine had described the avocado trees as "mature," and Rudy had been afraid he'd find that they were past their prime. But they were in good shape, topped off at twenty-five to thirty feet, nicely hedged. He sat at the dead man's desk with a cup of coffee, going over the records — irrigation, fertilization, crop production — that were kept in big cardboard boxes with orange backs. He'd seen boxes like that in lawyers' offices. These were labeled according to the avocado calendar in Texas: MARCH 1947–FEBRUARY 1948, MARCH 1948–FEBRUARY 1949, and so on. They were stored on gray metal shelves, the kind you expect to see holding old paint cans in the basement or the garage.

He could hear Maxine and Barney talking in the kitchen. Maxine, a gray-haired woman in her fifties, ten years younger than Creaky, kept coming in to fill up Rudy's cup. Barney had said she was considering several offers, but Rudy didn't believe him. She looked anxious, eager to sell. She was going to move to San Francisco to start a new life.

Rudy had done his homework. He'd studied the *Texas Avocado Growers Handbook* and gotten advice (much of it contradictory) from growers and shippers and brokers with whom he'd done business over the years. He'd brought a checklist with him and he went down the list item by item: parts per million of dissolved solids in the water supply, irrigation records, fertilization history, amount of allowable tip burn caused by the nitrogen in the fertilizer, production leaf analysis, chlorides and sodium in the irrigation water, the age and quality and type of irrigation system, the dollar returns per acre, market accessibility, labor, how much water necessary to leach the salts out of the soil. He'd gotten a soil profile and a history of low-register thermometer readings in the winter from the Soil Conservation Service of the USDA. Hasses and Fuertes won't grow in the Rio Grande Valley, but the Lula does well because it's salt tolerant. But neither the records of the grove, nor the Texas A&M Extension agent, nor the real estate agent, nor Creaky's widow could tell him what he really needed to know: *would he be happy here?* Would he find something final and self-sufficient? Aristotle's "supreme good," the end at which all actions aim?

He looked out the window. A tractor was pulling a wagon up a gentle slope; four men on ladders were snipping avocados with their avocado shears; the wagon disappeared into the trees. He put the boxes back in order on the shelves, right next to a big Latin dictionary, just like Helen's. Over the desk was an abstract painting that would have appealed to Helen. He'd never much cared for abstract art, but he liked this painting. The colors were too bright not to like it, the brushstrokes too strong, as if the painter had been mashing the brush into the paper. It wasn't signed, but he knew without asking that it was a Norma Jean.

The Texas A&M Extension agent was talking to the grove manager, Medardo, when Rudy came outside. He was pointing and gesturing. Barney and Rudy stepped down off the veranda and walked toward them, side by side. Barney was puffing. The agent, who'd been collecting soil samples with a tube, was speaking in Spanish. Rudy listened. They were talking about pH levels, which in the Rio Grande Valley were higher than they ought to be for avocados. As far as Rudy was concerned, the samples weren't necessary; he'd already felt the loose, loamy soil beneath his feet.

Maxine was in the kitchen making another pot of coffee. Rudy looked at his watch: 10:02. In fifteen minutes it would be sunset in Jerusalem. He gave a little laugh that came out like a hiccup. He wanted to make a joke about the Second Coming. He wanted to tell somebody, anybody, about the letter from his nephew, and about the radio program. But something stopped him, a counter-impulse. He turned and started to walk up the little hill where he'd seen the tractor disappear. "I got to take a leak," he said to Barney. He wanted to wait it out alone. Not that he thought anything was going to happen. Not that at all. But he wanted to think for a minute, by himself.

There were two groves, really, a lower grove and a smaller upper grove. The upper grove, about nine acres, was on the same "little hill" that had given the nearby mission its name, La Lomita. Creaky had his own five-horsepower pump to lift water from the lateral canal up to the sprinkling system. Rudy walked up the slope through the trees, which were loaded with fruit, even though Medardo's crew had been picking since late September. He was feeling sick and tired and hungover and uncertain, but when he came out of the dark grove into the sunlight, he thought once again of Plato's cave. The sun was so bright he could hardly see. The mesquite trees on the far side of the slope were covered with pale yellow spikes, and the ground was covered with yellowish pods. Through their airy foliage Rudy caught a glimpse of something shiny, a river, stretching from one horizon to the other, like a ribbon wrapped loosely around the earth.

A ribbon that hadn't been pulled tight, or that had worked itself free. He hadn't counted on this. The Rio Grande. This was the Rio Grande Valley after all. The Rio Grande was the source of the water in the irrigation canals. It was the reason he wasn't standing in the middle of a desert. But he hadn't counted on it adjoining the property. It wasn't like anything he'd ever seen. It was mud colored, but shining too, a smooth surface reflecting the bright sunlight. He seemed to see it not simply with his eyes, but with a more profound kind of vision that illuminated everything he looked upon. A slender, long-legged bird took to the air, crying *kip-kip-kip-kip* as it flapped its black-and-white wings to gain a purchase on the chilly air, and he was reminded once again of Socrates' comparison of the soul to a bird, for it seemed to him that the beauty he now beheld was a reminder of true beauty, and once again he had the sensation of sprouting wings. He was so overwhelmed that he forgot for a moment that he had to take a leak. He looked at his watch again: 10:12. If you were going to wait for the end of the world, where would you want to be? The radio hostess, Helen, had advised people to stay in their living rooms, but Rudy thought he'd found a better vantage place. He unzipped his pants and watered the ground, tracing a big *R*, for Rudy. 10:15. Two minutes. He watched the second hand on his watch, sweeping time before it, sweeping the seconds away, describing by its movement a mysterious dividing line between past and present. It was a long two minutes, like waiting for an egg to boil. What would it be like, Rudy wondered. The Second Coming, or a nuclear holocaust — which would be worse? He had forty seconds left to think about it. His mind suddenly started racing, traversing his whole life, his childhood: his dad jumping up on a truck to bid on a load of strawberries and then collapsing — dead of a heart attack before he hit the pavement; his high school graduation in the old school; the day the public library burned down, the morning of his wedding day, the births of his daughters, their first days of school, the day he and Helen signed the papers for the house, the night Helen died. And that only took up two seconds. He had thirty-eight seconds to go, an eternity. He started counting them — thirty-seven, thirty-six, thirty-five, thirty-four — but he was too impatient. He felt in his pocket for the keys to the rental car. They were there okay. His wallet was okay too, but it was too fat; there was too much junk in it. He took it out of his pocket and checked the hundred-dollar bill he'd folded up and stuck in the section behind his credit cards. Seven seconds to go. One thousand one, one thousand two, one thousand three, one thousand four, one thousand five, one thousand six, one thousand seven. Eight. Nine. Ten. He waited another minute, just to make sure, before heading back down the hill.

The adobe house was shaded by two large sugar hackberries with broad, spreading crowns. The extension agent, standing on the veranda on the south side of the house — which faced a large open area between an old gambrel horse barn and the garage — was jotting down something with a pencil on a pad of paper. The metal balustrades on the veranda, and those on the second-floor balcony, were painted dark green, like the trim on the narrow double-hung windows. Barney was lighting a cigar. Maxine Wilson was emptying her coffee cup over the balustrade. Rudy kicked a rock and they all looked at him, waiting for a sign. He shrugged. He didn't want them to know that he'd decided to make an offer on the property.

The River

Rudy closed on the grove on the sixteenth of March. After the closing, which took place in a lawyer's office in downtown Mission, he sat in the cab of the full-sized Ford pickup he'd bought from Maxine. (He'd given his old car to Molly.) He rolled the windows down and asked himself, *Now what?* And *What have I done?* Was it simply a bad case of buyer's remorse? It was three o'clock in the afternoon. He sat in the cab of the truck till four, watching people walk up and down Conway Avenue, the main north-south street: Mission Dry Goods, a furniture store, a movie theater, a bank, a tiny public library, a few homespun restaurants, a Rexall Drug Store, Spike's Motors. That was it. He shook his head, but he couldn't shake off the suspicion that he'd made a huge mistake. He didn't belong here; he was a Midwesterner; he should have stayed in Chicago. Seasick was the way he felt, as if he were on a ship pitching and rolling in the middle of the ocean. He was tempted to call the Robinsons, the new owners, to see if he could buy his old house back; tempted to call Becker and see if he could get his old job back. There were plenty of guys on the market like Plato's Thrasymachus, might-makes-right guys who didn't care how they jerked you around. But there were plenty of good guys too, honest men whose word was their bond. It had been a good life.

He was tempted to call the girls too, and say he was sorry. At the last minute they'd changed their minds about the sale. The house on Chambers Street was the place they'd always called home. Texas was too far away. What would they do about Thanksgiving? Christmas? Molly's wedding? Molly couldn't imagine getting married in Texas, and Meg had tried to buy the house herself, but she and Dan had just bought a house in Milwaukee and she couldn't talk Dan into relocating his medical practice. The two of them, Meg and Molly, had sat at the dining room table crying while they took down the chandelier — strings of Baccarat crystal ornaments hanging on the compass frame of an old Nantucket whaler — which had been excluded from the sale of the house. They'd barely been speaking to him, and they hadn't been especially pleasant to the people who'd come to look at the house. The dogs had growled too, as if they'd wanted to scare off prospective buyers, though they seemed to approve of the Robinsons, who had dogs of their own. Then the moving van didn't arrive on schedule. Rudy'd called the downtown office every half hour. It never did show up, and finally he had his stuff shipped in one of Becker's produce trucks.

And now, sitting in the cab of his pickup on Conway Avenue, he couldn't understand how he'd ignored or misread all these signs.

He bought a couple of blankets and a pillow at Mission Dry Goods. He'd checked out of the motel in the morning and was planning to sleep in the cab of the pickup till his furniture arrived.

He bought a loaf of bread and some sliced salami and a six-pack of Pearl beer at a small grocery store, Lopez Bros. All the avocados in the bins, he noticed, were Fuertes and Hasses from California. On the way home he stopped at the little trailer park, where a small crowd of winter Texans had gathered to watch the elephant paint. She stood at a heavy easel and painted with an assortment of brushes. Some of the larger brushes had special bent handles so she could hold them at the right angle. The smaller brushes she held right up inside her trunk. She wore a heavy metal anklet on her left hind leg. Rudy couldn't see that she was chained to anything, though there was a three-tiered electric fence surrounding the paddock behind her barn.

The winter Texans were getting ready to begin their annual migration back north and were there to buy paintings to take with them as presents. The paintings were on display in the stand by the road. Those on canvas were thirty dollars; the ones on heavy paper that could be rolled up and inserted into mailing tubes were twenty. There were also mailing boxes for the framed paintings, most of which were about two and a half feet by three feet. The titles were written on three-by-five cards and clipped to the upper right-hand corners of the paintings.

At four o'clock, Norma Jean finished a painting and her Russian owner led her back to the barn. The winter Texans looked through the paintings in the covered stand and made their selections while they waited for him to return. Rudy picked out a painting too — a swirl of bright colors — deep purples and greens and yellows that seemed to push up against the surface of the canvas. It was one of the thirty-dollar paintings: *Plum Blossom and Snow Competing for Spring.*

Rudy's new house had been built in the second decade of the century by a New England engineer who'd come to Texas to supervise the installation of the centrifugal pumps in the big pump house in Hidalgo and who'd stayed on to speculate in land and sugarcane. The double-hung sash windows in the living room still had glass panes that the engineer had brought with him from New England, but the original red roof tiles had been replaced with shingles, and Creaky and Maxine had converted a storeroom at the east end of the house into a big kitchen. Creaky's study, which had also served as his bedroom after the accident, opened onto the living room. All the doors on the first floor were extra wide to accommodate his wheelchair. The large downstairs bathroom was equipped with a whirlpool tub and an invalid's toilet on a pedestal, like a throne.

Rudy propped up *Plum Blossom and Snow Competing for Spring* on the counter next to the refrigerator and contemplated it as he ate a salami sandwich and drank a bottle of beer. What he knew about art he'd learned from Helen, because he'd seen all her slide lectures a dozen times and she'd quizzed him about what he'd seen, just the way she quizzed her students: Egyptian vs. Greek, Medieval vs. Renaissance, Mannerism vs. Baroque, Neoclassicism vs. Romanticism, Realism vs. Impressionism, Cubism vs. Surrealism. But he didn't always know what he liked. He'd depended on Helen for cues. She had a way of pointing out things that he hadn't noticed, like the way the Virgin Mary is holding her thumb in the book she's reading so she can get right back to it when the angel Gabriel is through telling her she's pregnant and that God is the father.

And he wondered about *Plum Blossom and Snow Competing for Spring*. Was it an accident? A blot? A Rorschach? Or was it a window on ultimate reality? On the Platonic forms? Probably an accident. Platonic Reality seemed to be receding into the distance, like a will-o'-the-wisp, no more meaningful, as Aristotle put it, than singing *la la la*. In any case, there were too many things in this world that required Rudy's immediate attention.

Rudy concealed his doubts and fears from Medardo, his grove manager, who pulled into the drive in the morning in a sky blue Buick Riviera and parked in front of the garage next to Rudy's pickup. The trees had been stripped in mid-March, before Rudy'd arrived, and Medardo had dressed the grove with nitrogen fertilizer. The new bud scales had separated and the trees were already starting to bloom. The avocados from the old harvest had belonged to Maxine, but Rudy wanted to go over all the records with Medardo, who also managed the little trailer park by the Russian's barn. Medardo was a good-looking man in his fifties whose springy mustache had been carefully trimmed to reveal his upper lip. He wore white linen trousers. Ringlets of curly black hair spilled over the collar of his pale yellow shirt.

Rudy knew from Barney, the real estate agent, that Medardo had been Maxine's lover for a time, after Creaky's accident, and had almost married her. In which case Medardo would now be the *patrón* and Rudy would be back in Chicago where he belonged. He wanted Medardo to know, however, that he was not a dumb city slicker, that he'd grown up on a farm and had thirty years' experience as a commission merchant under his belt, and that he would be keeping a sharp eye on everything — irrigation records, tree maintenance, weeding, fertilizer applications, yields, shipping records, labor costs. And *viernes culturales,* which Maxine had warned him about. "Cultural Fridays." What the hell were cultural Fridays? Maxine hadn't been very clear.

Rudy greeted him in Spanish, creating the impression that he spoke that language fluently, when in fact his high-school Spanish was limited to the indicative mood. They conversed in Spanish nonetheless, and Rudy learned what he wanted to know: that Medardo and a five-man crew had picked close to a million pounds of avocados last season.

He also wanted Medardo to know that he intended to open up a new market in Texas instead of relying so heavily on Becker in Chicago.

"Texas consumes more avocados than any state in the country," he said, "but if you walk into a supermarket all you find are California avocados."

Medardo agreed that it didn't make sense. But what was one to do? He shrugged his shoulders.

They were standing in Creaky's study, which was empty except for the metal shelves that held Creaky's grove records. Becker's produce truck hadn't arrived yet with Rudy's furniture.

"Something else that doesn't make sense," Rudy said, "are these *viernes culturales?* Cultural Fridays? You bring in guys from Texas A&M to give lectures?"

Medardo put his hand on Rudy's shoulder and explained. Once a month he took the boys — the pickers — across the border to Reynosa for a night on the town.

"And you expect me to pay for this?" Rudy said.

"You want to keep everybody happy, okay? You know what I mean?"

Rudy was determined to be firm with Medardo from the very beginning, to let him know who was boss, but he found it hard to be firm in a language he didn't know very well, and besides, the man was so handsome, his teeth so white, his smile so unforced, his animal spirits so contagious, his manner so generous, that Rudy couldn't bring himself to cancel the cultural Fridays.

"Yeah," Rudy said, "I know what you mean."

❖

Getting ready to live is easier than actually living, just as getting ready for a journey is easier than actually going on a journey. Rudy was anxious to get on with *Philosophy Made Simple,* but there was a lot to be done first. He replaced the uncomfortable invalid's toilet and seated a new one. He installed a shower. He bought a chain saw and, for the woodstove, cut up a couple of dead mesquite trees and a small ironwood tree that almost ruined the chain on his new Stihl saw. He slapped a new coat of calc on the thick adobe walls, and he arranged and rearranged the furniture when it finally arrived. There was no attic, no basement, no closets, but there were cabinets in the old tack room in the barn, where he stored his shotgun and fishing tackle, his Ampex tape recorder, Helen's slide projector, and the footlocker with his dad's magic stuff. He built bookcases in his study that had closed cabinets on the bottom, where he was going to put Helen's record collection, and five adjustable shelves on the top. He didn't have the pattern for Helen's Florentine curve, but he didn't need a pattern; that curve was fixed forever in his imagination. He drew it on a piece of cardboard and cut the top moldings by hand with his Japanese saw. He painted the bookcases forest green.

At the end of his third week in Texas, Rudy got Medardo, who'd stopped by on his way to Reynosa for a cultural Friday, to help him carry Helen's big post-office desk into the study and place it against the west wall so that he could look out the window at the upper grove and the rows of sabal palms that lined the drive.

They rolled out a threadbare Oriental rug that Helen had bought at an auction, and Rudy cracked open a couple bottles of

Pearl. Then he and Medardo unpacked the books and shelved them at random; Rudy didn't care. He could sort them out later. Right now he wanted to see what the room would look like full of books. It looked beautiful. The finishing touch was *Golden Flower and Jade Tree*, another Norma Jean, which Rudy hung between the two deep-set windows on the north wall. It was a beautiful room, a serious room where serious thinking could be done.

If Rudy and Medardo had been speaking English they would soon have exhausted their supply of conversation, but in Spanish things took time, and the beer and the fatigue made Rudy less self-conscious. In Spanish he was a different person — more relaxed, less impatient. Time slowed down in Spanish. A simple story about something that had happened on the market, which would take two minutes to tell in English, would take him fifteen minutes in Spanish. And there were topics he and Medardo would probably have avoided in English: Rudy's philosophical project or quest, for example. Rudy couldn't imagine giving an account of it in English, but in Spanish it seemed easy to explain to Medardo what he was trying to accomplish, as if he were spending Monopoly money instead of real money: to get some answers to the big questions, to settle on a rule of life. He drew a sketch of Plato's cave and showed it to Medardo, and he explained how he'd thought he'd caught glimpses of the realm outside the cave — on Christmas Eve and then again when he first glimpsed the Rio Grande.

Medardo examined the sketch of the cave. "These people in the cave," he said. "It's like they're sitting in a movie theater, right, or in front of the television set?"

Rudy nodded. "Something like that, but they're tied to their chairs, so they can't get up and look out the window."

"And you feel you were looking out the window? On Christmas Eve? And when you saw the river the first time?"

"That's what it felt like," Rudy said, "but Aristotle — Plato's star pupil — Aristotle made fun of Plato's ideal forms and said they were no more meaningful than singing *la la la*." He laughed. "*La la la*. That's very funny."

Medardo laughed too. "Señor 'arrington," he said, "Señor Aristotle was right about these glimpses of higher reality. You have to be careful. My cousin in Matamoros had a vision of the Virgin Mary, naked, and the bishop and a whole carload of priests came all the way from the cathedral in Monterrey. The church always investigates these things, you know, visions, miracles, things like that. They asked him all kinds of questions, and then they told him not to talk about it anymore."

Rudy opened two more beers. He could never be sure, in Spanish, when Medardo was pulling his leg.

"Do you think it was a vision?"

"I think he got his hands on a copy of *Playboy* magazine and it unsettled his brain."

"How about you, Medardo? Have you ever caught a glimpse of anything?"

Medardo leaned forward and put his hand on Rudy's arm. "Sometimes, señor, in the act of love . . ." He poured some beer in his glass and watched the foam rise and spill over the edge and run down the side. He wiped the side of the glass with a large white handkerchief. "Sometimes in the act of love I seem to *see* something, but then afterward, I think . . ." Medardo paused to light a cigarette. "Afterward I think I was only singing *la la la*."

Rudy found one of Helen's ashtrays in the desk and placed it on the arm of Medardo's chair. "My wife used to tell a story about Aristotle that you'd appreciate," he said. "When Aristotle was an old man he got a job as the tutor of Alexander the Great. He's giving young Alexander a hard time about his girlfriend, so Alexander gets his girlfriend, whose name is Phyllis, to dance naked right in front of Aristotle's window, where he's writing his book about ethics. Pretty soon Aristotle has such an *erección* he can't take it anymore and goes out and propositions Phyllis. Phyllis says sure, but she wants Aristotle to do her a little favor; she wants to play horsey — *jugar a caballo.*"

Medardo laughed. "What you want to say, Rudy, is *montar al caballito.*"

"*Montar al caballito,*" Rudy repeated. "In one of her lectures," he went on, "my wife used to show a slide of a medieval tapestry with a picture of Aristotle and Phyllis. Aristotle's wearing a bridle, and Phyllis is riding on his back, using a whip on the old man's bare rear end. Alexander's watching from behind a bush. You'd think Aristotle would be stuck. Here he is, caught with his pants down. But he was a smart old guy: 'If love can do this to an old man like me, a philosopher,' he says to Alexander, 'just think how dangerous it is for a young fellow like you.'"

The dean at Edgar Lee Masters had asked Helen not to show this particular slide, but Helen had ignored his request on the grounds that the slide was an integral part of her lecture on the iconography of education. *Iconography* was one of Helen's favorite words.

Medardo laughed. "It would make a wonderful *comedia,* don't you think? I'll play Alexander and you can play Aristotle, and we'll get one of the girls at Estrella Princesa to play Phyllis and ride on your back. What do you say? Ah, Rudy," he went on, without giving Rudy a chance to respond, "I hope your wife had many more stories like this one, but now I must be on my way." He smiled, revealing his large white teeth, and put his hand on Rudy's shoulder. "No, no, don't get up. I'll let myself out." He stood in the doorway for a moment. "Maybe you'd like to join me one of these days. When you get settled. For a *viernes cultural.*"

Aristotle's appetitive man, Rudy thought. "A man my age, Medardo," he said, blushing slightly. "I've put those things behind me."

"A man your age! Why, you're in the prime of life, Rudy. A man your age indeed." But Rudy waved him off and Medardo took his leave. Rudy could hear his footsteps in the passage that led to the kitchen, and then the sound of the door closing behind him, and then the sound of Medardo's car on the gravel in the drive.

No more meaningful than singing la la la, Rudy thought, *and isn't it better, after all, to follow Aristotle's advice and appreciate the wonder of the world around us, the wonder of ordinary experience, instead of wandering like Plato out to the edge of the universe in order to see what lies beyond?*

As he turned the pages, rereading the passages he'd underlined, he could feel Medardo's hand on his shoulder, strong and warm and human.

"*La la la,*" he sang, and laughed again.

Rudy was restless. He dug up a small garden next to the garage and put in lettuce, potatoes, a few tomato plants, some basil, some hot peppers, and then he made the garden bigger and planted broccoli and cauliflower, zucchini and cucumbers, more herbs. He wanted to plant arugula — Helen had been wild about arugula, which she'd tasted for the first time in Italy — but couldn't find any seeds. He bought a teach-yourself-Spanish book and a Spanish dictionary at a used bookstore in Mission, determined to master the conditional and the subjunctive. He walked across the international bridge to Reynosa three times in one week, on Monday, on Wednesday, and again on Friday, to practice his Spanish. On

Monday he ate a taquito at the Zaragoza market, surrounded by Mexican schoolgirls in their plaid uniforms; on Wednesday he ate the fixed-price *comida corrida* at Joe's Place — a run-down nightclub with pictures of William Burroughs and Jack Kerouac on the wall behind the bar — and on Friday he ate *cabrito* at a place called Casa Viejo, where the middle-aged waiters wore tuxedos. Rudy had hoped that raising avocados would be as enlightening, in its own way, as philosophy; he hoped it might teach him patience and wisdom. But it wasn't, and it didn't. The problem with avocados, Rudy discovered, was that they didn't make many demands on him. The Texas Lula doesn't have any natural predators and isn't subject to any diseases, so there was no need to spray. Most of the avocado growers also had citrus trees to keep them occupied, but all Rudy had to do from April to September was irrigate once a month. He spent some time on the phone with Harry Becker in Chicago, and with Nick Regiacorte, who handled avocados for the Graziano brothers at the Houston Produce Center. He paid visits to the Texas A&M Extension agent in Weslaco, who had put in a small experimental grove, and to the manager of the packing house in Hidalgo, who was going to ship his avocados. After that, there was no one to talk to except Medardo and the Russian, Norma Jean's owner, whose name he couldn't pronounce.

With Medardo he talked philosophy, trying to explain, in Spanish, whatever he'd been reading in *Philosophy Made Simple*. Medardo himself was a skeptic. Like Pyrrho, who'd served under Alexander the Great, he'd seen enough of the world to know that whatever people south of the border believed, the opposite would be believed by people north of the border. Rudy would always try to keep Medardo longer by offering him another bottle of Pearl, but Medardo would drink one beer and smoke one cigarette and then be on his way.

With the Russian he talked art, drawing on his memories of Helen's lectures. Rudy'd always preferred pictures that were pictures *of* something, and for the most part Helen had too — saints and popes and cardinals and naked women, horses and buildings and landscapes — but at the end of her life Helen had turned to abstract art — Jackson Pollock, Willem de Kooning, Mark Rothko — as if being free from pictures *of* something was liberating. At first the abstract paintings meant nothing to Rudy, but they seemed to open up for Helen a warm, silent space in which her spirit could rest, like a bird after a long flight, and that's what Rudy looked for in Norma Jean's paintings, a place to rest. But the paintings troubled him the same way the paintings that Helen kept returning to troubled him. Was there really something *there?* Was he looking at true Beauty or just at some paint splashed on a canvas?

The Russian could be found every afternoon in front of his little barn at the edge of Medardo's trailer park, sitting on a canvas chair while Norma Jean stood at her easel and painted. Rudy, who went into town every day to shop at Lopez Bros. Grocery and at a Lebanese deli in McAllen — to have daily contact with other people — would stop on his way home to watch. He bought several more paintings, and each time he bought one the Russian offered him a glass of vodka and they'd admire the new purchase together. The Russian had his own view of beauty: "Beauty is like death," he'd say, lifting his glass. "You can't understand it without vodka."

Rudy laughed. They were looking at a painting called *Ants Climbing a Tree.*

"Where do you get the titles?" he asked.

"I get them out of a Chinese cookbook."

"What happens when you get to the end of the book?"

"I just start over again. It take me about two years."

Afraid of chaos, afraid of disintegrating, Rudy spent a lot of time getting organized: kitchen, bathroom, bedroom, barn. He organized Helen's record albums on the lower shelves and then arranged and rearranged her books. There were art books, history books, a few novels, an edition of Shakespeare's plays, and the *Collected Poems of Robert Frost,* but there were also a lot of books that defied any kind of classification, even alphabetical order. What was he supposed to do with all the books on death that they'd bought at Kroch's & Brentano's when Helen got back from Italy? What was he supposed to do with *Woman's Day Home Decorating Ideas #1,* and with *Intimacy, Sensitivity, Sex, and the Art of Love,* in which the authors "explain the use of the 'bioloop,' the recently developed method of controlling mentally what had previously been thought of as autonomous bodily functions"? Where had these books come from?

When he'd finished arranging the books, he took up birding. His grove was located between the Santa Ana National Wildlife Refuge and the Bentsen–Rio Grande Valley State Park, right at the convergence of the Central and Mississippi flyways. Along the river in the morning, and again in the evening, the birds made a terrific racket. Rudy's mother had been a serious birder, a member of the Audubon Society who had over four hundred birds on her life list and who could imitate the sounds of dozens of birds. She participated in the Christmas Bird Count every year, and one fall she took Rudy with her to Michigan's Upper Peninsula to watch as thousands of migrating birds — raptors, waterbirds, songbirds — were funneled through a natural corridor to Whitefish Point. He'd started a life list of his own after the trip, but he hadn't kept it up.

He bought Peterson's *Field Guide to the Birds of Texas* and started a new list, getting up at four o'clock and heading over to the state park, a six-hundred-acre stand of subtropical vegetation only three miles upstream. Bentsen was home to almost three hundred documented species, and he soon had a list of seventy birds, but by sunrise every morning the trail that looped through the park was so crowded with birders searching for elusive "life birds" that he preferred to do his birding at home, sitting on the stump of an old mesquite tree that he'd cut up for firewood, near the spot where he'd waited for the Second Coming, and simply enjoying the society that presented itself to him: the great kiskadees that nested in the flowering mesquite trees and greeted him on his way to the river by calling out their name: *kis-ka-dee,* and the strange chickenlike chachalacas from Mexico who clattered like castanets; high-flying hook-billed kites, a pair of Harris's hawks, a family of least grebes who swam in Creaky's old swimming hole, a little cove carved out of the northern bank of the river; the belted kingfisher who guarded Rudy's stretch of shoreline, and the small green heron who crouched on the edge of the cove; the sandhill cranes who sometimes visited from the park. The kingfisher and the heron and the cranes, like other winter Texans, were getting ready to head north for the summer. The grebes and the kites and the hawks, like Rudy, would stay all year.

He was reluctant to call Meg and Molly too often because they were still angry. At least Meg was. She couldn't understand why he'd moved so far away from home. He wanted her to drive down with the dogs, but she didn't think it was a good idea. "They miss you, Pop. Just like the rest of us. But the kids love them." He figured she was holding them for ransom.

This was something new for Rudy. He'd never been at odds with his daughters before. He'd read all the articles in the Sunday papers about the problems that fathers had with their daughters, but he'd never experienced these problems firsthand. Oh, he'd had plenty of battles with the girls, especially when they were in high school, before Helen died, but they'd always been friends, that was the important thing, they'd always been good friends. He was beginning to look forward to Molly's wedding in August the way a child might begin looking forward to Christmas, even though it was only April, because he hoped it would mend the circle that had been broken. Molly and TJ were going to India in June, returning later in the summer. He wanted to put an end to this estrangement, which tugged at his heart, drew it down like a lead sinker on the end of a fishing line.

Early in the morning on the anniversary of Helen's death, April 22, Rudy was down by the river. As he turned to head back to the house, his arms aching pleasantly from the weight of his binoculars, he heard a distant trumpet blast. He thought it might be a whooping crane and his heart leaped up, but he scanned the horizon with his heavy binoculars in vain.

His fleeting experiences of beauty — and there were a lot of them — were so intense that they were painful rather than pleasurable. He couldn't figure out what to make of them. The birds, like Socrates' bird, reminded him of the soul, gazing upward and caring nothing for the world below. Norma Jean's paintings — there was one in every room now — opened like windows onto an uncharted inland sea. The Michelangelesque curves along the top of the bookcases stirred up an ache in him, like an old war wound, every time he took a book down off a shelf. Instead of becoming happy he became irritable and impatient. He lost his temper at material objects, as if he suspected that the universe was conspiring against him, playing tricks on him. He bumped into things in the dark, tripped over his shoes; he dropped things in the kitchen; he spilled his wine at dinner; the plastic garbage sacks tore when he tried to pull them out of the trash container he'd bought for the kitchen.

He was mildly depressed in the evening, not hungry at all, but he fixed a small panfried steak with a sauce made with garlic and balsamic vinegar. Fussing over food was important. It gave a shape to the day: breakfast, lunch, dinner; beginning, middle, end. He ate a Bosc pear for dessert and did the dishes. When the dishes were done, he sat at the kitchen table with a glass of Chianti and looked through his *Peterson's Guide*. According to the guide, the whooping cranes, or "whoopers" — there were only ninety-six of them left — would have departed in March on their annual migration to the Arctic Circle, so he'd probably been mistaken. But he browsed through the *Guide* anyway. None of the other birds in the valley made a "trumpetlike call." He was still looking through the guide when Meg called from Chicago. She'd just taken some flowers to Helen's grave in the southeast corner of Graceland Cemetery, far from the Fields and the Pullmans and the Potter Palmers, and was weepy as she remembered how her mother had mended her favorite dress after she'd torn it on a nail on the back porch, and how she'd never really thanked her properly, and so on. She'd been seeing a shrink, she said, who was helping her understand some things about her family. She didn't say what they were, and Rudy didn't ask. *You're only as happy as your unhappiest child*, he thought. And the pain he felt for his oldest daughter was like the longing he'd felt that morning when he'd heard the whooping crane, if it had been a whooping crane. He didn't know what to make of it.

He poured another glass of wine and sat for a while in the

dark, and then he went into his study. What he wanted to do now, he thought, was just lie low, "live unknown," as Epicurus advised. He'd wanted to make enough money to leave something for the girls, but maybe that wasn't important. He'd wanted answers to the big questions, but maybe that wasn't important either. Maybe what was important was just to live simply, to acknowledge one's insignificance in the larger scheme of things, to acknowledge no authority higher than reason and to subject one's emotions to this authority without complaining.

But he couldn't do it. *You're only as happy as your unhappiest child.*

He sat at Helen's desk and tried to sort out his thoughts. *Live unknown,* he wrote. He filled an entire page of the journal he'd bought to keep track of his progress. The ink flowed smoothly from Helen's eighteen-karat-gold nib: *Live unknown, Live unknown, Live unknown.* Then he put his head down on the desk for a minute, and when he woke with a start, the pen was gone. He felt a familiar sinking feeling, an athlete sensing defeat. He looked on the desk, examined every square inch of the sloping surface. He looked on the floor. He did a grid search of the floor, starting in the back corner under the desk and moving outward, past the wide door that opened into the bathroom, all the way to the opposite wall. He listened in his imagination for the sound of the pen rolling down the sloping surface of the desk and then hitting the floor. But he heard nothing. The pen was gone.

He looked everywhere. In his pockets. In the desk drawers. But he was very tired. The pen was gone. If Helen had been there, he could have called to her, and she'd have been able to tell him where to look without even coming into the room. She'd have known right where the pen was. But Helen wasn't there, and the sense that the universe was conspiring against him returned more strongly than ever. He experienced a surge of anger.

Why do you do this to me? he shouted inwardly. *Why?*

And in his imagination a voice responded, *No one is doing any-thing to you.* He recognized the voice of Epicurus, the voice of reason. *You've misplaced the pen, that's all.*

I haven't misplaced it, it's just gone. I've looked everywhere.

You're too tired to think straight. There's no point in getting angry.

I searched every square inch of the floor. I did a grid search. Do you know what a grid search is?

Well then, what do you think happened? Do you think the atoms that constitute the pen suddenly dissolved into other forms? That will happen eventually, but do you think it happened in the few minutes that you dozed off?

Rudy was reluctant to say it, but he really had no choice: *No.*

Very well, then, now go to bed.

Rudy acknowledged defeat, but he was too upset to go to bed. In the kitchen he poured himself a small glass of wine which he carried up the tractor path between two rows of trees.

The trees were in full bloom, so the grove was dark. It was a cloudless night and the moon was full and once he got to the top of the hill he had no trouble finding his way down to the little backwater or inlet — it looked like the head of an upside-down duck on the plat map he'd taped up on the wall in his study — where Creaky and Maxine used to swim, before the accident. There was only a trace now of the opening that Creaky had once cut in the dense chaparral that bordered the river. Helen would have loved to swim here. She loved to swim at night. The girls too. Rudy took off his shoes and shirt and pants and went down the bank. The chaparral was tough, tangled and thorny, but he managed to squeeze between two skeleton bushes and ease himself carefully into the cool water, water that had traveled all the way from the San Juan Mountains in Colorado. He was still holding his wineglass. *"If I was a headlight,"* he sang, softly, *"on some northbound train, I'd shine my light, on cool Colorado Springs."* He tossed the rest of the wine into the river and set the glass down on the bank. The drop-off was less than two feet. He walked out toward the main channel till he could feel the current, stronger than he'd expected, tugging at him. He started to turn around, but an inner voice — not the voice he'd heard earlier, the voice of reason, but a different voice — encouraged him to let go, and he did let go, leaned backward till he was floating. He could steer himself with his hands, and by raising his head from time to time — he was floating feetfirst — he could see where he was going, but he didn't care where he was going, and most of the time he looked up at the sky. On his left the North Star was a little lower than it was at home, and he couldn't locate Cassiopeia, which must have dipped below the horizon. The mesquite trees on the bank behind him were black shadows twisting in the moonlight. A barn owl coasted overhead. Silent. Something stirred in the brush, a bobcat or a peccary or a night heron. Mosquitoes hummed and bit his arms and neck, but the humming and biting didn't bother him. Had it been like this for Helen at the end? Being bitten by mosquitoes as you floated down a river? Is this what she'd wanted to tell him? But she hadn't wanted anyone to listen to the tapes she'd recorded, not while she was still alive.

It took him half an hour to reach the little mission chapel. From his position on his back in the river he could see just the tip of the steeple, but for the most part he gazed upward at the constellations. Rudy knew his constellations, because each one of his daughters had done a science project on them and they'd spent hours lying on their backs in the middle of the Edgar Lee Masters campus looking up at the sky. As the river bent to the south, he could see Virgo and Centaurus coming into view. At first they reminded him of true beauty, and he was overwhelmed. He knew that this heart-piercing ache, however painful, was the central experience of his life and that he would have to come to terms with it. No one — not Aristotle, not Epicurus, not Siva Singh — would ever convince him otherwise. But then it occurred to him that Virgo and Centaurus were just as arbitrary as the rudimentary classification system he'd used for his books — Helen's books. There were a lot of stars left out of the constellations, and nothing to stop you from drawing the lines in different ways to create different pictures. He wanted to lift his wings and fly, but he didn't have the power. He could only let the river carry him along.

In another half hour he reached Pepe's tavern, just before Anzalduas Park. He could hear the noise of drunken laughter before he could see the lights. *Aristotle's appetitive men,* he thought. *Appetitive women too, Plato's beasts, butting each other and feeding at a trough.* He remained quiet, afraid that someone might take a potshot at him if he made any noise. He rounded a bend, floated past the tables and lights on a small dock that stuck out into the river. The lights disappeared; the sounds of laughter grew fainter.

If he'd done nothing to stop himself, would he have floated all the way to the international bridge at Hidalgo? Or all the way to Brownsville and out into the Gulf? Probably not, but he didn't find out because he started to experience pains in his chest, as if someone had placed a weight on it and was twisting his left arm at the same time. He called out, no longer worried about getting shot, but he didn't think anyone could hear him. He turned over and tried to swim back to Pepe's, using an easy crawl, but the river, instead of holding him up, now seemed to be trying to pull him down. He could see the lights of the tavern, but he couldn't make any headway. After about five minutes the pain eased up and he was able to swim a little faster than the current that was carrying him downstream. As he approached the dock he called out "Help, help" and then "Hello, hello."

A handful of patrons gathered at the end of the dock, which bobbed up and down.

"Are you okay?" a woman shouted drunkenly. "Where are you? I can't see you."

"I don't have any clothes on," Rudy shouted back. "Would somebody bring me some clothes or a towel, please."

"This ain't a haberdashery." Laughter.

"I'm not armed," Rudy shouted.

"What are you doing in the river?"

"I lost my fountain pen," he shouted. "It belonged to my wife. She brought it back from Italy."

"Oh. You'd better come up on the dock," the voice said; "the ladder's over here, on the side."

Rudy swam up to the dock, which was strung with lights that looked like little red chili peppers. Hands reached out to help him, pulling him up. A towel appeared and then a glass of tequila.

"Say," someone said, "aren't you the guy that bought Creaky Wilson's place?"

"Did you find your pen?" someone else asked — a man dressed like a priest.

"Yes," Rudy said, taking the small glass of tequila, "I'm the guy. And no, I didn't, but it's all right. It'll turn up."

They helped him to a chair. Someone put some money in the

jukebox and a mariachi band began to play a soulful rendition of "Viva el Amor."

Rudy finished his tequila and chased it with sangrita, and then the man dressed like a priest drove him home.

"You want me to take you to the hospital?" the man said.

"No," Rudy said, "I'm all right now."

Irrigation

The idea that he might be dreaming when he thought he was awake had occurred to Rudy before — it's probably occurred to everyone — but he couldn't get too worked up about it personally. The possibility that the glass of red wine he'd drunk with his spaghetti the night before had been an illusion put into his head by an evil demon seemed equally remote, but the more he thought about it, the more he began to see that the French philosopher René Descartes might be right — at least about his "glimpses," as he'd started calling his visions. The front window on the house on Chambers Street wasn't a mysterious triptych; he wasn't a migratory bird; the river wasn't the river of Jordan. What had made him so sure it was time to move on and leave his old life behind? Besides, in the spring, migratory birds migrate back north.

It was the last week in April and already the temperature was in the eighties. You couldn't see any fruits yet — not till June —

but the trees were covered with beautiful blossoms and seemed to be fully committed to producing an excellent crop. It was time to irrigate. Medardo stopped by on Monday morning to say that he'd talked to the canal rider and that their water would be ready on Thursday. Rudy was glad to have something concrete to do. He'd been embarrassed about floating down the river, but in fact this little escapade had raised him in Medardo's estimation, and Medardo suggested that they drop the formal *usted* and address each other as *tú*. After Medardo left, Rudy went into town to buy a water permit.

On Thursday morning he waited for Medardo on the veranda, drinking coffee and doodling another sketch of Plato's cave with Helen's fountain pen, which he'd found folded into *Philosophy Made Simple*. It was seven o'clock. It would take almost twenty-four hours to irrigate the entire grove.

"Señor Filósofo," Medardo called to him from the drive to the veranda. "Any words of wisdom this morning before we go to work?"

Rudy smiled. "No," he said, "but I'm looking forward to getting my hands dirty. Finally." He didn't want to sound *too* excited as they walked down the drive to the lateral canal, but he didn't want to conceal his excitement either.

The water was lifted out of the Rio Grande at a series of pumping stations, like the one in Hidalgo, which he had visited. From the pumping stations it was released into the network of canals that irrigate the valley, which was not really a valley but a delta. The main canals carried the water as far as Alton and Edinburg, ten miles to the north, and the lateral canals, like the one that ran along the farm-to-market road at the north end of Rudy's property, carried the water east all the way to the Gulf.

It was seven thirty when they opened the gate at the lateral canal, but one of the seals on the pump that lifted the water to the upper grove was leaking and they had to close the gate and go into town to find a new seal. By the time they'd replaced the seal and opened the first two valves, at the edge of the grove, it was two o'clock in the afternoon. They opened the gate again and walked along the rows of trees to check the microsprinklers that were located under the canopy of each tree, and then Rudy fixed sandwiches and they drank beer on the veranda.

There were 110 avocado trees on an acre. Twenty-nine and a half acres times 110 equals 3,245 trees. Minus the skips, of course — trees that had died or stopped producing. One valve could irrigate 110 trees in an hour and a half in the upper grove, where the water was forced through a series of microsprinklers. One valve could irrigate two hundred trees in the same amount of time in the lower grove, which used a gravity system. You could open two valves at a time. Rudy couldn't figure it out in his head, but it took them five hours to irrigate the upper grove. Rudy fixed more sandwiches and they drank more beer on the veranda before going back to work.

They worked through the night opening and closing the individual valves that fed each row of trees. Each valve had its own personality, its own quirks. Medardo was familiar with them all. Some yielded to slow steady pressure, some to the tap of a rubber mallet. Some required a special wrench. A couple of the oldest valves (which should have been replaced long ago) turned clockwise, instead of counterclockwise, to open. They walked the rows of trees to check the aluminum irrigation pipes for leaks.

As they came up to the last valve, Medardo had to take a leak. Rudy fitted the wrench over the spoke of the valve wheel and struggled to open the valve by himself, but it was stubborn. Rudy strained too hard — he didn't want Medardo to think he couldn't manage it — and suddenly he felt as if he were being strangled. His chest tightened up like a fist, tighter than it had been when the river had taken hold of him, and he had to hang on to the valve so he wouldn't fall down. He could hear Medardo peeing in the dark, heard him zip up, like someone striking a match.

In spite of the pain, Rudy tried once more to open the valve, but it wouldn't budge.

"You're turning it the wrong way," Medardo said, shining his flashlight on the valve. "This is one of the old ones I was telling you about. You have to turn it clockwise."

Rudy let go of the wrench and lowered himself to the ground.

"You all right, Rudy?"

"Just short of breath."

Medardo turned the valve clockwise, and it opened easily.

"Medardo," Rudy said, "maybe that's what I've been doing all along, trying to turn the valves the wrong way."

"All along since when?"

"I don't know. Maybe since my wife died."

"Rudy," Medardo said, "you want to know what I think?"

Rudy nodded.

"I think you spend too much time worrying about what things *mean,* about the meaning of life. It's not good for a person. Now I'm going to speak to you as a friend."

"Of course."

"You asked me about the *viernes culturales,* do you remember?"

"Yes, I remember."

"And I invited you to join me. Now I invite you again. Next Friday, what do you say?"

"To a whorehouse in Reynosa?"

"A whorehouse? No no no. Not the Lipstick or the Tropicana, where I send the boys. Of course not. A man like you doesn't go to a whorehouse and pick a woman out of a lineup. No no no, nothing like that. I'm talking about a private club. At Estrella Princesa there is no lineup. At Estrella Princesa a man will always meet someone he knows — an uncle, a cousin, a friend. He can sit in a comfortable chair and have a drink and talk politics like a gentleman with a little *amiguita* at his side. It's all very civilized. And the women . . . These are not hardened professionals, señor; they're serious young women, very beautiful too, who wish to become dental hygienists or secretaries or even assist at the university. They are especially trained, of course, by Estrella herself. She teaches them how to shop, what clothes to wear, what books to read. They'll know how to help you out of your cave. And as the sun comes up, we'll sip tequila and weep at the sad songs sung by the mariachis who come over from the Plaza Morelos. What do you say?"

Rudy realized that this was not just a casual proposal but a special invitation that probably wouldn't be offered a third time, and he couldn't say that it didn't appeal to him. Beautiful young women, trained by Estrella herself. But he couldn't imagine his way, couldn't imagine himself walking into Estrella Princesa, talking politics, trying to explain American foreign policy to somebody's uncle with a little *amiguita* at his side. What was Medardo thinking of? It was out of the question. But how to decline? How to explain to Medardo that the senses *are* the cave?

"Think about it, señor. Consider. Your books . . . Plato, Aristotle. They cannot explain everything. You have to live."

Rudy wondered about Medardo's affair with Maxine Wilson. He couldn't imagine asking in English, but he felt free to ask in Spanish.

Medardo put his hand over his heart. "A man has one great love in his life, and she was mine. I confess this to you, and to you alone," he said. "She was a remarkable woman, a beautiful woman, and after Creaky's accident . . . It was a terrible thing, to be paralyzed like that. He could move only one arm, you know, just enough to use his special phone and manipulate the control of his electric wheelchair, and to smoke. He smoked all day. He had a clothespin that hooked onto the sleeve of his shirt, and Maxine'd light a cigarette for him and put it in the clothespin. She hated cigarettes and tried to get him to quit, but it was the only pleasure he had left." Medardo paused to light a cigarette. "Love is a strange thing, Rudy," he said. "It was not a matter of choice. You *norteamericanos* think that love is the source of security and peace and happiness, but in reality it is a source of suffering and anxiety. I was completely vulnerable. I even quit smoking for a while myself. It was a torture."

Rudy pictured the middle-aged, graying woman who'd shown him Creaky's files the first time he'd come to Texas, and who'd sat across from him in the lawyer's office at the closing, signing the papers with a ballpoint pen. "I'm sorry," he said.

"Your philosophers, Rudy," Medardo said, "what do they know about love and suffering?"

"Well," Rudy said, "I don't know about love, but Socrates was executed; and Aristotle had to leave Athens or he would have been executed too."

"Really? Executed? Philosophers? Why would they execute philosophers?"

"I guess they asked too many questions."

"Ah, Rudy," he said, dropping his cigarette and stamping it out in the sandy soil, "maybe you'd better be careful, no?"

"I don't think I'll be executed," Rudy said. "Not for a while, anyway."

Medardo stepped forward and gave Rudy a proper Mexican *abrazo*. It took a bit of doing to get the *abrazo* right — like learning to use his Japanese saw, or getting the curves just right for

Helen's bookcases — but in the end Rudy's right arm went over Medardo's left, his left under Medardo's right, and they tilted their heads to the left and administered a series of *palmadas*, little pats on the back, as if they were burping babies, an ancient and powerful means of expressing kinship and love, joy and comfort.

◊

What sorts of things did Medardo get up to at Estrella Princesa? Rudy had a vision of himself as Aristotle, bare-assed with some bare-assed whore riding on his back, while Medardo, like Alexander, watched from behind a bush. No, thank you. But he remained a little uneasy, nonetheless, about Medardo's invitation, which he had neither accepted nor declined. He felt that Medardo had been a little disappointed in him, and so he was trying to work out an explanation, trying to articulate the things he should have said on Wednesday night when they were irrigating. But what should he have said?

Rudy noodled his explanation all day Thursday and all day Friday, but when Medardo stopped by he had trouble putting his thoughts into words. "*Querido* Medardo," he said. "Forgive me, but my love for my wife was quite a different thing from what you propose. The pleasure you enjoy at Estrella Princesa is only a rough sketch of true pleasure, like my drawing of Plato's cave. It is mixed with pain. Only when your soul follows wisdom do you find true pleasure. Most men live like brute animals. They look down and stoop over the ground; they poke their noses under the table; they kick and butt each other with their horns and hooves because they want these animal pleasures. True happiness is only when the soul acts in harmony with virtue."

Medardo smiled. "So," he said, "you don't want to go?"

Rudy shook his head.

"The trees look good," Medardo said. "Did you notice how the leaves are opening up? They were starting to curl before we irrigated. Just a little. You have to know what to look for. Now they're fine." He waved from the window of his Buick Riviera as he drove off. In the late-afternoon sun his car looked black rather than sky blue.

A week later Rudy had a heart attack. If Norma Jean hadn't picked him up and laid him in the back of his truck, and if the Russian hadn't driven him to the hospital in McAllen, the date on his tombstone would have read May 3, 1967. And he wouldn't have cared.

He'd eaten a fiery chicken vindaloo at an Indian restaurant in McAllen, the Taj Mahal, and had spoken to the manager about catering Molly's wedding. He'd been prompted by a call from Molly, who'd found a hotel in Detroit that offered an assortment of Indian wedding packages.

Rudy was annoyed. "Are you trying to punish me?"

"Punish you? Papa, we just thought it would be easier for everyone. TJ's relatives live in Detroit. Our friends are in Ann Arbor. It just makes sense. All you'd have to do is show up. With your checkbook. The hotel will need a deposit fairly soon."

"It doesn't make sense to *me*," Rudy said, "and I'm the one with the checkbook."

"Just think about it, that's all."

"I've already thought about it," he said.

"Well then," she said, "suit yourself."

The manager of the Taj Mahal had been very accommodating, and had given him the business card of a pandit, a Hindu priest, who ran a small ashram near Bentsen State Park. Rudy studied the card:

Pandit Sathyasiva Bhagvanulu
WEDDINGS, FUNERALS, HOROSCOPES, PUJAS

"Is this the guy who's getting rid of the crows?" Rudy asked.

"Yes, he is a very remarkable man."

"I read about him in the *Monitor*," Rudy said.

"Precisely. I have a copy of the article in my office if you'd like to see it again."

Thousands of crows had been gathering in the downtown area, nesting in the trees, fouling the sidewalks and the car lots along Highway 83. The city had tried everything, including bringing in a falconer, but nothing had worked. The crows had mobbed the falcons, which had then refused to fly. Now the city had employed the pandit. The pandit refused to explain how he proposed to get rid of the crows — except to say that he wouldn't kill them; and he wouldn't allow anyone to observe him. This secrecy prompted people to watch for him, and various sightings were reported — in a car lot on Highway 83, on the municipal golf course, walking along the Mission Main Canal just north of the second lifting station — as if he were a rare bird, and in his bright robe, according to the article in the *Monitor,* he did look rather like a flamingo. There was a photo of him in the paper looking up at a dozen or so crows perched on telephone wires. The crows dispersed during the day to forage but gathered in the city in the evening, darkening the skies.

The manager also produced a scrapbook with photos of a number of Indian weddings he'd catered, one of which included, in addition to the photographs of the different dishes, several photos of an elephant that was all dolled up with costume jewelry and velvet trappings. In the background was a citrus grove.

"This is Norma Jean, right?" Rudy asked.

"Precisely." The manager shook his head up and down vigorously. "She is a very fine animal, very fine, very beautifully shaped, very well behaved. She did not cause one bit of concern. There were two hundred guests at this particular wedding, and we took care of everything. You won't need to be concerned at all."

Rudy spent most of the afternoon with the manager, drinking sweet tea and planning a menu that included tangy lentil soups, spicy vegetable curries, baked spiced fish, cucumbers in yogurt, hot bitter mango and sour lime chutneys, and platters of aromatic rice tinged with saffron. And the chicken vindaloo that Rudy had eaten for lunch.

It was almost five o'clock when Rudy left the restaurant. He drove straight to the Russian's to have a shot of vodka and chew the fat, and to buy three more paintings, one for each of the girls, and to see if Norma Jean would like to be in another wedding. The Russian was giving Norma Jean a bath outside her little barn when Rudy pulled into the drive. A portable radio was blasting the Beatles' new album, *Sgt. Pepper*, and Norma Jean was dipping her trunk into a big horse trough, sucking up water and then spraying herself so thoroughly that sheets of water covered her shoulders and flowed down her sides and onto the Russian, who was on his knees, scrubbing her stomach with a large brush. She had her eyes closed, and the Russian was doubled up underneath her, so they didn't see Rudy. Norma Jean struck Rudy as a being from the beginning of time, or maybe outside of time, like a Platonic idea, but at the same time he had the impression that he had intruded upon an especially intimate scene, as if he had intruded on a husband and wife in the privacy of their own bathroom. *This is happiness,* he thought as he watched the Russian scrub the big brush back and forth on Norma Jean's stomach.

He was about to clear his throat to announce his presence when a sharp pain in his chest took his breath away, as if he'd taken a bullet, or as if Norma Jean had sat on him. He opened the door and staggered out of the truck. He tried to hold himself up by putting his right arm through the open window, but he fell, belching loudly as he hit the ground. And then he was trying to tell the Russian, who was kneeling over him, that he just needed to lie still for a while, right there on the ground. He got his breath back for a minute; the clenched fist opened up. That's when he realized something else: that he didn't mind dying, didn't care, didn't give a hoot, as his dad used to say. He'd been a little frightened at first, but once the pain let up he didn't care one way or the other. He wondered if that was how Creaky'd felt. Or Helen. He just didn't want to die in Texas, that was all. He just wanted to go home.

He passed out again, and when he woke up in the Rio Grande Regional Hospital in McAllen, what he thought he remembered was the Russian lifting up his shoulders so that Norma Jean could slip her trunk underneath him and pick him up and lay him down gently in the bed of the pickup.

He tried to explain to the doctor the next morning: about trying to swim against the current in the Rio Grande, about straining to turn the valve that opened clockwise instead of counterclockwise, about the chicken vindaloo he'd eaten for lunch at the Taj Mahal, about the sensation of being shot in the chest, about the importance of the wedding . . . But the doctor wasn't listening. "You're lucky to be alive," he said. "You're lucky we've got one of the first CCUs in Texas."

"What's a CCU?"

"Coronary care unit."

"What's the diagnosis?" Rudy asked.

"Myocardial infarction."

"Why can't you just say 'heart attack'?"

"Because your heart didn't 'attack' you," the doctor said. "I'm going to give you a prescription for an oral arrhythmic and nitro-glycerin tablets."

"What's 'infarction'?"

"It's a blockage. Your heart's not getting enough blood. If you exert yourself too much, or get too worked up, especially after a heavy meal, then boom, you'll find yourself lying on the ground again. Your blood pressure will shoot way, way up and you'll de-velop diastolic hypertension."

"Avocados are supposed to reduce the risk of heart attacks," Rudy said. "Cancer too, and diabetes."

The doctor looked at him over the top of his glasses. "You need to watch your diet," he said. "No smoking. No alcohol. No rich foods — and that includes avocados. You don't want to clog up those arteries: no bacon, no sausage, no eggs, no butter, no cream, no driving for at least a month. The main thing is to keep calm. No emotional excitement. No conjugal relations."

"No conjugal relations?" Rudy said. "I'm not married."

"You're wearing a ring."

"I *was* married."

"You know what I mean," he said.

"What about the nitrogen fertilizer?" Rudy asked. "Could that have something to do with it? We got a couple of sacks of nitro-gen fertilizer in the barn left over from last winter."

The doctor shook his head while he wrote something on his clipboard. "You're barking up the wrong tree," he said.

Rudy didn't say anything. He didn't *like* hospitals — who does? — but he'd never really *minded* them. He'd had his tonsils out, and he'd been hospitalized once for pneumonia. He'd never particularly minded the dentist either. You went with your mother; you looked at a magazine. And whatever was wrong was taken care of. He hadn't even minded the shots, not the way his daughters had. In his arm or in his butt, it didn't matter. The doctor's office in St. Joe had been right in the doctor's house, and on their way home Rudy and his mother would stop at the drugstore in Stevensville to pick up a prescription and Rudy would order a cherry phosphate. His mother would have something too. It was hard to remember. He did remember spinning round on a stool. But then when Helen got sick . . . it was different. In and out of the Passavant Pavilion at Northwestern Memorial Hospital on Huron Street, right on the Gold Coast. Dr. Arnold in his office saying there was nothing more they could do. Helen had smoked for years, but it wasn't lung cancer that killed her. It was leukemia — attacking her lymph nodes, liver, spleen. She took a kind of perverse pleasure in that. At least they — Rudy and the girls — couldn't say "we told you so."

"And if I don't?" Rudy asked the doctor — back in Texas now. What did he care? He hadn't had a cigarette in ten years; he drank a glass of wine or two with dinner, it's true, but whom was he going to have conjugal relations with — he hadn't been with a woman since Helen died — unless he went with Medardo to Reynosa? Actually, he'd started to consider it. Rudy and Medardo: a couple of cockhounds, a couple of whoremasters. Better to die across the border in a whorehouse than in Texas.

"Don't what?" the doctor asked.

"Don't follow your advice."

"Your next one will be a lot worse," the doctor said.

"I'll think about it."

"You have to realize, Mr. Harrington, that dying is not like going to sleep. Very few people die with dignity. Five percent at most. For most people it's a painful struggle."

Rudy's father had died of a heart attack at the Benton Harbor market, keeled over while he was bidding on a load of strawberries, but his mother had died at home. There'd been a lot of coming and going, a lot of eating and drinking, even a bottle of whiskey, though his mother had been a member of the Women's Christian Temperance Union. But it was Helen he was thinking about now, how her body had shut down so that she no longer needed the morphine, how her breathing had slowed, how her lower jaw had jutted forward, how she'd slept with her eyes open because there wasn't enough strength in her muscles to hold her eyelids shut. There hadn't been much left of her at the end, and what was left had turned white. She'd lost her hair and looked like a marble statue or pillar in a museum. Rudy remembered the phone next to the bed ringing and ringing, though it was the middle of the night, and Margot coming into the room. She was working for a bookbinder in Hyde Park, on the South Side, just before she got a job at the Newberry Library. A boatload of black-market avocados — enough avocados to supply the entire Midwest — had left the Cayman Islands without the bill of lading, something that didn't seem important at the time, though it caused him a lot of grief when it docked in Hammond, Indiana, and he was almost arrested.

Rudy was inclined to argue with the doctor, calling him Doc: "A heart attack, Doc. A massive coronary. Bingo. That's it. Lights out. Doesn't sound too bad to me."

"If the lights don't go all the way out," the doctor said, "then you may run into some problems."

"What's the worst that could happen?" Rudy asked.

"The worst? You could wind up on a respirator, or paralyzed."

"I'd rather be dead."

"Suit yourself," the doctor said.

"That's what I used to say to my daughters," Rudy said.

❖

Rudy didn't mind dying; he just didn't want to die all alone. In Texas. He wanted to die in Chicago, in his own bed, with the dogs snoozing on the floor and the sound of his daughters moving around downstairs, or climbing the stairs to bring him a cup of tea or bouillon. The certainty that he'd made a mistake returned, washing over him, like a big wave, suffocating him. He didn't see how he could go on. The prospect of arranging an Indian wedding . . . The thing was impossible. All the talk of curries and chutneys and the elephant had been an illusion, a harmless fantasy. Better to let Molly arrange things with the hotel in Detroit. He lay back in the hospital bed and recited a litany of all the ancestors and relatives whose names he could remember and of the names of all the men he'd known on the market, and he tried to remember the street addresses and phone numbers of all the places he'd ever lived and of all the places his children had ever lived and of all the places he and Helen had made love.

Last Will & Testament

On Sunday morning — Rudy's second morning in the hospital — he woke up with a hard-on, not just a morning erection but the kind of pulsating ache that had visited him on Christmas Eve. When the nurse came in to give him a shot of lidocaine his prick was sticking out so straight he could hardly turn over on the bed. When he did manage to turn over he saw that Medardo'd brought a pair of pajamas and his dopp kit and his copy of *Philosophy Made Simple,* which he'd asked for on Saturday. Rudy was going to be in the hospital for a week and wanted something to read.

The nurse lifted his hospital gown and swabbed his left buttock with a bit of alcohol and put a bandage on it. "I'll be back this afternoon," she said.

What did it mean? What was his prick trying to tell him? What Rudy thought it was trying to tell him was this: he thought that his prick was mocking his condition; he thought that his prick was telling him that he'd never hold a woman in his arms again. He'd known that this might be the case ever since Helen died, but suddenly he knew it in a new way, and his chest tightened up and he thought he might be having another heart attack.

He closed his eyes, and when he did, he pictured the nurse coming back to give him another shot, only she was younger, and she was beautiful, and instead of a hypodermic needle, she had a glass of wine in her hand, and as she leaned over, one of her perky breasts poked out of her blouse and a nipple dangled above his lips, and his hand reached around behind her to caress a firm buttock.

He kept his eyes closed till he heard someone at the door: the nurse coming back into the room, naked, holding a glass of wine. Two glasses. But it wasn't the nurse, it was a priest. Rudy could smell tobacco on him and was overwhelmed with desire, a real knock-down, drag-out craving, for a cigarette.

"The doctor said you were pretty down, might want to talk," the priest said. "Father Russell, OMI, last of the Oblate Fathers of Mary Immaculate." He held out a hand. Rudy didn't feel like shaking it. The priest looked vaguely familiar.

"Might," Rudy said.

"I gave you a ride home the other night," the priest said. "From Pepe's. After your swim."

"That's it," Rudy said. "I thought you looked familiar."

"You know," the priest said, "sometimes pain is God's megaphone, his only way to get our attention."

"Hold it right there, Father. You got a cigarette?" It was the first time Rudy'd ever called anyone Father. He called his own father Dad, and his kids called him Papa or Pop.

The priest laughed and reached under his robe for a crumpled pack of Old Golds. Was he wearing a regular shirt under his robe, a shirt with a front pocket to hold cigarettes?

The priest pulled a silver lighter out of another hidden pocket, opened the top, and held the flame under the tip of Rudy's cigarette. The cigarette tasted wonderful, even though it made Rudy dizzy. But since he was lying down anyway it didn't matter. He hadn't had a cigarette in years. He'd quit when Helen and Margot were in Italy.

"You know, Father," he said, and he started to complain: about the job he'd left on the market in Chicago; about the house he'd sold; about the coolness between him and his daughters; about the GET-OUT-OF-HELL-FREE cards he'd find wedged under his windshield wiper every time he came out of the public library in McAllen; about the gun racks in the back of every pickup and the patriotic bumper stickers on every other car: AMERICA: LOVE IT OR LEAVE IT; about the call he'd gotten from an assistant warden at the Walls Unit in Huntsville, wanting some Texas avocados for a condemned man's last meal. "The man wants guacamole made from Texas avocados," Rudy said. "He ought to know they're not in season yet. The trees haven't even set any fruit yet, for Christ's sake. I asked if they could postpone the execution till mid-September. The assistant warden didn't think so."

"Why don't you just go back home?" the priest asked.

"To Chicago? Too late. I've burned my bridges."

"I understand, you don't want to lose face; but this heart attack gives you a perfect excuse to build them up again, your bridges. *Without* losing face, you see what I mean? No one would blame you now. You're off the hook. You don't have to prove anything anymore. Just live. All you have to do is live. Sounds like your daughters would be happy to have you back in the Midwest, unless there's something you're not telling me."

"No, no," Rudy said. "Just live. Just live. But how? But why? For what?"

"Why don't you come to mass with me at the seminary?"

"I'm not a Roman Catholic, Father," Rudy said, holding out a hand for another cigarette. The priest gave him a second cigarette and flipped open his lighter. "My wife used to smoke," Rudy said.

"Was your wife a Catholic?"

Rudy laughed. "She used to say that the Roman Catholic Church was the most corrupt institution in the history of the world, the number-one enemy of democracy and reason and freedom."

"You could believe that and still be a Catholic," the priest said. "But what about you?" the priest wanted to know. "What did you see?"

"What did I *see,* Father?"

"When you were dead, or almost dead, right after your heart attack."

Rudy tried to sit up: "Did you read that article in the magazine section in last Sunday's paper? 'Is There a Light at the End of the Tunnel?'"

Father Russell, OMI, nodded.

"Well, I'll tell you something, Father; it wasn't like that. I came as close to death as you could get; I came right up to the bank of the river and stuck my toe in. You'd think I would have caught a glimpse of the other shore, wouldn't you? Hell, the far shore of the Rio Grande is only ninety feet away. It's like standing in the batter's box and checking how deep the first baseman's playing. But I came back with nothing. What happened to the tunnel of bright light these people were talking about in the paper? With Helen waiting for me at the end? And my folks? Where was the welcoming committee? Where was the field full of flowers? Huh?"

Father Russell started to say something but Rudy interrupted him. "Maybe it was too dark," he said, "or maybe there was nothing to see. And not only that," Rudy said, interrupting himself, "I don't feel right now that life is especially precious. I don't value it any more than I did before. Maybe even less, in fact. I don't really give a shit, Father. One way or the other; take it or leave it. Epicurus says that death has nothing to do with us, because if you're alive, then death is not, and if death is, then *you're* not. Something like that."

"You've got a point," Father Russell said, and Rudy could see that the priest didn't know any more about death than he did.

The nurse came and threw the priest out. "Shame on you, you know you're not allowed to smoke in here." When he'd gone, she said to Rudy, "He hangs around the hospital because he's lonely. I'm not even sure he's a real priest. I think maybe he got in some kind of trouble over in Reynosa. Now they left him in charge of the seminary."

"Then he couldn't have been too bad."

"There aren't any students in the seminary, Mr. Harrington. It's empty. There's no one there. *Nadie*." She picked up the cigarette that the priest had left on Rudy's little table, snapped it between her fingers, and tossed it into the wastebasket.

That's when Rudy changed his mind and thought he'd go to mass with Father Russell after all.

Later that week he had another visitor, the Russian, who brought with him a copy of the *McAllen Monitor,* which had a picture of Norma Jean on page 2: ELEPHANT SAVES LOCAL GROWER'S LIFE. "She save your life," he said two or three times as Rudy was reading the article. "Now you do something nice for her."

"What do you want me to do?"

"I'm glad you see my point, because USDA inspector is coming along with all kinds of new regulations and rules. It is going to be a very difficult time for Norma Jean. I got to move the water faucet because she turn it on and off; I got to move the electricity wires that go over her head, because she can pull them down with her trunk. I got to make her stall bigger. I got to make her fence more volts so she don't run away . . . Twenty years we been living happy the way it is.

"Mr. Rudy, you got room at your place. You got three double-size stalls in the barn where Creaky used to keep his horses. You just got to move those old field bins Creaky left stacked up in there, unless you move them already, and tear down the inside walls. You got a paddock. You just need to put up a fence, three little wires. I do it all for you, and I stay there in the barn at first, is no problem. So many regulations and rules."

"You mean you want to board Norma Jean at my place?"

"Just while I fix up my little barn. Otherwise USDA is going to make me too much trouble."

"It's out of the question."

"Out of the question? She save your life, Mr. Rudy, how can you say no?"

Rudy tried to say no, but he couldn't do it.

After the Russian left, he read the article in the paper and admired the photo of Norma Jean.

Rudy spent a week in the hospital, and then Medardo took him home. On Friday morning, sitting in his bathrobe on the veranda, Rudy looked through the index of *Philosophy Made Simple*. There was nothing on sex, nothing to explain a hard-on. But there was a chapter on something called the mind-body problem, which went like this: on the one hand you've got the body, which is part of the material world. Matter: atoms, electrons, protons, neutrons, etc. These atoms and such don't have purposes or desires. They just whirl around according to the laws of physics. On the other hand, you've got the mind, and the mind wants all sorts of things. It's got all kinds of purposes and desires.

Well, how does the mind, which does not take up space or have any moving parts, make the body move? How do we crook our fingers?

Rudy tried it, held his finger up and counted to ten, and on the count of ten he crooked his finger. But how did he do it? He couldn't figure it out, and apparently no one else could either, not even Descartes, who wanted to say that it all happened in the pineal gland at the base of the brain, but nobody believed that anymore. And just think about how much more complex a penis was than a finger. A penis had a mind of its own. You couldn't boss it around the way you bossed your finger around.

He tried these ideas out on Medardo, who stopped by to see if Rudy needed anything — tried to get Medardo to crook his finger. But Medardo was skeptical and deliberately misunderstood him. "You can't just stand there and *come*," Medardo said; "you need *el frote*."

Later that afternoon Medardo returned with bacon, eggs, a sirloin steak, pork chops, potatoes, beer, and wine, but he drew the line at whiskey and cigarettes. No Jack Daniels for Rudy. No Old Golds.

When Rudy protested, Medardo waggled his index finger sideways. "What did the doctor say, Rudy? — no smoking, no drinking, no heavy foods, no sex. Am I right? I brought you bacon and I brought you a big steak. Enough is enough."

Medardo was on his way to Estrella Princesa. The groceries he'd brought were on the kitchen table. "You want me to help you put this stuff away?"

"I'll do it after you go. Listen, did I tell you the story about Aristotle and Alexander?"

"Two or three times, Rudy."

"Then let me ask you something: Is that the sort of thing you get up to at Estrella Princesa? Playing horsey? *Montar al caballito?*"

Medardo smiled. "Oh my, yes," he said; "it's exactly the thing." He laughed.

"Take me with you," Rudy said. "I want to go with you."

"Go with me? To Estrella Princesa? Whoa!" Medardo rubbed the back of his hand over his mustache.

"Not today, Medardo. In two or three weeks."

"Those Mexican whores would kill you, Rudy, a man in your condition."

"Do you know what, Medardo?" Rudy said. "I don't even care."

Medardo shook his head. "Those Mexican whores would kill you," he said again.

"What difference does it make now?" Rudy asked.

"You don't want me to have to tell your daughters that you died in a Mexican whorehouse, do you?"

"I thought this was a private club?"

Medardo held his hand out, palm down, fingers extended, and wiggled it back and forth, as if he had palsy.

"Do you know what, Medardo?" Rudy said again; "I don't care. I might even enjoy it, in fact. Can you think of a better way to go? *El orgasmo,* bang, that is it, it's all over."

"Well," Medardo said, "you've got a point. You've got your affairs in order, right? You got your will made out?"

Rudy shook his head.

"I want you to make out your will first, all right? Save your daughters a lot of grief later."

"My wife made out *her* will," Rudy said.

"Good for her."

"We got one of those standard forms from a stationery store. Maybe you could pick up one of those for me."

"I'll get one for you on Monday." Medardo got up to leave, but Rudy poured the rest of his bottle of Pearl into Medardo's glass. "One last drink."

Medardo waggled his index finger at Rudy a second time. "Not the *último trago*, Rudy. You mean the *penúltimo trago* — the *next-to-last* drink."

"Why's that?"

"The last drink, Rudy, that's the one just before you die, and that may be sooner than you think."

Rudy'd been out of the hospital for three weeks. He still hadn't told the girls about the heart attack. His own brush with death hadn't bothered him, at least that's what he told himself, and he didn't want it to bother them, but on Sunday he went to mass with the priest, Father Russell. He wasn't supposed to drive yet, so Father Russell picked him up in his old Pontiac.

Rudy figured he'd blend into the congregation, stay away from people who looked as if they might try to put him on a committee, and simply try to affirm, in the most general way possible, that our lives in this world, this universe, are not without meaning and purpose. But the nurse had been right; there was no one to blend in with: no seminarians, no congregation, no community. Rudy was the only one in the huge seminary chapel, except for the plaster-of-paris statues that lined the walls. He waited in the chapel till he got tired of waiting, and then he wandered back to the sacristy where Father Russell was struggling to get into some complicated vestments.

"I haven't said mass in six months," Father Russell explained. "You have to have at least one person in the congregation to say mass."

Rudy thought the mass was supposed to be in English, but Father Russell said it in Latin, and Rudy couldn't understand a word till Father Russell invited him, in English, to come up and take communion. He went. He knew that this was against the rules, but he went up anyway and knelt at the communion railing. He took the dry wafer on his tongue, but Father Russell didn't offer him any wine. Rudy held the wafer on his tongue, let it soften, the body of Christ. He could almost feel his heart getting stronger.

Afterward he was anxious to leave, to get out of there, but the priest didn't want him to go. Rudy could understand that. They ate in the huge seminary kitchen. The priest didn't know how to cook. They ate bologna and mayonnaise on white bread, and drank sweet sherry wine.

"What's the greatest tragedy in the history of the world?" the priest asked, pouring himself a little more sherry.

Rudy had no idea.

"Take a guess."

"The Holocaust?"

Father Russell shook his head.

"World War II?"

Father Russell shook his head again.

"I really don't have any idea," Rudy said.

"The burning of the library in Alexandria," Father Russell said.

"You mean in Egypt?"

The priest smiled.

"Are you serious?" Rudy asked.

"Mr. Harrington," he said, "the library had the medical manuscripts of Saint Luke. Cures for cancer. Cures for heart disease. Cures for leprosy. For everything. All lost. But I'm something of a healer too, a *curandero*. That's how I got in trouble with the bishop." He leaned over the table and put his hand on Rudy's chest.

How crazy can you get? Rudy thought. *It's no wonder they left him all alone at the seminary.* But he didn't push the priest's hand away.

◇

Medardo didn't bring the standard will form till Friday. His cousin — a justice of the peace from Hidalgo — came with him. Rudy opened three beers and they sat at the glass-topped table on the veranda.

"I'm going to arrange something with a woman who specializes in older men like you," Medardo said; "men with a heart condition."

Rudy didn't want to discuss these matters in front of a third party, but he had no choice. "How old is she?"

"Don't worry, Rudy. This is a beautiful woman. You'll thank me. But I'm going to stay right here and drink this beer while you fill out the will, okay?"

Rudy left everything he owned — the grove, the pickup, the two farm wagons, Creaky's old two-ton truck with slatted sides that they'd use to take the avocados to the packing house in Hidalgo — to the three girls. The only tricky thing was the piano. If Meg kept the piano, then each of the other girls would get five thousand dollars at the outset. Once that was taken care of, the estate would be divided three ways. Rudy signed the will and Medardo witnessed it, and Medardo's cousin notarized it.

"Now you won't have to worry," Medardo said. "No fighting over who gets what. And if something should happen, God forbid, your daughters will never know. The newspaper will say that you had a heart attack in a downtown club. That's all. Very discreet."

"I forgot about the chandelier," Rudy said. "The dining room chandelier was probably worth more than we paid for the house. It's up in Meg's attic right now, all packed up in newspaper."

"It's part of the estate," Medardo's cousin said. "Your daughters can sell it, or if one of them wants it they can have it appraised and settle it like the piano."

Rudy nodded. "One more drink," he said. "The *penúltimo trago.*"

But Medardo shook his head. He and his cousin were on their way to Reynosa for a cultural Friday.

The form for the will was, in fact, the same one Rudy'd gotten for Helen when she'd decided to make out her will. He'd been working on the side porch, tearing up the flooring so he could replace the sagging joists. It was 1960. Helen had less than a month left to live and had been making some tapes. Rudy played the guitar and did a little recording himself on an Ampex portable stereo recorder with a built-in amplifier, and he'd bought a punch-in/out switch so that Helen could start and stop the recorder with a click of a button. When he took a break and brought her a cup of tea, she told him she wanted to make out her will. She'd been recording, but she stopped when he came in. The microphones on their booms hovered over the bed like hummingbirds. She held the punch-in/out switch in her hand. She'd just finished a tape. Rudy held the iced tea for her so she could drink it through a straw, and then he put the tape in a box and threaded a new one in the tape recorder.

"You shouldn't be working so hard in this wet weather," she said. "This old house, it's like it's in motion. Every year you tear part of it down and rebuild it. Like Grandfather's hammer. The head's been replaced, and the handle's been replaced, but it's still the same hammer. And it's still the same house. It's like an enduring form, a center, a place that will hold our family for a while."

"I'm going to use treated wood for the joists," Rudy said. "It's expensive, but they'll last forever. Do you want me to rub your back?"

"Dying's harder than I thought it was going to be," she said. She had trouble rolling over so that he could reach her back. "I mean, I thought death was something that just happened to you, not something you had to *do*. I don't want to do it, but I don't want to miss it either. I feel the way I used to feel at my piano recitals: stage fright."

Rudy moved a microphone aside and sat down on the edge of the hospital bed he'd rented for her. "Oh, Helen."

"When I was a little girl," she went on, "my mother kept individual scrapbooks for my brother and me. She put everything in them: report cards, school programs, vital statistics, birthday parties, piano recitals, snapshots. We had a record of everything. I always meant to do that for the girls, Rudy, but somehow I never got around to it. My life has always been such a jumble, just like my mind is now, so when you listen to these tapes you'll just have to forgive me."

"There's nothing to forgive, Helen. You don't have to worry about that." Even at that point he couldn't ask her about Bruni. He didn't want to confront her in a hostile way, but oh, just, he didn't know, maybe get things out in the open. He wondered if she'd say anything about him on the tapes.

"I know that, Rudy, but I worry anyway. That's why I want to make a will, get everything in order. Maybe you could help me do that, Rudy. I'd ask one of the girls, but . . ."

"You mean get a lawyer?"

"No, I don't need a lawyer. You can get a standard form of some kind. I think they sell them at that place next to the deli."

He had no idea what she wanted to put in her will since everything they owned was held jointly. But he got the form for her, and the next afternoon he typed up the bequests on Helen's office Remington as she dictated to him. The form was still there in the box with all Helen's papers: "Last Will & Testament." He hadn't looked at it in years, but he got it out now. It was in a folder with her birth certificate, the letters she'd written to him when she was a senior at DePaul and he was working on the market on the other side of town, her diplomas, her teaching awards from Edgar Lee Masters, and a letter from Bruno Bruni that he'd found after her death in her desk drawer. It was written in Italian and Rudy'd never been able to read it, though he looked at it every once in a while.

- **I, HELEN ANNA HARRINGTON**, a resident of the City of <u>Chicago</u>, <u>Cook County</u>, <u>Illinois</u>, being of sound and disposing mind and memory, do hereby make, publish, constitute, and declare this instrument to be my Last Will & Testament, hereby intending to dispose of all the property, both real and personal, that I may own or to which I may be entitled at the time of my death, and by this instrument, hereby revoking all former Wills and Codicils thereto by me heretofore made.
- **FIRST:** I hereby direct that my Executor shall pay all of my just debts, funeral expenses, the expenses of the administration of my estate, and any estate or inheritance taxes from my residuary estate, without apportionment or right of reimbursement from any beneficiary or transferee of property.
- **SECOND:** I give and bequeath the following property and amounts to the following named persons:
- Fra Lippo Lippi's *Madonna and Child* to my oldest daughter, Meg, as her absolute property, because she's going to be such a wonderful mother;
- Antonio del Pollaiuolo's *Dance of the Nudes* to my second daughter, Molly, as her absolute property, because she dances so beautifully and is destined to have many adventures;

- Donatello's *David* to my youngest daughter, Margot, as her absolute property, because from the back there's such a remarkable resemblance, though she probably doesn't know it. It's hard to see your own backside;
- Piero della Francesca's portrait *Federigo da Montefeltro* to my husband, Rudy, as his absolute property, because he's as handsome as Federigo.

"Oh, Rudy," she said as he pulled the finished form from the typewriter. "I wish you'd wear that red hat I bought for you, from the Abruzzi. Then you'd look just like Federigo."

"I think it's up in the attic somewhere. I didn't throw it away."

"I know, Rudy. You've never thrown anything away."

They were looking at a reproduction of one of de Kooning's untitled abstracts when the notary came that evening to notarize the will. Ribbons of bright color. Rudy was beginning to understand, or at least to get over his fear that there was something to understand that he didn't understand. When he heard Meg answer the door downstairs he adjusted Helen's head scarf — she'd lost all her hair — and her face seemed to grow clearer, almost translucent.

He helped her sign the will with her fountain pen — *una cosa di bellezza* — and the notary, one of the secretaries from Rudy's office, stamped it with the official seal of the state of Illinois. And then he held up the recent *New Yorker* — with a picture of a man walking through leafy trees in Central Park on the cover, at least he thought it was Central Park — and turned the pages so she could look at the cartoons.

When he went up to bed that night, he stood outside the bedroom door and listened. He didn't want to go in if she was talking into the tape recorder, because she wouldn't record anything if someone else was in the room. He could hear her voice, but he couldn't make out what she was saying. And he never did find out, because the tape recorder had malfunctioned. The tapes had been blank.

At the thought of the tapes, which he kept on the shelf at the back of his desk, Rudy's chest tightened up. He put one of his nitroglycerin tablets under his tongue and sat at the desk till the pain went away.

A Cultural Friday

Estrella Princesa was tucked away on a side street, like a small, old-fashioned hotel. There was no sign, only a bronze plaque on the wall, the sort of plaque on which you expect to find the name of a famous person who'd lived in this place a long time ago. A traffic cop in a brown uniform stood under the dark green awning, as if he were a doorman, and men were getting in and out of green taxicabs. Rudy and Medardo passed under a low colonial arch into a courtyard where parrots roosted in neatly trimmed flowering trees and a fountain bubbled and Peruvian flutes lilted softly, a pleasant contrast to the raucous mariachi music of the Plaza Morelos.

In the lobby, comfortable chairs were arranged around small tables that were cluttered with glasses and colorful plates. Rudy's idea of Mexican food was chips and salsa, beans and rice, tacos and burritos filled with ground beef, which is what you got at the Mexican restaurants in Mission, but a buffet by the bar offered a wonderful array of tempting hors d'oeuvres: marinated shellfish and abalone, barbecued meats, fresh shrimps, pickled hot peppers, plates of little turnovers. Everyone — the old men, the young women, the waiters, the musicians — seemed happy to see Medardo, who was dressed in a chocolate-colored pin-striped linen suit and a pale yellow shirt with French cuffs, and who had an engaging smile on his broad face.

At first Rudy felt out of place in his old, all-purpose sport coat — inelegant, awkward, not at all like the men sitting in the comfortable chairs with *amiguitas,* their little friends, by their sides. Most were men his own age, but they were nothing like the pale-faced golfers pictured in the *Golden Age Digest* he'd looked through on the plane on his first flight down to Texas. These were men whom the sun had burnished to the color of the fine cigars they were smoking, men who looked as if they had left all their cares behind them and were looking forward to whatever pleasures the evening might hold in store. The *amiguitas* were truly beautiful. Did they really want to become secretaries and dental hygienists?

Medardo spoke briefly to a man who'd come out of the adjacent card room to greet him, his playing cards fanned out in his hand, and then ordered a glass of champagne at the bar. Rudy hesitated between a Cinzano and a Campari — he could never remember which it was that Helen had liked — and ordered Campari. *"Con sifón?"* the barman asked. Rudy nodded. He listened indifferently to the hum of conversations and the slap of playing cards and the click of the balls that came from the billiard room. He thought of slipping away, but Medardo held him by the arm and introduced him to one patron after another, men who greeted him with soft Mexican handshakes and who seemed to know him, or rather to know that he had had a heart attack recently and had been lifted into the back of a pickup truck by an elephant. The story, with the photo of Norma Jean, had run in *El Mañana,* the Reynosa paper, as well as in the *Monitor.*

María Gracia, the woman who specialized in older men with heart conditions, had just bought a flower shop — a *floresteria* — with a small inheritance, but she was still meeting some clients at Estrella Princesa, including a wealthy art dealer who flew down from San Antonio once a week just to see her. Rudy noticed her as soon as she came through the door in a black spaghetti-strap dress and began exchanging greetings with people. Everyone knew her; everyone was glad to see her, as they'd been glad to see Medardo. It took her twenty minutes to angle her way across the room and join them at the bar. Once she reached them, she began to rummage in her purse for a package of cigarettes. Rudy, his heart accelerating, lit her cigarette for her — an Embajador — and took one for himself. She pulled the smoke deep into her lungs and then exhaled with obvious pleasure.

"Well," she said, in English. "Now we can talk." She kissed Medardo and held out her hand to Rudy, who shook it.

"So," Medardo said, also in English, "how is your book coming?" He touched Rudy's arm and explained: "María's writing a book about her adventures. She's got everyone very worried."

It was the first time Rudy had heard Medardo speak English. His slight accent was charming. Rudy wondered if his own accent was charming when he spoke Spanish. Somehow he doubted it.

María laughed.

"Are *you* going to be in it?" Rudy asked Medardo.

"No, but *you* might. Just be careful, and keep your nitroglycerin pills handy."

"I only *say* I'm writing a book," María said, "so that everyone will be nice to me."

Medardo left them and they smoked their cigarettes.

"Medardo warned me not to fall in love with you," Rudy said. This was the same advice that the Italians who worked for

Becker had given him at the Casino, on Roosevelt Road, before he'd gone upstairs for his first time, with a girl named Shirley, who later became the mistress of a prominent politician. But he'd fallen in love with Shirley anyway. That was the summer before he'd met Helen.

"That's probably good advice," María said. "When you're in love you're defenseless. And," she went on, "Medardo told *me* that you're a *pensador,* a *filósofo,* a lover of wisdom. Men like you are greatly admired in Mexico." She adjusted one of the straps of her dress. "Why don't you say something wise and then we'll go into the dining room."

"Something wise?" Rudy said. "I don't know . . ."

"A *pensador,* a *filósofo* . . . you must have plenty of wisdom."

"How about this?" Rudy said, holding his hand up and crooking his finger.

"Is this a secret signal, Rudy?"

"No," he said. "But it shows how little we know. How can the mind, which is immaterial, move the finger, which is material? That's Descartes, and that's just the beginning. Have you ever heard of Bishop Berkeley?"

"An American?"

"No, he was a British philosopher. Two hundred years ago. From Ireland, actually."

"Oh," she said. "And this Bishop Berkeley?"

"If Bishop Berkeley is right," Rudy went on, "we can't even be sure the finger exists. Outside the mind." He crooked his finger again, and María crooked her finger too. "We don't know anything, María. And if we can't understand how we crook our fingers, all the big questions . . . love, death, beauty . . ."

She put her cigarette down in the ashtray and touched his hand. "Let's eat," she said. "I can't think when I'm hungry."

❖

"Tell me something," she said when they'd been seated in the dining room, a bottle of white wine open on the table between them, "that you've never told anyone before."

Rudy filled her glass. He hesitated for a moment — he was too old for this — but then he let himself go: "My wife fell in love with Italy," he said, filling his own glass and setting the bottle down. "And she fell in love with an Italian."

María added a splash of jalapeño sauce to her abalone cocktail and passed the bottle to Rudy. "Here's all the Italian I know," she said, when she'd finished chewing, and she used her index finger to pull down on the cheekbone under her right eye. "How about you?"

Rudy shook his head. "The problem was," he said, lifting his glass and then putting it down again without drinking, "that she had this way of talking about Florence — Helen did, my wife, after she got back — that always bothered me. She talked as if just to be in Florence were enough to make a person happy. As if you didn't need anything else. Just to *be* there. And she ate like an Italian, scraping her food onto her fork with her knife and raising it to her mouth with her left hand. For a while, after she got back, she answered the phone in Italian, as if she were still in Florence — I'd call home and she'd say 'Pronto' — and she dated her checks in Italian, with the day of the month first and then the name of the month, in Italian, and then the year. She made her ones like sevens and put a crossbar through her sevens so no one would mistake them for ones. But that wasn't the problem. The problem wasn't mistaking sevens for ones but ones for sevens, which happened all the time, and caused a lot of grief with the bank. It was silly."

"But that's the way you're eating, Rudy," María said. "That's the way I'm eating."

"Maybe so."

"Not maybe, Rudy. That's the way you're eating right now."

"There's more to it than that," he said. "I can't figure it out. It permanently altered her, made her into a different woman."

"More confident, more sure of herself?"

Rudy nodded.

"Livelier in bed?"

Rudy nodded again. "Then at the end, just before she died, she made these tapes for me. For the family. I've got them in my study out at the grove. But something went wrong with the tape recorder. The punch-in/out switch that I bought so she could turn the recorder on and off from the bed was activating the tape recorder without activating the recording heads."

"And?"

"I've always thought she must have said something about Bruno Bruni; that was her lover's name. About what happened. Some explanation. I don't know what. But something. Something I could hang on to. The truth."

"I'll tell you what the truth is, Rudy. She wanted a little *aventura*. Every woman does. It's human nature. And all by herself in Italy . . ."

"A little *aventura*," he said as the waiter served their seafood enchiladas. "I suppose you're right."

"Now tell me about your daughters," María said, cutting off one end of an enchilada with her fork and lifting it to her lips.

He told her about his daughters, and when he was through she said, "Look at me, señor. I'm not a young woman anymore. But I'm still beautiful. This is why you're here. Can you put aside everything else and enjoy this evening? Now, this Bishop Berkeley," she said, smiling. "I'm sorry, Rudy, but I have to smile when you tell me that you can only experience things in the mind . . ." She crooked her finger at him and laughed. He touched the little bottle of nitroglycerin tablets in his shirt pocket.

"It's more complicated than that," Rudy protested. He took a bite of his enchilada, which was filled with creamy seafood, like something you'd find in a French restaurant.

She shook her head. "No, Rudy. No, it's not. Don't drive yourself crazy with these questions. Look at Medardo. He's happy, you're not happy. Why is that?"

Rudy didn't answer.

"Seriously, Rudy. Answer me. Why is Medardo happy and you're not happy?"

Rudy'd already given some thought to this question. "I think," he said, "it's because he's got the right touch on life. I think the Italians on the market in Chicago had it. Maybe all Italians. Certainly Bruno Bruni. Maybe that's what Helen was looking for."

"The 'right touch on life,'" she repeated. *"Alegría."*

"Yes," he said. "That sounds right. That's a musical term, isn't it."

"Let me tell you something," she said, still leaning forward, "that I think you already know. So your wife took a lover in Italy — it doesn't really matter. What if she fell in love with him? A little *aventura,* that's all. Does it matter now? She came home. That's what matters. Look right at me."

"Sorry," he said. He realized he'd been looking down the front of her dress. He looked *at* her and she smiled.

"This is it, Rudy. This is what you're looking for — *alegría.* The embrace of a woman. And the love of your daughters, your three lovely daughters. Rejoice in them, and remember your wife with love. Your whole world is full of love, Rudy, and I think you know that. *Gratitude* is the word that should be on the tip of your tongue. Not 'I'm worried I'm worried I'm worried,' but 'Thank you thank you thank you.' For your daughters and the good times you shared with your wife, for hot water in your bathroom and this good wine, and for these wonderful enchiladas. Don't be afraid." She stuck her fork into the last bite of her enchilada, pointed it at him, and then stuck it in her mouth.

Rudy didn't know if she was offering him the accumulated wisdom of a civilization older than his own, or if she was tempting him to abandon his quest.

Meg

A man with three daughters will never run out of stories. At the beginning of June Margot called from London to say that she'd just auctioned off a book of erotic drawings she had found in the convent where she'd been working. She'd restored it herself and sold it at Sotheby's for a quarter of a million dollars. She wanted to know how to set up a trust for the convent. Rudy tried to explain. Two weeks later Molly called from India. Someone had handed her a dead baby in front of the Kalighat in Calcutta; she'd placed a garland on the shaft of the great black lingam at the Golden Temple in Benares, where she'd met the King of the Dead — down at the burning ghats; a rhinoceros had wandered into the tea garden in Assam, and Nandini, TJ's mother, had shooed it away with a broom; she'd been riding Nandini's elephant, Champaa, through the jungle every morning, before the rains came, and they'd been to see the erotic sculptures in the museum temple of Shakti in Madan Kamdev.

"What did you do with the dead baby?" Rudy asked.

"I handed it to someone else."

"And the King of the Dead? What sort of guy was the King of the Dead? How did you meet him? Did you just bump into him on the street and he invited you in for tea?"

"There're two of them, actually," she said. "Two brothers — two kings — but they don't speak to each other. They're the richest men in India. They take on the bad karma of the people they burn."

"Doesn't sound good to me," Rudy said. He didn't ask about the great black lingam or the erotic sculptures.

Both these phone calls ended on a sour note: "You sold the only place I ever called home," Margot said to him when he suggested that she might like to come to live in Mission. And Molly, who had a dozen more names to add to the guest list, wanted him to reconsider having the wedding in Detroit. She'd landed a role as a dancer in an independent film about life in Assam on the eve of independence, part of which was going to be filmed at a neighboring tea garden, and she wouldn't be back in time to make the arrangements — they'd have to have the wedding in September instead of August. TJ's aunt would take care of everything if they had the wedding in Detroit. Texas was too inconvenient.

But Texas was convenient for Rudy, who'd already ordered a hundred wedding invitations, and he refused to budge, even though he'd have to order new invitations with the new date — Saturday, September 9. He wanted his daughters to come to Texas, wanted them to see the grove and the river and the house with its thick adobe walls that kept it cool even in the hottest weather, wanted them to see the garden and the barn and the elephant.

Meg had a story too, but he wasn't sure what it was. She called at the end of the month, right after lunch, as Rudy was about to go into town to pick up the new invitations. She wanted to tell him more about the shrink she'd been seeing. Her theories — or the shrink's theories — made Rudy so upset he'd had to put the phone down and take a pill. That's when he told her about the heart attack. It was the only way to stop her. He didn't want to hear what he'd done to her, how he'd screwed up her life as well as Molly's and Margot's. This was unfamiliar territory. She said she'd be there the next day, Friday. He tried to talk her out of it because the Russian was bringing Norma Jean on Saturday, and that had gotten her going too.

"An elephant? Listen to me, Pop — you need someone to look after you. I'm coming down there tomorrow."

He tried to dissuade her, but she was determined. So he canceled his cultural Friday and met her at the airport. As soon as he saw her emerge from the door in the side of the plane and start down the steps to the apron, he forgot that he was annoyed. She was wearing a suit with shoulder pads that made her look like a football player, and even at this distance he could see dark shadows under her eyes. Her hair was pulled back so tight he thought it must be hurting her scalp. He waited for her to detach herself from the crowd of passengers walking across the tarmac.

"Imagine, having a heart attack," she said, before he could even embrace her, "and not telling anyone for two months."

He put his arms around her. "I didn't want to worry you."

"You weren't going to tell us at all, were you?"

He shrugged. "Someday."

He could see two men on the apron behind her, unloading the luggage from the small DC-10 that had brought her from Dallas to Miller International Airport in McAllen.

She bought a copy of the *Monitor* and glanced through it while they waited at the baggage claim.

"Have you tried your theories out on your sisters?" Rudy asked as they walked across the parking lot to the car. Rudy offered to carry the suitcase, but Meg wouldn't hear of it.

"They're not theories," she said. "They're insights."

"Let me see if I've got this straight," he said, once they were in the car. "Molly could never settle down with one man because I was always too affectionate with her, so she kept falling in love with men like me. It begins with an all-consuming passion, but then the incest taboo kicks in and causes her to lose interest?"

"It's more complicated than that, but that's the general idea."

"And Margot . . . I was too protective of Margot, I treated her like a baby, and that's why she's so dependent?"

She nodded.

"Have you noticed," he said, "that Molly's getting married? To one man?"

"We'll see," she said.

"And that your little sister's been having an affair with a married man in Italy."

"And you think that's a healthy declaration of independence?"

"Well," he said, "at least it's a good story. And it's just the beginning." He told her about the book of erotic drawings, and about the auction at Sotheby's, and he told her about Molly's adventures too — the dead baby, the King of the Dead, the rhinoceros, the elephant.

Meg didn't say anything.

"They're wonderful stories, Meg," he said. "Imagine finding a book of dirty pictures in a convent and selling it for a quarter of a million dollars so you can set up a trust for the nuns. Imagine shooing away a rhinoceros with a broom. TJ's mother just walked right up to it and started batting it." He shook his head in disbelief. "But it's *your* story that keeps me awake at night, Meg, do you know why?"

"Why?"

"Because a father's only as happy as his unhappiest daughter, and right now that's you. Do you want to tell me what's going on?"

"We've got to get you out of here, Pop. That's what's going on. Get you back home where you can be near a good hospital. Dan says you shouldn't be relying on nitroglycerin, that you ought to be taking something for the long run, phenobarbital for anxiety and a blocking agent like propranolol. You can't stay down here all by yourself. You abandoned ship. You've had an adventure. *You've* got a good story to tell. Now it's time to come back home. You can move into the apartment over the garage, Dan's already started fixing it up. New hot-water heater. The kids would love it. We would too. And the dogs."

"You've been holding the dogs for ransom, haven't you. I should have driven down with the dogs instead of flying."

"Don't be ridiculous. It just wasn't possible. Besides, the kids love them."

"Is this your best offer?" he said.

"I'll forgive you for saying that, Pop, because I know what's in your heart. But it's a good offer. And it comes from *my* heart."

"Meg," he said, not sure what he was going to say. But he didn't have to say anything, because she interrupted him.

"Oh, Pop," she said. "Just look at this. Have you seen tonight's paper?" She batted the open newspaper with the back of her hand. "This is incredible."

"The pro-war rally?"

"You knew about it?"

"Just what I heard on the radio this morning."

"Your local congressman's announced that he's introduced a bill to jail professional agitators and flag desecrators."

They were driving through an area of small truck farms — cabbages, carrots, onions, broccoli, cantaloupe, watermelon, sugar-cane, corn, citrus. Small birds crowded the fences and telephone wires, but no crows.

She kept on: "*Kill a Commie for Christ.* Oh, Pop, this is horrible. There's a picture of a kid wearing a T-shirt that says *Kill a Commie for Christ.* How can you stand it?"

There was more in the paper, and he let her go on without interrupting. But when they turned in the drive, he asked her, finally, if everything was all right at home.

She shook her head.

"Is Dan having an affair?"

She started to cry.

Rudy was back in familiar territory. Now he knew what to do, what to say, knew how to handle the situation. Good advice started to bubble up inside him. But it wasn't so simple. It turned out that *she* was the one having an affair, not Dan. She told him the story as she helped him fix supper. This was their traditional mode of discussing matters of importance. They kept their hands busy, wiping mushrooms, slicing them, mincing garlic, washing the last of the lettuce from the garden.

Rudy wondered, as she talked, what she'd think if she knew about his cultural Fridays at Estrella Princesa.

"Look at me, Pop," she said. "I'm not who you think I am. I'm no better than Mama."

"No better than Mama? How can you say such a thing? What are you talking about?"

"I don't know what to do, Pop."

"This man . . . who is he?"

"A civil-rights lawyer. He's one of the leaders of the antiwar movement in Milwaukee. That's what I'm doing. Counseling draft resisters, getting the paperwork done for marches and demonstrations."

"Married?"

She nodded. Rudy took a deep breath. Margot's married Italian was one thing; a married American was something else. "Does Dan know?"

She shook her head.

"Does he suspect?"

"I don't think so."

Rudy was at a loss again. He cut little slits in the fat on a couple of pork chops so they wouldn't curl up when he browned them. Meg dried the lettuce in a salad spinner.

"Now I know what Mama must have gone through in Italy."

"What do you mean 'what Mama must have gone through'?"

"Bruno Bruni."

Rudy was surprised, embarrassed. "I didn't know Bruno Bruni was public knowledge. Did Mama . . ."

"No, Pop. Mama never said a word. Margot figured it out. A couple of years later, when she went back to Florence for a year and lived with the Ciprianis. Mama had an affair with Bruni, the man who helped them get settled. I didn't believe her at first."

"I didn't know *she* knew," Rudy said. He wanted to tell Meg the truth about the affair, but he didn't know what the truth was. He'd never been able to pin it down.

"You called from Chicago," he said, "after you went to Mama's grave. Were you alone?"

"I was when I called."

"But in Chicago? Did you go down there with the lawyer?"

She nodded. "We stayed at the Palmer House. He had a meeting."

"Are you in love?"

"I don't know, Pop. I don't understand anything anymore."

"You know, it's not the end of the world."

"It is for me . . . Don't be angry, Pop."

"I'm not angry."

"I'm an adulteress."

"But at least you haven't been *taken* in adultery."

She laughed, and then she started to cry again. "Do you re-member Laura Chamberlain's wedding? Laura's little sister started to sing a solo right at the beginning and then she broke down and cried?"

"I remember."

"That was okay. She was just overwhelmed. But nobody went up to help her, to put an arm around her. The accompanist kept starting over, and she kept starting to sing and then she'd start crying again. She just stood there and cried, and I couldn't figure out why one of the bridesmaids didn't go over to her, they were right up there in the front of the church, but they just stood there and let her cry and cry, and finally Mama got up and went up and put her arms around her. I feel just like that little girl, Pop."

And suddenly she is that little girl; she's fifteen years old and the boy who was going to ask her to her first dance has asked someone else. She's sitting at the kitchen table. She's come home from school early. Walked home. Stunned. He wants to offer her the conventional wisdom, that there are plenty of fish in the sea, that she'll have plenty of opportunities, that any boy who'd treat her like that wasn't worth her time anyway . . . But he doesn't say any of these things because he knows that they're like the advice he reads in Ann Landers — good advice as long as you don't need it, perfectly sensible as long as you don't have any use for it.

"When you stayed at the Palmer House," he said, "what was it like? Ecstasy?" It was awkward to say things like this, to his daughter, to this beautiful woman. But he wanted to know, and so he said them anyway as he waited for the pasta sauce to cook down a little: zucchini from the garden, sliced thick and cooked in butter and garlic.

"Pop, I'm sorry. I didn't mean to unload on you. I didn't, really.

That's not why I came down here. What am I going to do? What did *you* do, Pop?"

"Ecstasy?" he asked again. "Is that what it was?"

She smiled. "I guess so. Pretty close anyway."

"How often do you get to experience ecstasy?" he said. "I don't want to damp it down. I don't want you to damp it down."

"Pop." She seemed offended. "My marriage is at stake here."

She wants me to scold her, he thought, *she wants to be punished;* but he was determined not to dispense any conventional wisdom, not to punish her. "Everybody wants a little *aventura.* That's what they call it in Spanish — a little *aventura.* It's perfectly normal. It's human nature."

"Do you really believe that, Pop? Is that what Mama wanted? A little *aventura?*" She was standing at the sink with her back to him.

He drained the pasta, added the sliced zucchini and some Parmesan cheese.

"I don't know what I believe, Meg. We never talked about it," he said. "Not really. We should have, but we didn't. The rector of the American Church in Florence wrote to the dean at Edgar Lee Masters, and the dean called me, asked me to come up to his office. That's how I found out about it. He said that Mama'd gotten involved with a man who preyed on American women. I was afraid she'd lose her job. I almost wished she would. That's when I decided to go to Italy."

What he experienced now was the same shame and humiliation he'd experienced in Italy. He could feel it in his face and in his neck and in his arms. He didn't want his daughter to see him like this, but she turned toward him.

"Oh, Pop. Pop. I don't know what to say." She reached across the table and took his hand. "And it never evened out? You never . . ."

"No," he said. "Well, actually, I've been seeing a woman over in Mexico. Once a week. She's a lovely woman. You'd like her. But it's not ecstasy, Meg. It's comfort, that's what it is. Comfort. That's the best I can hope for now. Comfort."

He served up the pasta and they sat down to supper.

◆

After supper they walked down to the river. It was late, but not quite dark yet. He put his arm around her. "When the time comes, you'll know what to do," he said.

"That's the sort of thing Mama used to say," she said.

"Let me try again: whatever you do, the feeling will follow."

"Mama again!" She laughed.

"I've got Mama's fountain pen in my pocket," he said. He took the pen out of his pocket and showed it to her. It was too dark to read the inscription, but she held it in her hand as they walked.

"Do you wish you'd never found out?" she asked. "About Bruni?"

"No," he said. "I can't imagine not knowing." When they reached the river Rudy turned off the flashlight and they stood in silence, listening to the night sounds: peepers, cicadas, king rails, the *wheet wheet wheeeer* of the pauraques, the whistle of a screech owl on the other side of the river.

"I suppose," he said after a few minutes, "if Mama hadn't had the affair with Bruni, she'd have become someone else. But I didn't want her to be anyone else. I just wanted her to be who she was."

"Did you become a different person too, Pop?"

"I guess I did," he said. "I hadn't thought of it that way."

"You were a saint."

He shook his head.

"But who knows about Dan," she said — a statement, not a question.

"Maybe you'll find out," he said, "and maybe you won't."

He told her about floating down the river on the anniversary of Helen's death, the day she'd called from Chicago and told him she'd been seeing a shrink. He told her about letting go and just floating.

"And then you had a heart attack," she said. "Oh, Pop. You're as crazy as Mama. And tomorrow you're getting an elephant. Remember the chicken that Mama adopted?"

Rudy laughed. "Chicky-chick was some chicken, except she turned out to be a rooster. And Norma Jean is some elephant."

He turned the flashlight on again and they walked back to the house in silence. What he knew now he'd known from the beginning: that if Helen hadn't gotten sick, hadn't been diagnosed with leukemia right after Easter, she wouldn't have come home. What she'd had wasn't a little *aventura*. It was the real thing — ecstasy. He'd seen it in her face when he went to Italy. She was going to send Margot home in June, but she was going to stay for the summer. To do research, she said, but he knew that she wanted to stay so she could be with Bruni. He should have had it out with her then, in Italy, should have forced her to choose between him and Bruni, should have challenged Bruni to a duel, should have hunted the man down, the son of a bitch. Instead he'd backed away, let it ride. He *had* become a different person. He'd become the person he was now.

Meg and Rudy drank coffee on the veranda in the morning while they waited for the Russian to arrive with Norma Jean. Molly, off in India, had left the wedding arrangements up to her father. Meg didn't think it was right, but Rudy could see that she was glad to help out, glad to have a project.

"All Molly wants," she said, "is plenty of good champagne and lots of the frozen *Saint-Cyrs* you always made for special occasions."

"Don't forget the sacred fire," Rudy said. "And the *mandap*. That's the wedding tent."

Meg had the brochure from the Detroit hotel, so they had something to start with. "You're sure about this, Pop? It'd be a lot easier to do it at the hotel in Detroit. You just had a heart attack . . . and what do you know about Indian weddings?"

"I know that you need a *mandap*," he said, "and a sacred fire. I've talked to the manager of the Taj Mahal about the dinner, and I've got the phone number of a pandit. I've got his card, in fact. What more do you want? An elephant? We've got an elephant too. How hard can it be? I put on a terrific wedding for you, didn't I? A hog roast? Two big turkeys?"

"That was different. That was a *Midwestern* wedding."

Rudy shrugged his shoulders. "Here's the Russian," he said; "I can hear his truck."

The Russian pulled into the yard towing an open horse trailer behind his pickup. Norma Jean was looking over the side of the trailer.

Meg shook her head and stood up. "This pandit," she said, "is this the guy you were telling me about? The one who got rid of the crows?"

"Right."

"Well, he must have something going for him."

Meg and Rudy walked down the drive and watched as the Russian pulled the ramp for Norma Jean out from under the bed of the open horse trailer. When Rudy approached, to help the Russian lock the ramp into place, the elephant reached over the side of the trailer with her trunk and grabbed his wrist. He tried to pull his arm back, but she held his wrist tightly and lifted it slowly to her mouth, as if she were going to bite his hand off.

"Is okay," the Russian said. "She want you should pet her

tongue. Is very big honor. Is how elephants greet each other, only you don't have no trunk. You got to use your hand. She remember how she save your life."

Rudy closed his eyes and let his hand rest on the huge tongue.

"She like if you move your hand around back and forth," the Russian said.

Rudy stroked the elephant's tongue. It was rough and smooth and slippery all at the same time, and it was attached at the front as well as at the back, so that instead of flapping up and down, like a human tongue, it undulated with a gentle, rhythmical movement, like a wave humping up over a shoal. When she'd had enough, Norma Jean took his wrist in her trunk and removed his hand from her mouth. She rumbled her appreciation and raised her foot and stomped the floor of the trailer. Rudy wiped his hand on his pants. The Russian checked the ramp and opened the gate.

"*Peachay,*" he shouted, and Norma Jean began to back down the ramp. "*Peachay,*" the Russian repeated. "It take her a while to get used to new place," he said to Rudy. "We take slow and easy." Norma Jean backed off the ramp, trumpeted, and looked around. The Russian took her on a little tour, showing her the house, Rudy's garden, the garage, the big sugar hackberries at the south end of the house, and finally the barn.

The Russian was going to sleep in the old tack room, which still smelled of soap and leather, though it hadn't been used in years. The three horse stalls had been extra large to begin with, so Norma Jean had plenty of room in the barn, and in the day she could stay outside in the old paddock. Rudy didn't like the look of the three-tiered, five-thousand-volt electric fence that he and the Russian had shifted from the Russian's paddock, but he didn't want Norma Jean running loose, and there didn't seem to be any alternative.

The sight of Norma Jean's bulbous head, her big eyes, her trunk, which she waved at him, made Rudy smile, but when he stood beside her and put his hand on her shoulder and felt her strength, he experienced something close to awe. He had expected her skin to feel leathery, like a basketball, but it was soft and hairy, like the thick Pendleton blanket he'd given to Molly one year for her birthday.

"Now we inspect her new home," the Russian said. *"Agit, agit."* But Norma Jean balked when the Russian tried to lead her into the barn.

"She know something up," he said. He got an ankus out of the cab of the truck and tugged on the loose folds of skin along her leg. She trumpeted loudly. He tugged again, pulling harder this time with the curved hook of the ankus — *"agit, agit"* — and she lumbered slowly into the dark barn and into her stall, which had been covered with straw bedding.

"Is good," the Russian said, cutting the twine on a bale of alfalfa and spreading it out.

Meg stood next to Rudy and watched while Norma Jean explored her stall, testing the latch with her trunk.

"We put in a special latch," Rudy said to Meg. "Elephant-proof."

Norma Jean tugged on one of the eyebolts in the back of the stall and then reached over the wall of the stall and turned on the hose. The Russian said something to her and she turned it off and then tried to unscrew a nut, but Rudy and the Russian had tightened everything with a wrench.

"You want to pet her?" the Russian asked Meg. "You come over here. She like if you tickle her."

Norma Jean looked at them with amber-colored eyes. Her lashes were long and wiry. Meg approached cautiously and touched her trunk.

"Go on ahead," the Russian said. "Tickle her nose. Ha ha ha. Is all hairy."

Norma Jean pulled her trunk back and reached up under Meg's left armpit. Meg jumped back.

"She like tickle you too," the Russian said, shaking with laughter. Norma Jean seemed to be laughing as well, a deep elephant chuckle.

"I got her things in the truck," the Russian said. He opened a sack of oranges and tossed one into the stall. Norma Jean mashed it with her foot, mixing it in with a little alfalfa before scooping it up and flipping it into her mouth. Rudy and Meg watched her while the Russian went out to the truck and came back with a soccer ball and an oversized plastic harmonica. "Maybe we take a quick look outside," he said, "so she can see everything before she have her lunch." A door at the far end of the barn opened into the paddock.

Out in the paddock Norma Jean swiveled her head around, raised her trunk in the air, shot it out straight, and exhaled sharply at the Russian, who responded by blowing into the end of it.

"She be happy here, you'll see. You be happy too. There are elephant with good disposition and elephant with bad disposition. Norma Jean have good disposition."

The Russian went back to the truck to unload her easel and her paints and brushes. Norma Jean galloped over to a couple of scrubby acacia trees at far end of the paddock and pulled off a branch, which she used to scratch her back. Then she walked the perimeter of the paddock and came back to the barn.

"It's a little scary to see her out there," Rudy said, "to see how fast she can move."

"So, she saved your life, Pop?"

"Lifted me right up into the bed of the truck. The Russian couldn't have done it by himself."

Norma Jean ambled toward them and stopped. She lifted her trunk and touched Meg's hair. Meg held very still.

"It's all right," Rudy said. "It's all right."

◇

That night Rudy woke up about three o'clock, as he often did, and couldn't get back to sleep. He went into Meg's room and sat on the edge of her bed for a while and stroked her hair. He went back to bed and turned on the radio, which was tuned to the local station. Bob and Helen had put their failed predictions of the Second Coming behind them, though they hadn't lost interest in the subject. Tonight they were taking calls about the pandit who had gotten rid of the crows. Where had the crows gone? callers wanted to know. What did it mean? Who was this pandit anyway? Rudy was interested. He had the man's card in his pocket, after all.

One caller suggested that the pandit might be the Ancient of Days, but Bob and Helen didn't think that was likely, because the Ancient of Days wore a snow white robe, whereas the pandit's robe was saffron colored. Another wondered if the coming of the crows and their subsequent disappearance might be a sign of the Last Days and reminded listeners that only Jesus saves — not Bob and Helen, not the Ancient of Days, not the pandit. Only Jesus. Only Jesus. A car dealer called in to say that he didn't care who the pandit was, he'd gotten rid of the crows and now he didn't have to wash the crow droppings off his fleet of four hundred cars every day.

Rudy turned the radio off and got up to go to the bathroom. He looked at himself in the mirror while he washed his hands. The knot of anxiety in his stomach showed in his face. He knew better than to turn on the radio in the middle of the night. He'd think he was immune to Bob and Helen, but they always managed to upset him.

He didn't know much about the Ancient of Days, but he could hear an old hymn ringing in his head:

> *O Worship the King, all glorious above,*
> *O gratefully sing, his pow'r and his love,*
> *Our shield and defender, the Ancient of Days,*
> *Pavilioned in splendor, and girded with praise!*

He heard a trumpet blast from the barn. Norma Jean was awake too. He went downstairs and stepped out onto the veranda for a minute. He caught a whiff of elephant dung — fruity, not unpleasant — and sensed a throbbing *phut phut phut*, like the pulse of a freight train in the distance — the infrasonic sounds that elephants use to call to each other over long distances. He couldn't actually hear these sounds, but he could sense them, and he thought that Norma Jean was trying to communicate something to him, trying to tell him that soon he would see clearly and that everything would be all right.

Rudy took his oldest daughter out to lunch at the Taj Mahal. While they were waiting for their chicken vindaloo they sat side by side in a booth and looked through the chapter on India in *Weddings of Many Lands*. They wondered what TJ would say about the elephant; they talked about where to put the *mandap* and where to put the sacred fire, about whether the ceremony should be in the house or in the barn or outside in front of the barn; they discussed the original menu with the manager, who recommended a few changes. But they didn't talk about Meg's affair, or Helen's. They'd said all they needed to say.

"You are inviting Norma Jean elephant to this wedding?" the manager asked as they were leaving.

Rudy nodded. "I don't see why not."

The manager smiled. "Every elephant, you know," he said, "is a manifestation of Lord Ganesh, our elephant-headed god, the remover of obstacles. He is always invoked at the beginning of any great undertaking, such as this one. If you invoke Lord Ganesh, everything is sure to be very fine indeed."

"Sounds like good advice to me," Rudy said,

"I'm sure you will be very, very happy," the manager said to Meg.

"No, no," she said. "It's my sister who's getting married. She's in India right now with her fiancé."

"Well then," he said, "I'm sure your sister will be very, very happy. She is already very lucky to have a good sister like you and a good father to concern themselves with all these matters."

"I'm sure she will be," Meg said, "and yes, she is."

The *Ding an Sich*

After Meg left, Rudy spent more and more time with Norma Jean. He helped the Russian exercise her every morning. She understood more than forty commands, which the Russian barked out in the old language of the mahouts as they walked around the paddock. He was teaching them to Rudy, not Norma Jean.

At nine o'clock the Russian would leave Norma Jean out in the paddock so that he could work on bringing his barn by the trailer park up to USDA specifications. She'd take a long drink at the big watering trough by Rudy's barn and kick up some dirt or play with her soccer ball, which she batted around with her trunk, and her oversized plastic harmonica, which made a sound like a kazoo, before heading out to the acacia trees. Sometimes Rudy went with her, to practice his commands. He could get her to go forward (*agit*) and backward (*peachay*), to the left (*chi*) and to the right (*chai ghoom*), and to raise her trunk (*oopar dhur*). But he couldn't seem to master the most important command of all: stop, or *dhuth*, which you were supposed to pronounce "dutch," only without the *ch* sound at the end. Rudy couldn't quite get it.

On the way back to the barn he'd shout "duth," "dutch," "dhuth," but she'd keep right on going until she reached the watering trough, which Rudy kept full. She'd dip her trunk in, suck up several gallons of water, and blow a fine spray over her back and on her belly, and sometimes over Rudy too.

She'd take a little snooze in the afternoon, standing up, and when the Russian came back they'd set out her paints, big cans of tempera paints — children's finger paints that came from a school-supply wholesaler in Houston. She looked forward to these sessions and would get testy if she had to wait too long. After the painting session, Rudy and the Russian would hose her down and scrub her with two big brushes and then pumice stones, and the Russian would clean her toes.

"Who cleans elephants' toes out in the jungle?" Rudy asked.

"They clean them themselves with a stick," the Russian said, "just like they draw pictures."

They fed her in the morning and again in the evening: a bale of hay, a bale of alfalfa, rolled oats, specially formulated grain that the Russian bought from the zoo in Brownsville, a sack of potatoes, and ten to twenty pounds of fruit. She was very partial to potatoes and oranges. She ate the potatoes whole, but she mashed the oranges with her foot. She consumed a hundred and fifty pounds of fodder every day, half of which she deposited, like steaming loaves of bread, in the front of her stall, where it could easily be mucked out. The Russian shoveled the manure into the back of his truck and sold it to a citrus grower north of town.

Rudy cooked for the Russian and they ate on a card table out in the barn. The Russian had been with his father when his father'd bought Norma Jean at the *hathi* bazaar in Sonepur, and he demonstrated how his father had bargained with the vendor, their hands under a blanket to conceal the negotiations from curious spectators. If the buyer pressed the first two joints of the first finger of the vendor's right hand, he said, taking Rudy's hand and pressing his finger, that would mean he was offering five thousand rupees. If the vendor wasn't satisfied, he'd pinch the first joint of the buyer's next finger to raise the price by five hundred rupees, and so on. After his father's death, the Russian and Norma Jean had traveled for years with a Russian circus in eastern Europe and then in South America. He liked to reminisce about her adventures, and Rudy liked to listen to his stories: Norma Jean loose in the streets of Mexico City; Norma Jean swimming all the way across Lake La Barea, near Guadalajara; Norma Jean tapping a keg of beer on the circus train from Chihuahua to Ciudad Obregón. Then, fifteen years ago, the circus went belly-up in Reynosa, just across the river, and the Russian had simply taken off one night and walked the elephant across the international bridge, passing out *mordidas* to the border guards so they'd look the other way. Her Indian name had been Narmada-Jai, but he'd changed it to Norma Jean, Marilyn Monroe's real name, because she was so beautiful. He pronounced Marilyn Monroe as one word — Marilynmonroe. What times they'd shared together, good times and bad times, but he was an old man now, he said — he didn't know exactly how old — and he was worried about what was going to happen to her when he was gone. He offered to sell her to Rudy for five thousand dollars.

Rudy laughed. "I can remember when her picture was on all the magazine covers at the same time. Marilyn Monroe's picture. That was the summer Helen went to Italy for the first time and I started doing all the cooking."

The Russian poured a small glass of vodka for each of them and they drank.

"I can remember the day she *died* too," Rudy said. "August fifth, nineteen sixty-two. My youngest daughter had just gotten a job as a book conservator at the Newberry Library, and Molly — the one who's getting married — was getting ready to take off for Ann Arbor to study modern dance."

"You can't understand it without vodka," the Russian said, pouring two more glasses.

"I guess that's true of a lot of things," Rudy said.

That night, as he was drifting off to sleep, Rudy could hear Norma Jean, through his bedroom window, stirring in her stall, making her presence felt — an occasional trumpet blast followed by a full-throated roar.

Sometimes after lunch, while Norma Jean was snoozing, Rudy'd read *Philosophy Made Simple* out in the barn. He read and reread the chapters on Berkeley and Hume, underlining key passages with Helen's fountain pen till there were no more passages left to underline, but he couldn't find the flaws in the arguments that led, step by step, to the following conclusions: that the external world has no palpable existence apart from our perceptions; that the self itself is nothing but a bundle of these perceptions; that causality is psychological, rather than physical — a habit of mind based on the laws of association and constant conjunction.

And yet these arguments changed nothing. When he looked out his kitchen window in the morning, the sugar hackberries and the barn were still stubbornly there, and so were the sabal palms along the drive; when he looked inside himself he could still catch a glimpse of the boy who'd eaten the entire peach crop with his dad, three years in a row, back in the twenties; and when he turned his key in the ignition of the pickup, electric current flowed from the battery through the coil to the distributor and from the distributor to the spark plugs, and the engine started.

He found Kant's blend of rationalism and empiricism much more to his liking than Berkeley's idealism and Hume's skepticism, though the chapter on Kant was very difficult. *There's something "out there" after all,* he thought, *beyond the realm of phenomena, beyond the world of appearances.* He was back where he'd started, in Plato's cave, trying to make sense of the shadows.

But what was out there, in this realm beyond the cave, which Kant called the noumenon? The *Ding an sich,* that's what was out there. The "thing in itself." That's what Rudy wanted. Not the appearance of the thing, not the representation of the thing in his mind, but the thing in itself, reality.

But the problem was, you could never get at this reality, this *Ding an sich.* It's like a camera, Siva Singh explained. How do you know that the pictures you take are going to be black-and-white? Kant's answer is simple: because you have black-and-white film in the camera. It doesn't matter how you set the f-stop or adjust the shutter speed. It doesn't matter where you stand or how you hold your camera or how you shade the camera lens. You're going to get black-and-white photos. It's the same with people. How do you know that the next thing you see is going to exist in space and time? Answer: because you've got space-and-time film in your camera. It doesn't matter what you do, you're never going to get a picture of the *Ding an sich.*

Rudy could see the sense in this, but it bothered him anyway. He couldn't stop himself from taking mental pictures, turning his imaginary camera every which way, trying different light settings and shutter speeds, hoping to capture on film a glimpse of the *Ding an sich,* like the glimpse you get of Marilyn Monroe's underpants in *The Seven Year Itch.* He and Helen had seen *The Seven Year Itch* when it first came out in 1955, at the Biograph Theater up on North Lincoln, and the image was still as clear as a bell — the billowing skirt, Marilyn's laughter as she tries to hold it down, and then the little glimpse of white panty, like a star glimpsed through a gap in scudding clouds. There had to be *some* way to get color pictures. Why not just load color film in your camera?

And then one night, about eleven o'clock, he was taken by surprise. He was standing at the edge of the grove. It was dark under the avocado trees; the moon was hidden by clouds. He could see, in the beam of his flashlight, the narrow, silvery mesquite leaves on the trees on the far side of the slope, and he could feel the pods on the path under his feet. He was halfway down the slope when he saw a mysterious light coming around the bend in the river, heard mysterious music, music and soft laughter that rippled through the dark: the *Ding an sich.* He fumbled with the switch of his flashlight. He wanted to see what it looked like. *"Hola!"* he shouted, aiming the beam of the flashlight at the light on the river, the source of music and laughter.

The light went out, the music stopped, the laughter ceased. The flashlight sent a feeble beam into the darkness. He could see faces, wide-eyed, and a girl's bare breasts. It was his neighbor's son, floating down the river in his new pontoon boat, with his girlfriend.

"So," María said, when Rudy told her about it on his next cultural Friday. "You thought for a minute you got a glimpse of this *Ding an sich? La cosa en si misma?* Like a vision of the Virgin Mary?"

"Something like that." Rudy laughed. "Just for a minute. What do you think?"

"Maybe," she said, laughing. "Probably as close as you're going to get."

◆

Armed with the brochure from the hotel in Detroit and with *Weddings of Many Lands,* Rudy met the pandit at El Zarate, a coffee shop in downtown Mission. The pandit had three white stripes running across his forehead, and a red dot just over his nose — not one of the little *bindis* Rudy'd seen Indian women wearing, but a bright red spot the size of a silver dollar. A chain of large beads, wrapped twice around his head, kept his white hair out of his eyes but allowed it to hang down over his shoulders; his long beard covered his shirtfront and concealed his mouth. He was drinking tea. He was, he explained, a *baba* — a guru, a teacher — as well as a pandit. He approved of Rudy's intention to ground his daughter's wedding in ultimate reality, in the *Ding an sich.*

"Ceremonies are in place," he said, pausing to blow on his tea, "with roots that reach down very deep, Mr. Harrington, all the way down into the *Sivaloka,* the causal plane, the quantum level of the universe where the gods guide the evolution of the worlds."

"Did you say *worlds?*" Rudy asked.

The pandit nodded.

"My daughter's fiancé has just published an article about parallel universes in an important journal."

"Yes," the pandit said, "western science is beginning to catch up with what the great sages have known from the beginnings of time."

Rudy offered to send him the articles in *Time* and *Newsweek,* but the pandit waved the offer away. He may have been pleased with Rudy's intentions, but he was not at all pleased with Rudy's answers to his questions about Molly and TJ.

"*Kanyadan,*" he said, shaking his head. "*Kanyadan.* The greatest gift a man can bestow is the gift from which he will acquire the most *punya* — the gift of a virgin. The gift of your daughter in marriage . . ." He fixed Rudy with a glance as sharp as a needle. "'On this auspicious day,' you must say, 'I give away my daughter who is pure and in perfect health and beauty to this groom.'"

"There's nothing to be done now," Rudy said. "They've been living together for six months."

"You should be ashamed to say such a thing to me," the pandit said.

"I'm sure that all Hindu brides are virgins," Rudy said.

The pandit brushed this observation aside. "The key concept here is *prem*," he said, "what you call love. But let me explain that while *prem* is an aspect of traditional Hindu marriages, it is not the mainspring, and it does not play any role in the marriage negotiations. The aim of marriage, Mr. Harrington, is to unite two families, two lines. *Sangam*," he said, "the auspicious confluence of two mighty rivers. It is not necessary that the individuals love each other at the beginning. It is not even necessary that they know each other. From what you've told me, however, your daughter is entering into a love match, a grand, individualistic passion based entirely upon *prem*. It has nothing else to support it. Such a union is cheap and immoral. It will fail because its very foundation is illusory and impermanent."

"But how do you ever get to the foundation?" Rudy asked.

"Supreme Consciousness," the pandit said, leaning forward. "All our spiritual practices have Supreme Consciousness as their ultimate goal. But it is not a parlor game; it is not for those who are mentally and emotionally unstable."

"Like me?"

"I did not say that, Mr. Harrington." He finished his tea and pushed the cup away from him. "I want you to sit comfortably."

Rudy adjusted himself in the booth.

"Keep your back straight."

Rudy straightened his back.

"Now close your eyes and relax. Breathe naturally, through your nose. Let the breath come in and out of your nostrils without forcing it. Breathe deeply. And stop fidgeting. This won't hurt you. Don't worry about other people looking at you, just do as I say."

Rudy took a deep breath and let it out slowly. Then another.

"Now," said the pandit, "I want you to focus your awareness on a point right between your eyebrows, do you understand?"

Rudy nodded.

"Now bring your awareness in, slowly, till it's about three inches inside your head, inside your brain, and just let it rest in the silence. If images start to appear, don't fight against them. Just let them recede into the shadows."

Rudy waited. No images appeared, but the sounds of the coffee shop grew fainter and fainter.

"Now ask yourself," the pandit said, "who is aware of your own awareness? What is there? What is not thinking, not doing, just watching? And who is aware of your awareness of your own awareness?"

Rudy felt a hand on his shoulder. The pandit was shaking him. He took a sip of his tea, but it had grown cold. He felt alive, clear-headed.

"If you connect regularly with your atman," the pandit said, "even if only for an instant, your heart will be healed. You will be calmer and less fearful."

"My heart," Rudy said.

"Yes," the pandit said. "I read about your heart attack in the *Monitor*. You were very fortunate that the elephant was there. Norma Jean. I believe her real name is Narmada-Jai. I have several of her paintings at the ashram. In any case, we shall begin, as I have explained, with an invocation to Lord Ganesh. The elephant-headed god."

"Norma Jean's staying at my place for a while this summer. The USDA inspector is after the Russian to make some changes in her barn. I was thinking we could work her into the wedding. Maybe TJ could ride on her from the house down to the barn, wherever we set up the *mandap*."

"A white horse would be more appropriate," said the pandit, "unless you're a king or a maharajah."

"Well, I'm not a king or a maharajah," Rudy said.

"An elephant is always an auspicious presence at a wedding," said the pandit, softening his tone, "but her function should be not to carry the groom but to greet your guests." He laughed. "It would probably be best," he went on, "if I performed a short version of the traditional ceremony. If you wish, you can let me know in a week or two and I will cast the horoscopes and determine an auspicious date and we can proceed from there."

"What would an abridged ceremony be like?"

"It would be shorter. Not two or three days, but an hour. And it would be comprehensible to non-Hindus."

"That's good," Rudy said.

"It must take place outside. You'll need a *mandap,* as you already know, and some carpets to sit on, or even folding chairs. At the front and in the center we'll position the sacred fire, which can be in a brazier, or even a charcoal grill. But you need not trouble yourself with these details now. The Taj Mahal can provide the *mandap,* and I'll take care of the rest."

Rudy nodded again.

"And I'll need their natal charts."

"Natal charts?"

"Their birth dates and the precise times of their births, so I can cast the horoscopes."

"I'll see what I can do.

"One last thing, though, Mr. Harrington. A *mangalashtak,* or poem, must be presented on this occasion. You could perhaps compose the *mangalashtak* yourself, if you're inclined that way. Or you could choose something suitable."

"I'll see what I can do," Rudy said again.

"Mr. Harrington," the pandit said, standing up, "you know, I suppose, that Lord Ganesh — the elephant god — in his aspect as Ganesh Mahodara, the big-bellied one, is the dispeller of *moha*, which is infatuation or delusion. He is the remover of obstacles."

"Well," Rudy said, "I read a little about Lord Ganesh in *Weddings of Many Lands,* but we've put some obstacles in his path."

"No obstacle is too great for Lord Ganesh," the pandit said.

"I'll remember that," Rudy said, picking up the check. "By the way. When you asked me to focus on that spot in the brain . . . atman. Was that Supreme Consciousness?"

The pandit almost choked on his tea. "Mr. Harrington," he said when he'd recovered himself, "you are full of surprises. You are not a king or a maharajah, but you want your son-in-law to ride on an elephant at your daughter's wedding. And now, having taken one small step on a journey that will occupy a sage for many lifetimes, you ask me if you have achieved Supreme Consciousness!" He extracted a napkin from the napkin holder and wiped his eyes. "Excuse me," he said. "I sometimes forget where I am."

"In Texas, you mean?"

The pandit nodded.

"One last question," Rudy said. "How did you get rid of the crows?"

The pandit took hold of his wrist, like Norma Jean. "Mr. Harrington, Mr. Harrington. We all have our secrets. This is mine."

That night Rudy got out Helen's correspondence folder and went through her letters — the ones she'd sent him before they were married, and then from Italy — till he found the poem he was looking for, a *mangalashtak* for his daughter's wedding. The letter was dated June 12, 1931, six weeks before they were married. Helen was working as a secretary at DePaul, her alma mater, taking one course a term toward a master's degree in art history, reading poetry, studying French and Italian. It was the second year of the Depression. No one had any money, but people still needed to eat. Rudy was working sixty to eighty hours a week on the South Water Market, living up on the second floor of Becker's warehouse on Fourteenth Street. His job was to round up a crew of dockwallopers — winos from the St. James Hotel on Twelfth Street — and pay them a buck apiece to unload the boats, loaded with produce from the big farmers' market in Benton Harbor, that docked at the piers just south of Congress Street.

The summer days were long. The last boat would usually dock just before midnight, and he had to have his orders filled by four o'clock in the morning and, at five, start his rounds in the city. But he was young and strong, and at least once a week he'd take the El up north to Fullerton to see Helen and they'd walk in the little park at the end of Shakespeare Street and she'd smoke a cigarette and blow smoke rings and tell him about her classes. Or he'd meet her at the Art Institute, and when it closed at five o'clock they'd have a soda at the big Walgreen's across the street. One night she stayed downtown and they went dancing at the Oriental Dance Emporium on State Street. She rolled her stockings down to her knees and fastened them with elastic bands that nearly cut off her circulation. The next day her uncle, the referee who'd introduced them and who was anxious to marry her off, came over to Becker's, where Rudy was stacking flats of avocados onto a pallet, and hinted that it was about time for Rudy to clarify his intentions.

She'd been writing to him at Becker's, and the secretaries and the bookkeepers had never stopped kidding him. She told him how much she loved him, and she sent sketches she'd done of the buildings at DePaul or the animals in the Lincoln Park Zoo, and she copied out poems that she especially liked. The poem Rudy was looking for was by Edna St. Vincent Millay. Helen had heard Edna read at the Arts Club a couple years earlier and now, she'd written to Rudy, Edna was having an affair with the University of Chicago student who'd introduced her at that reading. The poem had been written to him, the student, George Dillon. Rudy hadn't really understood it till Helen explained it to him, but he'd folded it up carefully and carried it in his billfold for years, till the creases had worn down to nothing and the paper itself was smooth and shiny, and he was afraid it was going to fall apart. He took it out of the folder and smoothed it out carefully on Helen's desk:

> *Not in a silver casket cool with pearls*
> *Or rich with red corundum or with blue,*
> *Locked, and the key withheld, as other girls*
> *Have given their loves, I give my love to you;*
> *Not in a lovers'-knot, not in a ring*
> *Worked in such fashion, and the legend plain —*
> Semper fidelis, *where a secret spring*
> *Kennels a drop of mischief for the brain:*
> *Love in the open hand, no thing but that,*
> *Ungemmed, unhidden, wishing not to hurt,*
> *As one should bring you cowslips in a hat*
> *Swung from the hand, or apples in her skirt,*
> *I bring you, calling out as children do:*
> *"Look what I have! — And these are all for you."*

Sitting at Helen's desk, he read the poem, saying the words out loud, as if he'd just opened her letter and were reading it for the first time, as if their life together still lay ahead of them, as if all he had to do was take the Howard Street El north to Fullerton and she'd be there in the station, standing at the bottom of the stairs, or sitting on a bench at the trolley stop, her head in a book, waiting for him.

He folded the sheet of paper carefully and put it in his billfold.

In the third week in July, the Russian went to visit his sister in Mexico. He hadn't been able to visit her in fifteen years, he told Rudy, because he hadn't been able to leave Norma Jean. He mucked out the elephant's stall and filled it with a load of fresh straw for her bedding, and he brought plenty of fodder. He tacked up a list of addresses on the side of the barn, out of reach of Norma Jean's trunk: the local vet, the large-animal vet at the zoo in Brownsville, the farmer who sold him the alfalfa, the citrus grower who bought Norma Jean's poop. He kissed Norma Jean good-bye and headed out the drive.

Rudy was sorry to miss his cultural Friday, but María, who was going to do the flowers for the wedding, had already visited twice that week, to have a look at the barn and at the veranda, and on both occasions Rudy had cooked for her and she'd spent the evening. Besides, it was the first time Rudy'd had Norma Jean all to himself for a whole day and a whole night. What he really wanted to do was take her out for a walk by himself, without the Russian — not in the paddock, but up around the house, maybe down to the lower grove. After all, he'd mastered over twenty commands. But what if he couldn't get her back into the barn? The prospect was too daunting, and he had too much to do. He opened the back door of the barn and let her out into the paddock. Maybe later, he thought, when he came back from the post office.

He spent the rest of the morning addressing and stamping the last of the wedding invitations, and most of the afternoon on the telephone, talking to the manager of the Taj Mahal, who had decided he wouldn't be able to provide the dishes he and Rudy had selected at the price they had agreed upon, and to the pandit, who called to say that he had cast the horoscopes and determined that Saturday, September 9, was an inauspicious day and that therefore the wedding would have to be postponed.

Rudy didn't know what to do. There were no other Indian restaurants in the area, no other pandits. And Molly wouldn't be home till the first of September. The shoot was behind schedule because the monsoons had come early. If they hadn't finished the movie by the end of August she'd have to go back *after* the wedding. Rudy tried to interest her in some of the more serious wedding problems, but she told him she had to go. TJ's uncle Siva would be arriving early to help with the arrangements, she said. He'd deal with the pandit and the manager of the Taj Mahal.

When he got back from the post office, he set up Norma Jean's easel and her paints and listened to the radio while she painted. The news of the great world seemed to be coming from a place as far away as India, maybe even from another planet.

In the evening, when the sun finally went down, he grilled a pork chop and drank a couple of beers, and then he went out to the barn to say good night to Norma Jean. It was dark in the barn, and he didn't realize at first that she was crying. But when his eyes got used to the dark, he could see that her head was lowered, her powerful trunk hanging loose, and big tears were flowing from under her wiry eyelashes and running down her elephant cheeks and splashing onto the floor.

Rudy knew just how she felt. "It's going to be okay, sweetheart," he said. "You're going to be all right. Your friend will be back tomorrow night. I'm here with you now. It's just for a little while. I'll take good care of you, don't worry."

Her tears upset Rudy. Were they really tears, or just some kind of natural discharge? Could she be in musth? But he thought that only male elephants went into musth.

She kept on crying, letting it all out now, sobbing, her whole frame trembling. Rudy climbed up on the rails of the stall so that he could reach her head. He rubbed the two humps, softly rounded like breasts or buttocks. He leaned over and kissed the hump nearest him. "It's going to be all right." He scratched her neck and her rough trunk. She used her trunk to put his hand in her mouth, and he stroked her tongue, which seemed to calm her.

He went up to the house and brought back his guitar, which he'd hardly played since he came to Texas. It was an old small-bodied Gibson that he'd picked up on Maxwell Street the first time Helen went to Italy. He sat down on a bale of alfalfa, and began to sing:

> *Winds on Lake Michigan,*
> *Lord, blow chilly and cold,*
> *Winds on Lake Michigan,*
> *Lord, Lord, blow chilly and cold,*
> *I'm going to leave Chicago,*
> *Go back to Vicksburg, that's my home.*

Did she remember her old home, he wondered? Did she remember her mother and her elephant aunties? The *hathi* bazaar at Sonepur, where she'd been sold to the Russian's father? The circus, the travels in Russia and then Poland, the long trip to South America in the hold of a ship? The trains in Mexico?

Crossing the international bridge from Reynosa to Hidalgo, on foot, in the middle of the night?

Rudy remembered his old home, and Helen. If Helen were here . . . They'd talk things over at the kitchen table — the manager of the Taj Mahal, the pandit. A couple of jokers, a couple of wild cards. If Helen were here, he wouldn't give them a thought, and he wouldn't give a damn about the *Ding an sich,* or about the failure to get his hands on it, about the probability that his quest would come to nothing. That it was all foolishness. Like thinking that the lights and music on the river were coming from beyond the realm of appearances, when it was just a couple of kids making out in a pontoon boat. His excitement at reading the chapter on Kant had waned. What good was the *Ding an sich* if you could never get your hands on it? It seemed to him now that all the great questions were unanswerable. The things that matter most to us are unknowable, and this unknowability weighed him down. Death, beauty, love, sex, pain. What can we know? How shall we live? What happens when we die? He didn't know any more about these things than when he'd been sitting at Helen's desk back in Chicago.

"If I get lucky, babe," he sang, "and find my train fare home, I'm going to leave Chicago, go back to Vicksburg, that's my home."

He sang the songs he used to sing to his daughters when they were sad: "Key to the Highway" and "Sittin' on Top of the World" and "Wimmin from Coast to Coast":

> *Sometime my baby wear a hat,*
> *And sometime she wear her tam,*
> *Sometime my baby wear a hat,*
> *Sometime she wear her tam,*
> *She got them great big legs*
> *And they shaped like Georgia hams.*

He kept playing till Norma Jean stopped crying, and then he took his shoes off and lay down on the Russian's cot in the tack room. There was no tackle left now, nothing but the storage cabinets and the old hooks and an old raincoat, stiff with age, and the Russian's duffel bag next to the cot. As Rudy faded into sleep, Norma Jean made her presence felt, a great gray shape, moving gently like a shadow in the dark.

The Übermensch

None of them had ever encountered a real philosopher before, much less an Übermensch, and they were all a little
apprehensive when they heard the car in the drive. When they
stepped outside onto the veranda, TJ's uncle Siva, who'd called
from the Starlight Motel, was climbing out of the car he'd rented
at the airport, a shiny blue-black Mercedes. It was hot. The temperature had been in the upper nineties all week. The thick
adobe walls kept the house comfortable, and Rudy'd installed a
big exhaust fan in the roof of the barn to draw off some of the hot
air. The Russian, who'd gone to visit his sister again, had been
hosing down Norma Jean twice a day. Rudy's zucchini plants had
collapsed, but the herbs were doing well and he had all the
tomatoes and cucumbers he could eat.

Uncle Siva shaded his eyes, though he was wearing sunglasses, and surveyed the grove before turning toward the house.
He wasn't a big man, but he carried himself like a big man and
wore his suit jacket over his shoulders, like the men Rudy'd seen

in Italy when he went to confront Helen about Bruni, men who walked around the piazzas like kings or popes, men whose faces showed up in the pictures in the big Uffizi museum there — Frederick Montefeltro, or Pope Leo, or Lorenzo the Medici. This was the way he'd always pictured Bruni, walking around with his jacket over his shoulders. And this was the way he'd been picturing Nietzsche's Übermensch. What did these men know that he didn't know? What made them so sure of their place in the world, their place in the great scheme of things?

Uncle Siva had written very forcefully about these supermen in *Philosophy Made Simple* — these men who step outside traditional moral values, these men who dispense with ordinary notions of good and evil and create their own versions of life — and it was clear to Rudy that Siva regarded himself as a member of this select club. But how did you do it? How did you join? And how did you know when you'd been accepted as a member? And was it a good thing to do in the first place?

Rudy'd been planning to discuss these questions with Siva privately, but he was a little apprehensive, and at the last minute he invited Medardo and Father Russell and María to join them for dinner. Safety in numbers. María would have to leave early because the art dealer she'd been seeing was coming in that evening instead of Saturday. The art dealer owned two galleries — one in San Antonio and one in Austin — that specialized in southwestern art, and Rudy'd been wondering if he might be interested in some Norma Jeans.

In spite of the heat, Uncle Siva wasn't sweating, though his high brown forehead shone as if he'd polished it. He removed his sunglasses and turned to look at Rudy, and Rudy could see that he was a force to be reckoned with, which was just what he needed: a man who could deal with the manager of the Taj Mahal and with the pandit.

In the kitchen Medardo and Father Russell rose to shake hands with the philosopher. "You must be used to this heat," Father Russell said.

"It's been very hot in New York," Uncle Siva said, "but it wasn't bad in California."

"I was thinking of India."

"It doesn't get this hot in Assam," Siva said. "Not up in the hills, but it rains a lot."

Rudy took a tray of Italian meringues out of a slow oven. He was working on the last of the frozen *Saint-Cyrs* he'd planned for the wedding reception. He'd spent a lot of time with Norma Jean in the afternoon and was running late, and the meringues were taking a long time to dry out because of the humidity.

María had brought a bouquet of brightly colored flowers from her *floristería*. Rudy didn't have a proper vase and she was arranging them in a tall beer glass. "Irises," she said, smiling. "These sword-shaped leaves symbolize the sharpness of the Virgin Mary's pain at her son's suffering." She was wearing tiny emerald earrings that matched the color of the leaves.

"My mother always called them 'flags,'" Rudy said.

"Rudy says you're some kind of superman," María said, looking at Uncle Siva.

There it is, Rudy thought — *out in the open.*

Siva smiled. "Yes," he said, "but not the kind who can fly and leap tall buildings at a single bound."

Rudy closed his eyes.

"Not superman," Father Russell said. "Übermensch. It's a German word —"

Rudy interrupted the priest to explain: "I've been reading the chapter on Nietzsche in *Philosophy Made Simple,* and I have to tell you, I have a lot of trouble with the Übermensch. Does noble morality really begin with an affirmation of the self?"

Uncle Siva looked at Medardo and then at Father Russell and then at María and then at Rudy. "Yes," he said. "The answer to your question is yes." And then he started to laugh. "I had no idea what I was getting myself into," he said. "This is really astonishing. Why, I've just come from a conference at Berkeley where no one would dare put such an important question so directly, but here in this out-of-the-way . . ."

"So," Medardo said, "you *are* a superman?"

"Let me put it this way," Siva said, removing his linen jacket and loosening his plum-colored tie. He rolled up his sleeves. "I've lived life my own way, on my own terms. I never wanted to be a conventional academic philosopher. I wanted to cut down jungles, not irrigate deserts. Once I saw New York, I knew exactly what I wanted from life. What I wanted was to live on the Upper West Side, somewhere in the sixties, write books, make enough money to entertain my friends and to go to the theater or to a concert at least three or four nights a week, to fall in love with a series of beautiful and interesting women, and to spend a month in Paris every fall. And that's exactly what I've done. I support myself by writing books — *Philosophy Made Simple,* my maiden voyage, has been a real gold mine, if I may say so — and by producing television shows for educational television and for the BBC in which I interview contemporary philosophers about important philosophical issues: pragmatism and ethics, the pluralistic universe, logical atomism, the new logic, the verifiability principle, ordinary language philosophy, Kierkegaard's solution to the Socratic paradox, how Heidegger would have responded to Nietzsche, and so forth." He spoke with a British accent, saying "loife" for "life" and "contempree" for "contemporary."

"And what about Paris?"

"Ah, Paris. I'll be leaving for Paris shortly after the wedding. A few things to take care of in New York — my sister Nandini is coming — and then . . ."

"Well then," Rudy said, dotting a strip of waxed paper with butter and fastening it to the inside of a plastic ice-cream container. "You're the perfect person to take care of a couple of little problems." He explained the grief he was getting from the avaricious manager of the Taj Mahal and from the crazy pandit. He poured a bit of chocolate mousse into the bottom of the container and arranged a series of meringues around the edge. "These are supposed to look like the ribbons on the hats worn by cadets at Saint-Cyr," he said, "the French military academy."

"My sister is much better at that sort of thing," Siva said, laughing. "She'll take care of everything. You'll see. I'm hopeless at these domestic problems. Besides, I'm flying down to Oaxaca in the morning. Nietzsche, you know, wanted to visit the high plateaus of Oaxaca, where he could look down on the Pacific. In a way I shall be his surrogate."

"You can't see the ocean from Oaxaca," María said. "Not from the city. You'd have to go to Puerto Angel or Santa Cruz Huautuico."

"Oh."

"Your sister . . . ," Rudy said, adding a layer of crumbled meringues over the chocolate in the bottom of the container. "My daughter says your sister chased away a rhinoceros with a broom."

"Oh, yes, but it would have been a one-horned bush rhinoceros, not a savanna one. The bush rhino has very bad eyesight. A savanna rhino is a very different matter."

"Still . . ."

"Don't worry — she's quite capable of dealing with restaurant managers and pandits. And she's very fond of your daughter. You don't have to worry on that score either. I spoke to her just last week. She's even teaching Molly to ride Champaa, her old elephant. It's not impossible that she will move to the States herself, now that our father has died — it's been two years. Nothing would make me happier. She has two thousand coolies to manage, so it's not an easy life for her. Life on a tea garden is very tedious. And there are *dacoits* and kidnappings, and there's always trouble brewing with the native tribes. So it's not only tedious, it's quite dangerous, rather like Schopenhauer's vision of human life — boredom on the one hand, anxiety on the other. I'm here in the States, her son is here, and besides, she would like to remarry."

"What are *dacoits?*" Rudy asked.

"Bandits. She can't leave the garden at night without armed bodyguards."

"Why can't she remarry in India?" María asked.

"There's almost no chance of that. For a widow . . . it's almost impossible. Damaged goods. Especially for my sister. She married out of caste to begin with. What we call *prem,* a love match."

"So your sister's not happy in India?"

"Not entirely. She has been not exactly ostracized — she's a *zamindar,* a landowner, too wealthy to be ignored; too powerful — but . . ." He started to laugh. "I shall put in a good word for you, Rudy. Maybe I can arrange something. My aunt has arranged several appointments with prospective suitors in Detroit, and I've turned up a couple of eligible bachelors in New York, but perhaps I'll propose you instead."

Rudy started to protest.

"Seriously, Rudy. My sister is an extraordinary woman. Not a great beauty, but something better — she enjoys the imperfections that make a work of art more striking. Like the extra limbs in some of Rembrandt's drawings."

"What kind of imperfections? You don't mean she's got an extra arm or leg?"

"Red hair, for one thing."

"My wife had red hair," he said.

"It is not really red, of course," Siva said. "But there's a hint of reddishness: *laal*. She could never live up to the ideal of the *pativrata*, the wife who worships her husband like a god, but of course that doesn't matter in the United States. And I can say that we would be in a position to promise a significant dowry. Think about it, Rudy. I believe in being straightforward in these matters. Also, I think she would like this place. Quite frankly, I think she would prefer it to New York or Detroit."

The mousse in the bottom of the ice-cream container kept the meringue ribbons from slipping. Rudy added a layer of crumbled meringues, then more mousse. Then another layer of meringues. More mousse. Another layer of meringues. More mousse. Another layer of meringues, till the container was filled. Uncle Siva fell silent as Rudy poured in the last of the mousse and took a deep breath. "I don't know why I get nervous when I do this. There's not much that can go wrong. And I enjoy working in a kitchen full of people. It reminds me of home."

"That's because you're concentrating fully," Uncle Siva said. "Like a true artist."

"I never thought of it like that," Rudy said. "You see the ends of these meringues sticking up?" Everyone looked. "If I bent them now, they'd break; but once they're frozen you can bend them right over. That's what I'll do. For now I'm going to have to cover it with a piece of tinfoil instead of putting the lid on it."

"I had a slice of a *Saint-Cyr* in Paris once," Uncle Siva said, "at the Grand Véfour in the Palais Royal; it was served with *crème Chantilly*. Quite extraordinary. I never expected to eat it again in Texas."

"I made a small one earlier — for tonight," Rudy said, putting the newly prepared mousse in the freezer. He didn't know what *crème Chantilly* was, but he didn't ask.

"I've got two bottles of good claret in the car," Uncle Siva said suddenly. "I don't want them to cook."

Rudy sent Medardo out to the garden for some fresh tomatoes and put on the water for pasta while Uncle Siva went out to the car to rescue the wine. María went to freshen up.

"You're awfully quiet," Rudy said to Father Russell.

"I think this man is dangerous," Father Russell said. "I think you need to be very, very careful."

By the time Rudy served the pasta, they'd finished the first bottle of wine and started on the second. The wine was certainly better than what Rudy was used to drinking, though it didn't really stand up to the puttanesca sauce, which he'd made with tomatoes from the garden. When Uncle Siva asked if there was any Parmesan cheese, María put her hand on his arm. "Be careful, Uncle Siva. You don't want to make *brutta figura.* You'll upset Rudy."

Siva looked at Rudy and then at María.

María explained: "You're not allowed to put Parmesan cheese on pasta that has anchovies in it. Right, Rudy?"

"You don't want the cheese to interfere with the flavor of the anchovies," Rudy said. Siva gave a mock frown to cover his embarrassment. "Besides," Rudy added, "this is a southern Italian dish. They didn't even *have* Parmesan cheese in the south."

Rudy got a small bowl of leftover Parmesan out of the refrigerator and put it on the table in front of Uncle Siva. Siva looked at the cheese but didn't put any on his pasta.

"For heaven's sake," Rudy said. "Go ahead and use the cheese. It's a silly rule anyway."

Siva hesitated — Rudy could see he was tempted — but finally decided against it.

◆

For dessert Rudy served four wedges of a frozen *Saint-Cyr* and a bottle of the Pol Roger that he'd bought in Brownsville to sample for the wedding.

"Have you ever eaten at the Grand Véfour?" Siva asked, looking up from his plate.

They all shook their heads.

"I had the *lamproie à la bordelaise* and my companion had *pigeon Prince Rainier III,* with cognac and some kind of meat glaze. It's all coming back to me. This a very Proustian moment, really. An involuntary memory. Monsieur Oliver himself brought the *Saint-Cyr* to our table," he said, refilling his glass. "I can see him now, I can see the back of his head reflected in the big mirror in the corner behind our table. And I can see the back of my companion's head too, in the mirror, her long hair falling free." He paused. "Rudy," he said.

Rudy started to say something, but Siva held up his hand. "In moments like this, moments of bliss, as in sexual congress, the mind is steadied, focused on the present moment. Past and present converge, so to speak. The taste of this wonderful *Saint-Cyr,* for example, circumvents the senses and goes directly into the atman. The Veil of Maya is lifted."

Rudy used his finger to wipe up the last bit of chocolate on his plate. He put his finger in his mouth and looked around at the others. They'd had so much to eat and drink that they were all looking around at each other in a trancelike state. After a moment of silence Rudy said, "I forgot to serve the salad. It's in the refrigerator. Tomatoes and cucumbers and basil from the garden." But no one wanted salad now, not after *le Saint-Cyr, glacé.*

◇

Rudy put on a pot of espresso, but María had to leave to pick up her art dealer at the airport, and Medardo . . . It was not too late to put in an appearance at Estrella Princesa. Rudy showed Uncle Siva and Father Russell some of Norma Jean's paintings while they drank their coffee, and then took them out to the barn to see Norma Jean herself.

"My sister is going to be very pleased," Siva said, putting his hand on Rudy's shoulder as they walked across the gravel drive. "She's very fond of elephants. Very fond. When my grandfather was alive, we kept four elephants. The oldest one, Raja, a big tusker, helped clear the land for the Assam Railway and Trading Company. But there is only one elephant now, Champaa, who's like part of the family. She comes to the kitchen every morning and puts her trunk in at the window, and my sister gives her a banana. Her mahout can't move her away until she's had her banana."

"Shhh," Rudy whispered, "she may be asleep. Norma Jean."

Rudy didn't turn on the light when they entered the barn, and it took them a while for their eyes to adjust to the darkness. What they could see, after a minute or two, was a large shadow, dark on dark, Norma Jean. She was awake. She stretched out her trunk to Rudy and kneaded his shoulder.

Siva put his hand on Rudy's other shoulder. "Schopenhauer, you know," he said, "says that the idea of the elephant is imperishable."

"You mean like a Platonic form?"

"Very like a Platonic form."

"Or the *Ding an sich?*" Father Russell asked.

Siva started to laugh. "Very like the *Ding an sich,*" he said.

"Every time the Russian goes to visit his sister," Rudy said, "I'm tempted to take her out for a spin, but I've never had the nerve. We could do it now. You know a little something about elephants."

Siva sobered up immediately. "Not a good idea," he said. "Definitely not a good idea. An elephant without its own mahout? Believe me, I do know something about elephants, and I know this is not a good idea. Perhaps if my sister were here. Perhaps. But none of my grandfather's elephants went anywhere without their own mahout."

"I know a little something too," Rudy said, opening the gate of Norma Jean's stall. He was feeling a little light-headed, but not out of control.

"I think Uncle Siva's right," Father Russell said, but Rudy was already giving the command: *"Agit, agit."* And Norma Jean, as if by magic, began to glide forward slowly. Rudy picked up the ankus, which was hanging on a nail, and touched her, and she turned toward the front door of the barn into the open area that separated the barn from the house and the garage. *Agit, agit. Chai ghoom, chai ghoom. Right, right.* Norma Jean turned to the right. *Chi, chi. Left, left.* Norma Jean veered to the left. Rudy wasn't aware of Uncle Siva now, nor of the priest. His heart was pounding the way it had pounded when he'd driven his dad's Packard for the first time alone. *"Dhuth, dhuth,"* he said firmly, but he still didn't have the pronunciation quite right and Norma Jean ignored him.

His parents had been asleep and he'd taken the keys from the hook in the kitchen and after he'd started the car, which his dad had left out by the packing shed, he'd waited five minutes, ten minutes, to make sure they hadn't woken up, and then he'd driven to Silver Beach, the amusement park on US 12, his hands trembling on the wheel, afraid to go more than fifty miles an hour. At first. And then goosing it up to sixty, seventy, eighty, so that the car left the pavement and soared into the air when he went over the viaduct north of Stevensville. His dad was waiting for him in the kitchen when he got back. He thought he was in for a whipping, but his dad poured them both a little tot of whiskey, in jelly glasses, and asked him not to take the car again without asking. It was Rudy's first taste of whiskey. "Your mother doesn't need to know about this," his dad said, and Rudy didn't know if he meant the car or the whiskey.

Rudy took Norma Jean past the sugar hackberries by the house, past the septic tank, past the garden, and around the garage before heading back, past Siva's Mercedes and Father Russell's Pontiac. Someone had turned on the light in the barn, and he could see the priest and the philosopher standing in the big doorway. He couldn't get Norma Jean to stop, but he maneuvered her into the barn — tugging at her loose skin with the ankus, the way the Russian did — and eased her into her stall, like a pilot bringing a big liner into port. He took a deep breath and opened up a bale of alfalfa for her and emptied a sack of potatoes onto the floor in front of her.

Uncle Siva, who had an early-morning flight, was anxious to leave. Father Russell stayed behind to have a nightcap and to chat while Rudy washed up the dishes.

"You still think he's dangerous?" Rudy asked, handing Father Russell a dish towel.

Father Russell laughed. "Now why in the world," he asked, putting down the plate he'd just dried and shaking his head back and forth, "would an Übermensch care one way or another about whether or not it's okay to put Parmesan cheese on a plate of spaghetti? Why, you're more of an Übermensch than that phony."

Rudy slept in the barn that night, as he always did when the Russian went to visit his sister. It was hot, but he covered himself with a flannel sheet. He was too excited to sleep, too aware of his own strength. How Helen would have enjoyed this evening. Now there was an Übermensch, or an Überwoman. Helen. How her face had glowed when she told him she wouldn't come back to Chicago with him. It was a beautiful apartment, in the center of Florence, but there was a nightclub on the first floor and the music started up as they were talking, the noise echoing in the air shaft and filling the courtyard. Margot was already asleep. They were talking in the kitchen. Helen was standing in front of the stairs that led up to a rooftop terrazzo. She'd charted her course, and it was only because of the cancer that she'd altered it later on. But she had chosen her own way then too. She'd come home with Margot in June and taught for another three years. When she became too sick to teach any longer, she'd organized her *self* around something other than splenic irradiation and courses of busulfan and radioactive phosphorus — around old photographs and old memories, around her art books and the cartoons in *The New Yorker,* and around her record collection, mostly operas, and the slides that she'd used in her art history classes. Rudy moved the record player upstairs so she could listen to music, and he bought a new screen and set up the projector in the bedroom so that they could look at the slides together in the evening. So much beauty, it was overwhelming: Italian operas; Greek temples and sculptures; medieval cathedrals and manuscripts; Renaissance paintings; the Impressionists; the Modernists. She never complained. She was cheerful if not happy. She was in a lot of pain, but not in too much pain to smile at the *New Yorker* cartoons that Rudy held up for her to see, not even at the end, when he had to describe them for her and read the captions.

Helen would have put Parmesan cheese on the spaghetti. She

put Parmesan cheese on everything and didn't worry about making *brutta figura.*

How funny Uncle Siva had looked, like the donkey who can't decide between two equidistant bales of hay. Rudy would find no help in that quarter. But he didn't think he'd need it. He thought maybe the priest was right. He had a bit of Übermensch in him.

Molly

The thing Rudy enjoyed most about walking Norma Jean, which he did every chance he got — and the Russian, far from objecting, actually encouraged him — was the sense of power. He couldn't get enough of it. He'd read about the life force and the will to power in the chapters on Schopenhauer and Nietzsche, and he thought this was what he was tapping into, though what he experienced with Norma Jean was not blind and impersonal, but gentle. A soft command, a touch of the ankus, and the elephant would turn to the right or to the left, guided by his own will.

It didn't occur to him to ride her — the Russian never rode her, never talked about riding her — till Molly arrived on Saturday, a week before the wedding. Siva had come back from Oaxaca the night before and had eaten supper out in the barn with Rudy and the Russian, who was leaving again in the morning to pay another visit to his sister. Rudy thought Siva might hold the elephant walk against him, but the philosopher was in good spirits. They drank some Pölstar vodka, which the Russian bought by the case in Reynosa, and told stories. The Russian told Norma Jean stories that Rudy'd heard before but never tired of hearing. Siva told Oaxaca stories: he'd climbed the pyramid at Mont Alban, and he'd met a woman in a little *posada* in a canyon right on the beach at Puerto Angel who was going to join him in Paris at the end of September. Rudy told about seeing the river for the first time and about mistaking the mysterious lights on the river for the *Ding an sich,* but he kept his own counsel about the life force and the will to power.

The Russian left about ten o'clock in the morning. He took his time, fussing over Norma Jean, kissing the bridge of her trunk and her big elephant cheeks while Rudy stomped around, impatient for him to be off. Molly had called from the airport; she was going to drop TJ and Nandini off at the motel and come right over. Rudy was making a cup of Constant Comment tea when he heard her car in the drive.

"Oh, Papa," she called to him when he stepped out onto the veranda, "this isn't so bad. I thought . . . But where's the river? Where's the elephant?"

"The river's over there," he said, pointing at the upper grove. "You can't see it from here, and the elephant's in the barn."

He was tempted to scold her when she told him she was going back to India after the wedding to shoot the big dance scene at the neighboring tea garden, but then he was always tempted to scold her. Meg, who needed prodding, brought out the reckless devil in him, but Molly, who needed restraint, brought out his more cautious, play-it-safe self. *Don't go back to India, for Christ's sake,* he wanted to say. *Go back to Ann Arbor with your husband. Forget about the movie. This is your honeymoon.* He'd felt an upsurge of joy when he first saw her, but now he was annoyed, and he was angry with himself for being annoyed. It was a kind of jealousy or resentment, actually. Of the way she lived for the moment, her motives and desires transparent. There was no more guile in her than in Norma Jean. But his negative feelings — the impulse to scold her — soon vanished. The morning air was fresh and not so humid. A breeze was blowing in from the river, though he knew it wouldn't last. He had her all to himself, for a few minutes anyway. He put his arms around her.

"So," he said, holding her out at arm's length to have a good look. "As beautiful as ever, even after traveling for almost thirty hours. I was getting a little worried."

"You know me."

He thought he did, but he wasn't sure what she meant. He knew that the impulse to scold would come back again — *How could you just stay in India like that and not come back to plan your own wedding?* — but he wasn't going to let it interfere with his present happiness.

"The elephant's out in the barn?"

"Just hold on," he said.

She said she was sorry about coming back so late, but he could see that she wasn't sorry at all. She was pleased with herself. Rudy was pleased with himself too. He showed her the freezer, which was packed with frozen *Saint-Cyrs* in different-sized plastic containers.

They walked out to the barn, holding mugs of hot, milky tea, which Molly said was the way they drink tea in India.

"So," Rudy said, "you're going back to India?"

"Yup."

"And how do TJ and his mother feel about that?"

"Well, TJ's not too thrilled, but Nandini is more progressive in her way. One of the few female mahouts in Assam. Well, she's not a mahout really, but she knows how to handle an elephant better than the mahouts. And she's one of the only female elephant owners. The mahouts say that elephants don't want to be ridden by women, because women menstruate, but they must have made an exception for Nandini. The elephants, not the mahouts. And for me too. I've been riding almost every day. She's taught me a lot about elephants."

"That's what her brother said. What about your real estate license? I thought you already had a desk lined up in a good office?"

"Selling real estate? I don't know, Papa. It's not much better than selling insurance. All these horrible people, worried about their middle-class lives. Comfort, security . . ."

"That's what *I* worry about," Rudy said. "Money. Security. Mortgage payments. Putting down roots in a new place, creating a home."

"I know, Papa. A house is the biggest investment most people will ever make in their lives, but . . . I've tried a lot of things, Papa, but you always encouraged us to try new things. And Mama too. It's not me — selling real estate."

"You sold *our* house."

"That was the hardest thing I ever did, Papa. It was terrible. It was a huge mistake. I cried all the time."

"You encouraged me to move, remember? 'This old place is too big for you, blah blah blah.'"

"But we didn't know you'd move so far away."

"Here's what I've figured out," he said. "That old house — our house — held so many memories . . . It would have been too easy to sink down into them, like sinking down into that old sofa we had up in the attic. That's what I was doing. I didn't realize it at the time, but I was starting to hear a door close now and then, or someone taking a shower, and I'd wait for one of you girls to come downstairs. I needed to break away from that old life. I needed a life with a future, a last fling."

"Quite a fling," she said, laughing and looking around her. "I guess I wouldn't have had an elephant in my wedding if you'd stayed in Chicago."

Rudy put his arms around her again. "Don't go back to India," he said. He couldn't help himself. He thought he was a bit of an Übermensch. After all, he'd taken his fate into his own hands when he decided to buy the grove. He hadn't just drifted downstream with the current, he'd shaped his life according to his own heart's desire. But then his older, more cautious self kicked in: "Go back to Ann Arbor with your husband. It's your honeymoon."

"We're taking our honeymoon in January," she said. "TJ's giving a paper in London. Besides, we've been living together for six months. It's not like it's the first time for us."

"This is your shot at a normal life," he said. "You've made it this far; you're almost an adult; don't go backward now. What if this trip is a deal breaker?"

"You mean, don't upset the apple cart, don't rock the boat?"

"That's exactly what I mean."

"Papa, you worry too much. TJ knows how important this is to me. How many chances will I get to be in a movie? I'll get a credit. We've talked it through. I'll be gone only a week, two at the most."

He was thinking, not for the first time, that he was glad she was marrying TJ, who seemed sensible, smart — maybe even brilliant — and stable. And he was thinking about her string of disastrous boyfriends: high school dropouts with tattoos, cigarette packs rolled up in the sleeves of their T-shirts; a disc jockey who was ten years older than she; the guy she wanted to go to California with on a motorcycle. That was in 1954, right after she graduated from high school. And later she did go to California with a guy, a different guy, on a motorcycle. There was a baseball player too. Married. He gave her free tickets to all the Cubs home games and introduced her to all the players: Ernie Banks, Billy Williams, Ron Santo. She could have gone to Italy with Helen and Margot, but she hadn't wanted to. And then there were the men she met when she was teaching at the dance studio on Jackson and Wabash, after she dropped out of Edgar Lee Masters. If he closed his eyes he could still see the hand-lettered sign, up in the second-story window:

LEARN TO DANCE
$5 AN HOUR

When they reached the barn, Molly peeked in at Norma Jean. "Oh, what a beauty," she said. "Aren't you a lovely elephant. You sweetheart."

"Shall we take her for a spin?" Rudy asked.

"Fantastic."

Rudy wanted to show off a little, but Molly upped the ante. Why walk when you could ride? "I've been riding Champaa almost every day," she said. "There's nothing to it."

"By yourself?"

"With Amma — Nandini — or with Punchi — the mahout. But they don't do anything, they just walk along beside. You don't have to worry, Papa. All we have to do is put a rope around her neck. Something to hang on to."

But Rudy wasn't worried. He was excited. "I know the commands," he said. "I just haven't ridden on her, that's all."

There was a coil of heavy rope on the wall behind the tractor, next to a six-foot tow chain. Molly looped the rope around Norma Jean's neck.

"How are you supposed to get up on her back?" Rudy asked. "Do we need a blanket or a pad?"

"I never use one," she said. She was already in Norma Jean's stall. She tossed the rope over Norma Jean's head and tied it under her chin while Norma Jean checked Rudy's pockets for sweets.

"*Buy toe,*" Molly said loudly. "That's the command for 'kneel.'" Molly repeated the command several times, but Norma Jean ignored her.

"Never mind," Molly said, climbing up the side of the stall and scrambling onto Norma Jean's back.

"Do we need the ankus?" Rudy held the ankus up so Molly could see it.

"You can bring it along, Papa, but don't worry. I know what I'm doing." She kicked her shoes off and put her feet behind Norma Jean's ears.

Rudy opened the stall door and climbed up the side of the stall and onto Norma Jean's back behind Molly. There was nothing to hang on to except Molly, who started giving commands: *Agit, agit.* Norma Jean shuddered and moved out of the stall. Norma Jean was like Ernie, his grandfather's draft horse, but bigger. They left the barn and stopped for a while in the warm sun. Norma Jean looked around, raised her trunk and sniffed the air.

"Where do you want to go?" Molly asked.

Rudy tried to get comfortable. Norma Jean's back looked like a nice broad space, big enough for a picnic, but it felt more like straddling a rail fence. Norma Jean pawed, or footed, the gravel in the drive, and then she headed toward Rudy's garden by the garage, where she stopped to snack on a couple of tomatoes.

"Let's go up to the house," Molly said.

"*Agit,*" they both said at once, and laughed.

Norma Jean started toward the house. "You steer her," Molly

said, "by commands and by pushing your heel on the soft spot behind her ears and by flicking your toes. Left foot for left; right foot for right. It's hard on your toes at first, but I'm used to it."

"I know about the commands," Rudy said. "But she's wandering all over the place."

Molly may have been used to riding an elephant, but she didn't have very good control, and neither she nor Rudy could stop Norma Jean from lumbering on past the house and investigating the chinaberry trees that Creaky had planted along the farm-to-market road, like a row of beach umbrellas. Norma Jean tasted some of the yellow berries but then spit them out. She wandered all the way to the pump house, where water from the lateral canal was lifted up into the upper grove, and then reversed her course and headed back across the open courtyard toward the upper grove. The farm-to-market road and the pump house were familiar territory, but Rudy'd never taken her into the grove itself.

As Norma Jean was about to enter the upper grove, Rudy heard a car in the drive, and then a second car.

Norma Jean heard it too — at least she trumpeted. *"Chai ghoom,"* Molly shouted, *"chai ghoom,"* but Norma Jean didn't change direction.

Molly continued to shout out different commands — *chai ghoom, chai ghoom, chai ghoom, chi, chi, chi, dhuth, dhuth, dhuth, dhuth, dhuth* — but Norma Jean didn't pay any attention to her. Rudy started shouting too: *dhuth, dhuth, dhuth, dhuth.* But Norma Jean ignored him as well, and they disappeared into the grove. The trees were covered with green globes, thicker than ornaments on a Christmas tree.

"African elephants have two fingers," Molly said, as if she were a docent at a zoo, "on the tip of their trunk. Indian elephants have only one."

"That's what the Russian told me," Rudy said, looking down at the ground. Norma Jean was not a large elephant, as elephants go — standing on tiptoe Rudy could reach the top of her head — but they seemed to be pretty high up.

"And the ears of Indian elephants are shaped like India," she said.

"Before or after partition?"

"She likes avocados," Molly said, ignoring his question.

"They're not ripe yet," Rudy said. "I mean, they don't ripen on the tree. You've got to pick them first."

"Norma Jean doesn't seem to mind."

Rudy minded, though. The full sun was beating down through the trees, and neither one of them had thought to wear a hat. Rudy's legs were cramping. But the thing that bothered him most was the loss of control. His will counted for nothing. His ship was rudderless. He didn't know what to do. He'd been too arrogant and now he was going to pay the price, about to make a fool of himself — *brutta figura.*

Finally they heard a shout. Rudy recognized Medardo's voice. Better Medardo than Uncle Siva.

"What do we do now?" Rudy said to Molly. "Shall I try the ankus?"

"I hear them coming," Molly said. "TJ will kill me."

Rudy turned and caught his first glimpse of Nandini, in a sari the same shade of green as the avocados, coming down the row between the trees behind Medardo. When she got closer he could see that her face was the color of walnuts, or dark tea. Her features were like her brother's, but she was animated rather than handsome or beautiful, and her hair was not really red, but it had a slight reddish cast, as Siva said. She raised her arms and took a deep breath, as if she were about to sing an aria, but then he saw that she was laughing.

"I think you are finding yourselves in maximum difficulty,"

she shouted. Siva was wearing a broad smile, but TJ, standing behind his mother, wearing a University of Michigan baseball cap, was not amused. "What are you doing?" he shouted. Nandini touched him.

"We're just going for a ride," Molly said.

"Norma Jean stopped for some breakfast," Rudy explained.

Norma Jean stretched out her trunk to reach a particularly large avocado, high up. Molly was pushed back against Rudy and her short skirt rode up to her waist. The men glanced up at her legs and looked away. She pulled it down without saying anything and kept on shouting commands at Norma Jean, who pretended not to hear her. The avocado she wanted was so large she couldn't get a purchase on it with the tip of her trunk, so she grabbed the branch and snapped it off the tree.

Nandini reached up and touched Molly's leg, squeezing herself between Norma Jean and the branches of an avocado tree, heavy with fruit. She whispered something in Norma Jean's ear. She adjusted her sari with one hand and held out the other hand to Norma Jean, who greeted her with her trunk, though she didn't put Nandini's hand in her mouth. *"Utha, utha,"* she said. Her voice was softer and more musical than the Russian's sharp barks, but Norma Jean understood her perfectly and raised her right front leg. "You can come down, Molly," Nandini said.

Molly held on to the elephant's big ear, swung her legs over the elephant's back, and stepped down onto the raised knee. The leg went down slowly, like an elevator, and Molly stepped off. "Thank you, Amma," Molly said, and then she introduced them: "Papa, this is Nandini. Amma, I'd like you to meet my father, Rudy."

TJ was still upset, embarrassed: "How could you do this?" he said. "Go off with someone else's elephant? It's like stealing a car . . . In India . . ."

"It's my fault," Rudy started to say, but this was between Molly and TJ.

"Don't scold me, TJ," Molly said. "Maybe in one of your parallel universes I'll be your *pativrata,* but not in this one." She walked off, back toward the house, through the burgeoning trees. TJ hesitated for a moment. Nandini said something to him in Hindi, and then he followed Molly.

This was exactly the kind of situation that Rudy'd been afraid of. He understood TJ's embarrassment. But he knew something that TJ didn't know — he knew you shouldn't scold Molly, though in fact he could never stop himself from scolding her.

"Lord Ganesh," Rudy said, looking down from Norma Jean's back, "removes all obstacles."

Nandini put her hands over her head and raised her shoulders and let out a long sigh. "I am happy to hear you remind me so," she said. "Lord Ganesh is surely the most accommodating of all the gods. *Utha, utha,*" she said, speaking directly to Norma Jean. And then to Rudy: "Now you must climb down, following the example of your expert daughter."

Medardo and Uncle Siva headed back to the house. Rudy and Nandini led Norma Jean up the slope toward the end of the row, about the length of a football field, where they'd have room to turn around. Nandini carried the ankus, but she didn't use it.

"I'm sorry my son is becoming upset," she said.

"Molly sometimes has that effect on people," Rudy said.

"They both have nerves. It's such a very big step."

"Do you think they'll be all right?"

"'It is easier to control a wild elephant than this girl,'" she said, laughing. "An old folk song. I think Lord Ganesh will remove all obstacles. But you already are telling me this. You know, we always say our first prayer to Lord Ganesh, at our morning puja."

"Lord Ganesh sounds like a very nice god."

"He is the maximum best god, Mr. 'arrington. Everyone in India will tell you so."

On the way back to the barn she asked questions about avocados. Polite conversation, Rudy assumed at first, but she seemed genuinely interested in everything. In the irrigation system, for example, not just in Rudy's grove but in the entire valley. Her father-in-law had established a similar system of canals in Punjab, she said, and she'd like to see the pumping station in Hidalgo. He explained that the agricultural extension agent advised stripping all the trees in November, but that Medardo preferred to spread the harvest out till the end of February or even mid-March.

All the trees had been grafted, he explained, because avocados don't come true from seed. "You don't know what you're going to get if you plant a seed, so you take the scions from the stumps of cut-back trees and graft them onto the rootstock. These avocados, Lulas, are a West Indian–Guatemalan hybrid, vigorous, uniform, salt tolerant, disease resistant." He pulled off a leaf, rubbed it between his fingers, and held it to her nose. "Anise," he said. "Or fennel. A little bit."

"*Ajwain,*" she said, breathing in deeply. "*Saunf.*"

"All avocado trees have two series of flowers," he went on. "The two series open at different times during a two-day cycle, once as females and once as pollen-bearing males."

"Then you must need to plant two different *kalam,*" she said. "I don't know the word in English, when you make a variety by choosing breeding."

"Cultivar," he said. "You do in California, but not in Texas, because with Lulas — the kind of avocados we grow here — the cycles overlap."

"Most convenient! And how many trees per hectare?"

He couldn't answer because he didn't know how big a hectare was. So he couldn't estimate the size of her tea garden either.

"Tea is just the opposite of avocado," she said. "It is in March that the cropping begins."

He pulled a medium-sized avocado off the tree and cut it open with his pocket knife to expose the three concentric layers. The drama that had been unfolding under his nose now unfolded a second time in his memory: the scales separating to reveal the tiny buds, so irresistibly soft that he'd rolled them back and forth, absentmindedly, between thumb and forefinger, and touched them to his lips; the buds plumping and turning into flowers; the bees humming as they did the work of pollinating the flowers; the flowers that contained in their ovaries the germs of hard seed and soft, buttery flesh; and now the clawlike hands of the trees holding the set fruits in magician's fingers. He'd been buying and selling avocados for thirty years: squatty green Fuertes with flat bottoms; knobby, dark-skinned Hasses; pear-shaped Zutanos; long-necked Jims; smooth, oily Pinkertons; handsome, shiny Texas Lulas; but now he felt that for the first time he was waking up to the mystery.

"Most of the edible flesh," he said, pointing with the tip of his knife, "is in this middle layer, the endocarp. It's got more starch and more oil than the outer layer, the mesocarp — you see this greenish yellow band under the skin. But the mesocarp is good too. We'll take a couple back and leave them in the kitchen. If they soften up in a week or so, then we'll know they're ripe. I don't think these are quite ready yet, though." He picked two large avocados and carried one in each hand.

She wanted to know how many kilograms to expect from a single tree; how much it cost to irrigate; how many men he employed and how much he paid them. When he got home, he looked up *hectare* in a dictionary, and then he did the conversions: hectares to acres and acres to hectares, kilograms to pounds and pounds to kilograms. A tea garden of 1,500 hectares would be 1,500 x 2.47 = 3,705 acres. An avocado grove of 29.5 acres would be only 11.943 hectares. It didn't occur to him till later that she'd been asking questions like a prospective buyer, and he wondered if her brother had suggested to her that he, Rudy, might be a prospective seller.

The Bath

In the morning, Rudy and Nandini walked to the river to see if Rudy's little cove might be a suitable spot for giving Norma Jean a bath. The Russian hadn't returned on Sunday night and Rudy was starting to worry, but Nandini seemed to have a perfect understanding of Norma Jean, and Norma Jean seemed to have a perfect understanding of Nandini. When they came out into the open at the end of the last row of avocados, they could see the river through the feathery leaves of the mesquite trees. Rudy wanted to surprise Nandini, just as he had been surprised when he first visited.

"Look, Mr. 'arrington, wild *suar.*"

"Pigs?"

"Yes, that's the word. Pigs."

A herd of javelinas was feeding on prickly pear.

"These are javelinas. They're not really pigs."

"They look like pigs to me."

"They have four toes instead of three on their hind feet."

She held up four fingers. "How does that make them not pigs?"

"Well, they're different from domestic pigs, anyway."

"I thought pigs have hoofs. Can you have toes and hoofs at the same time?"

"Hooves *are* toes," Rudy said. "They smell pretty bad — the javelinas. Like polecat."

"What is polecat?"

Rudy tried to explain that too. A kingfisher rose from the water with a fish in its beak. The kingfisher she recognized, and the green heron fishing in the little cove, and the hoarse chuckle of a yellow-billed cuckoo — *ka-ka-ka-ka-ka-ka-kow-kow-kowp, kowp, kowp.*

"Is maximum beautiful, Mr. 'arrington. You must be very happy here."

He didn't answer that question, but he did explain some of the "obstacles" that remained to be removed: the disagreement or misunderstanding over the menu with the manager of the Taj Mahal, the pandit's insistence that the wedding be postponed because September 9 was an inauspicious day. And he'd learned from Father Russell that the deadline for applying for a wedding license had passed. Something would have to be done on Monday.

Rudy picked up a stone and threw it at the javelinas, which scattered and disappeared. "They scatter in all directions," Rudy said, "so usually one of them seems to be chasing you."

"But this time, no," she said. "So we are safe to walk to the river."

They walked down to the river, to Rudy's little cove. "I've cut back some of the chaparral," he said, "the rough brush along here. There ought to be room for her to get through, and the drop-off here is only about a foot."

"Elephants can't jump, you know," she said, "but a foot is less than one half meter, right? So she should be able to manage this step."

"Right. About a third of a meter."

They walked back up the slope. When they reached the top they paused and looked back.

"I don't know about the wedding permission," Nandini said, "but there is always something that can be done, and my brother can deal with the restaurant manager and the pandit. He is very good at these things."

"He told me that *you* were the one who was good at these things." She laughed, and seeing that she was not as worried as she ought to be about these obstacles, Rudy put his own worries aside for the moment. They turned and headed back to the barn. Nandini's attitude toward Norma Jean was puzzling. On the one hand, she seemed to regard her as a god — a manifestation of Lord Ganesh — but on the other she talked about her as if she were an old draft horse, not something set apart from ordinary life, but at the heart of it. Rudy supposed this was like his feelings about avocados. On the one hand, they're a good, nourishing fruit — the source of his livelihood for many years, and of his daughters' science projects too. On the other, many people regard them as exotic, weird, something for foreigners. He tried to explain this to Nandini. "When I was growing up," he said, "no one ate avocados. Avocados were for Mexicans. People thought they made you . . . well . . . hot-blooded. The name comes from an Indian word for testicle — *ahuacatl*."

"An Indian word?" she asked. "I have never heard of this word before."

"South American Indian," Rudy explained. "Nahuatl."

"Yes, of course."

"Well, anyway," Rudy said, "Norma Jean certainly likes them. Did I tell you her Indian name is Narmada-Jai?"

"Yes, I believe she must be coming from Kerala. You see her long trunk and her big ears and the two domes on her head, and her nice round shape, like a barrel. Her back is making a perfect arc. Or maybe from Bihar. Do you know that the festival of Lord Ganesh will be coming soon? Ganesh Chaturthi, the birth anniversary of Ganesh, the son of Shiva and Parvathi. We don't celebrate Ganesh Chaturthi in Assam, but I have seen pictures that my uncle brought from Bombay one time, of boats and clay images that they are sending into the river. I think it would be very nice, don't you? We could do it right here." She nodded at the river.

"Yes, why not? The pandit suggested something like that. Clay images. You know," he went on, "I had a kind of vision when I decided to buy this place. I was standing right here." And he told her about the radio show about the end of the world. "They thought the Second Coming — that's when Christ comes back at the end of the world — was going to be the next morning. I was talking to the Realtor and the widow of the owner. I seized up inside. I had to get away. It was supposed to happen at ten seventeen, when the sun went down in Jerusalem. I didn't believe it, of course, but I wanted to be by myself anyway. I climbed up on the rise and saw the river. I hadn't even realized it was here. This is where I waited, right where we're standing, for the end of the world."

"I know about this Second Coming," she said, "because there are many missionaries in Assam, among the tribal peoples. But it didn't happen, did it?"

"No." Rudy laughed. "We're here, aren't we? They must have got their calculations wrong." He didn't mention that he'd taken a leak, hadn't wanted to be blown into Kingdom Come with a full bladder. "I knew then that I was going to buy this place. Maybe that wasn't really a vision. I mean, I didn't *see* anything.

But I had a sense of *understanding* something. *Seeing* in that sense. *Understanding*."

"And what did you understand?"

"That's just it. I don't know. I was hoping your brother could explain it to me, but probably it was nothing at all."

"Perhaps a sign from Kshipra Ganapathi. It is very beautiful. I can understand how pleased you were when you saw the river."

"You have a big river near you, don't you."

"Yes, the Brahmaputra. In places, you cannot see the far shore."

"I told my daughters I was thinking of selling the house in Chicago. I was trying to scare them, but they thought it was a good idea. So I put it up for sale, and then they changed their minds. But I was too stubborn. I had this idea of starting a new life."

"Molly is telling me this story."

"There was something else too. That night in the motel, the people on the radio were encouraging listeners to call in and leave a message for someone they loved if they were separated or estranged. People were calling in. And I called in too. I had a message for my wife."

"Your wife?"

"I'm sorry," he said. "She's been dead for seven years. I shouldn't be telling you these things. It's embarrassing. I hardly know you."

"It's quite all right, Mr. 'arrington."

"I'll try to pull myself together," he said. "We'd better get back."

In the afternoon, Molly and Nandini went into McAllen to do some shopping. When they got back Nandini wanted to take Norma Jean to the river. There was a certain amount of stomping around and trumpeting as they brought her out of the barn. Nandini commanded her to kneel so that Molly, in a very revealing bikini, almost nothing at all, and TJ could ride on her back. While they were mounting the elephant, Rudy walked on ahead with the chain saw to widen the opening in the chaparral along the bank of the river. The saw roared and the blade dug down into the dirt to cut the tough brush close to the ground. He'd just sharpened the chain, and now he'd have to sharpen it again, but he didn't care. A pair of snowy egrets, who sometimes wandered up from Bentsen, flapped their wings and moved to the duck's-bill end of the cove and resumed feeding. Looking up, he saw Uncle Siva walking next to his sister, who was leading Norma Jean. She was wearing her green sari and TJ's dark blue and gold University of Michigan baseball cap to protect her face from the sun.

Rudy pulled the trigger on the saw and cut into the heart of a horse-crippler cactus with nasty red spikes. He didn't want Norma Jean to step on it. The saw caught hold of the cactus roots and fired dirt and blue smoke into the air. When he released the trigger he heard Nandini shouting at him. "Please, you are going to upset Norma Jean. She does not like this noise."

It was hot. Rudy was sweating, and Norma Jean, who had stopped at the last row of trees to eat a few avocados, was flapping her ears like fans. The bumps on her head had swelled up, but she didn't look upset to Rudy. As she approached the river she started coiling and uncoiling her trunk and squealing, as if she were returning to a favorite swimming hole of her childhood. Nandini held her back, shouting *"Dhuth, dhuth."* Norma Jean's whole body began to vibrate with excitement, and Rudy thought she might charge ahead, but instead she began to kick at the short grass along the riverbank, uprooting it with her toes before gathering it up with her trunk. It was only when Nandini released her that she stepped down into the water.

The egrets took off but then circled back to watch. Norma Jean kept moving forward till the water almost reached her stomach and then stopped. TJ and Molly jumped feetfirst into the water.

Rudy took the chain saw back to the barn. He went up to the house to put on his swimming suit. When he returned, Norma Jean was squirting everyone with trunkful after trunkful of water. Nandini's sari was completely soaked and he could see the outline of her new American bathing suit underneath it. He had brought the Russian's bucket of scrub brushes and sponges from the barn and now passed them around. Nandini spoke to Norma Jean, and the elephant lay down on her side in the shallows, trunk up, while they scrubbed one side. At a word from Nandini, she turned over so they could scrub the other side. The Russian had hosed her down every night, but even so, the cracks in her skin were caked with dirt. Rudy patted her head.

When they'd finished scrubbing Norma Jean's sides and her head, Nandini removed her pleated sari — one end of which was draped over her left shoulder, the other knotted just above her waist — and tossed it on the bank, along with her U of M baseball cap, and began to wade out of the cove into the main channel of the river. Rudy thought for a moment that she'd been pulled under by the current, and a fantasy in which he swam to her rescue took him by surprise. This fantasy was as vivid as any he'd ever experienced, but then he realized that she was swimming, that she was in fact a strong swimmer. He swam after her but couldn't catch her before she reached the opposite shore, where the bank was steeper. They steadied themselves by hanging on to a low branch of a live oak tree that provided a little shade.

"Now you can say you've been to Mexico," Rudy said. "Like your brother." Looking back, he could see Uncle Siva standing by himself, the sun gleaming on his Humpty Dumpty forehead. Was he looking at them? He was shading his eyes, but he had his sunglasses on, so Rudy couldn't tell.

Nandini reached out and touched the steep bank. "Who lives here?"

"Mexicans."

"No, I mean here." She touched the bank again.

"No one. It's just desert — creosote, mesquite, cholla, prickly pear. But wildflowers too."

"I'm sorry for scolding at you, Mr. 'arrington. My brother is explaining to me about the cactus, how it could hurt Norma Jean's foot."

"Your brother knows everything, doesn't he?"

"Oh yes," she said, "he is quite a know-everything." She looked at Rudy and smiled. "But he has reminded me," she said, "that elephants are quite extraordinary in this country. I know that. I mean, I have seen many books, I am not a village person. I have seen American films and television programs. I have visited in Paris and London, but I am tired from the trip. I am forgetting that not every American is so fortunate to have an elephant, especially such a good elephant as Norma Jean."

"She's not mine," Rudy said. "She'll only be staying for a few more weeks."

"Elephants have always been important in my whole life, since I was a little girl, and my grandfather have elephants."

"But you married and moved to the city?"

"That's true. Yes. For three years. I am twenty-nine and TJ is only three when my husband is killed."

"What was it like after living out in the country?"

"Oh, it is very nice in Guwahati. There are so many things to see. And my husband was a lovely man. From Punjab. There are no elephants in Punjab." She laughed. "My grandfather give us a lovely house near the Fancy Bazaar, and we are very happy in Guwahati. We have a baby and want to have another baby. Then my husband is killed in an accident at refinery, and I take my son and go back to my home. By this time my father have his own generator for electricity and we have running water. My grandfather is still alive and my mother is needing help to take care of him, and my father is needing help with tea garden. I understand the elephants. I know all the mahouts, Punchi and Mohammed and Ali. There's a special tribe where the men become mahouts.

"My father is wanting to expand, to anticipate independence. He is wanting to buy more land, two thousand hectares of new land that has never been planted, but he knows it has good tea soil. The British people are leaving. We clear two thousand hectares with just elephants. My grandfather is supervising all the clearing."

"And now you have just the one?"

"Just the one, yes — Champaa, and she is very old. My grandfather, long ago, is having four at one time. They work very hard, but they enjoy life too. He is operating a kind of postal office for the British tea planters. Only elephants can go through when the rains come. He is like a king."

"What do you do with Champaa?"

"We still do some logging, and I rent her out to nearby towns and villages for weddings and festivals, like a temple elephant, and for clearing land sometimes." She looked up and shaded her eyes. "My brother is watching us," she said.

"Then we'd better be careful," Rudy said.

"Oh, I do not think my brother is caring," she said, laughing. She waved at her brother and then pushed off against the steep bank. Rudy followed her.

Norma Jean was reluctant to leave the river, but Nandini spoke to her firmly and she climbed up the bank and everyone else followed. Rudy went with Nandini, who had wrapped her wet sari

around her, to get Norma Jean settled in her stall. Siva went up
to the house with Molly and TJ. Nandini was starting to shiver.
Rudy poured some of the Russian's vodka into a paper cup and
handed it to her before pouring a cup for himself.

"You should put on some dry clothes," Rudy said.

"I will in a moment, please."

Norma Jean kept shifting around, reaching out to touch
Nandini's hair with her trunk. She was starting to get hungry,
and Rudy was becoming increasingly anxious about the Russian.

"Elephants are very fond of alcohol, you know," Nandini said.

"I didn't know that."

"They raid the villages," she said, "if they are brewing beer.
And when my grandfather's favorite elephant is dying, Khush,
we give him bottles of Old Monk rum, and we mix his oats and
gur with rum too."

"What's *gur?*" Rudy asked.

"I don't know the English word. Maybe molasses."

They walked up to the house, sipping from their paper cups.

Molly and Siva and TJ were sitting at a card table on the veranda, working on a jigsaw puzzle Molly had brought from India.

Siva rose to greet them, holding a glass of red wine. He raised
his glass in a mock toast. Rudy and Nandini raised their cups.
Siva said something in Hindi that made Nandini blush, but she
didn't explain what her brother had said.

Rudy served leftovers for supper. The Russian had not returned
yet, and Rudy was worried.

"Where does his sister live?" Siva asked.

"Somewhere in Mexico."

"You don't know where?"

"No. It can't be too far, because he's never been gone more than one night before."

"That narrows it down some."

"But not a lot."

"I think I'll drive over to his place," Rudy said, hoping that Siva would offer to join him, which he did.

The weather was hot but not unbearable. They drove with the windows down in the pickup. There was no sign of the Russian's truck, and the little house he rented from Medardo was dark. Rudy caught a glimpse, in the headlights, of something white taped to the door, and he knew what it was without getting any closer. It was a letter addressed to him, and he didn't have to open it to know what it said. They sat in the pickup and Rudy turned on the cab light. Siva read the letter aloud: "Dear Rudy, I am very sorry to leave you without saying good-bye, but I have too many years to be making repairs on my old barn. I leave my oldest and best friend in your care because I know she love you, and I know you take good care of her. I leave many paintings in the barn for you to buy food for Norma Jean."

It was signed, "Your friend, Vasily Vsevolodovich Czutzimir."

Rudy was stunned. His chest constricted. He had trouble breathing. He took a nitroglycerin tablet out of the little bottle in his shirt pocket and swallowed it without water. The taste was bitter.

"Do you want to look in the barn?" Siva asked.

Rudy couldn't talk. He could only shake his head. He handed Siva the keys to the pickup and they traded places so Siva could drive. Rudy tried to breathe deeply on the way home. Siva parked the truck in the drive.

"I need to be alone for a while," Rudy said. "You go on up to the house." Siva nodded.

Rudy sat in the barn with Norma Jean for a few minutes and

then opened the door of her stall and started shoveling her big turds into the wheelbarrow. About fifteen minutes later Nandini joined him. "My brother is telling me you are upset because this Russian is going away."

It was dark in the barn, but he could see her standing in the doorway. She was still wearing TJ's University of Michigan baseball cap. He could make out the gold letters. She walked to the door of the stall and put her hand on Norma Jean's trunk.

"One thing is clear for Norma Jean," Nandini said. "She is excellently disposed, all good things an elephant can be: kind, friendly, big-hearted, barrel-shaped, very fragrant, like sandalwood. And I can see that this Russian he is taking good care of her. And she is very smart too. You see how she lays down all her *leed* in one corner to make it easy to clean up after her."

"Very smart," Rudy said, dumping another shovelful of turds into a wheelbarrow. "The Russian sells these to a local citrus grower for fertilizer," he said. "I'm thinking they might be good for avocados too. I've started a pile in the northeast corner of the lower grove."

Nandini laughed. "You see how she listens to us now?" Norma Jean, her head cocked to one side, flapped an ear and began to massage Rudy's shoulder with her trunk while Nandini poked around in her mouth. Nandini talked to her all the while, telling her to please hold her trunk still.

Rudy turned on the lights.

"She has good strong teeth," Nandini said, "and you see how pink her tongue is, no black spots, and good strong toenails, just the right length on all eighteen toes." Rudy looked at her feet. He hadn't counted her toes before. She had five on her front feet, four on her back. "And she is very fond of you," Nandini went on. "I am thinking more than just fond of you. She loves you. Is very unusual. I think it is because she is saving your life."

"I haven't forgotten that," Rudy said. "But I can't take care of an elephant. If the Russian doesn't change his mind and come back by tomorrow, I'm going to call the zoo in Brownsville."

"I don't think Norma Jean is going to be happy in a zoo, Mr. Rudy." She shook her head. "And I am thinking that you might consider about this in a different way. I am thinking it is a stroke of maximum good fortune for you if this Russian does not come back."

"Looking after her's a full-time job," Rudy said. "It was one thing to have her around for a few weeks, but now the harvest is coming up."

"She can help you pick your avocados. This is clearly a *shubhkaal* for you, an auspicious time."

"Of course," Rudy said, "and I suppose she can pull the wagon when this old tractor gives out."

"All the tea gardens," Nandini said, "used to have elephants instead of tractors."

The tractor, an old Case 500 diesel that needed a new clutch, was parked in the back corner of the barn, next to the door that opened onto the paddock. Rudy needed this tractor to get him through his first season, because he couldn't afford a new one. But replacing it with an elephant?

"You remember how I am explaining to you about Lord Ganesh," Nandini went on, "our elephant-headed god. There is also Rina Vimochaka Ganapathi, who aids people who are in debt. And Durga Ganapathi, who helps us through in our difficulties. This form has eight hands with *ankusha*, tusk, *akshamaala*, arrow, bow, *kalpalatha*, *jambhuphala*, and *paasha* respectively in each hand. This form of Ganapathi is adorned in red cloth. I think Durga Ganapathi will come to your aid in this time."

"He's got his work cut out for him."

He heard a car in the driveway and thought for a moment that the Russian had come back after all. But when he went to the door he saw it was Father Russell's Pontiac. Rudy watched without saying anything as the priest got out of the car and walked up to the house.

"Now I am showing you something you must learn very soon," Nandini said. "There are four ways to mount an elephant, but this is the way you must learn, so you will be more expert even than your expert daughter. This is such a way that is most comfortable for the elephant."

"My expert daughter didn't do so well the last time we went for a ride," Rudy said. "And I made a fool of myself."

"It requires you to have more experiences, but you have to start at some time. You don't just drive a car once and then they give you your driving permission. Now please remove your shoes and stockings."

Rudy took off his shoes and socks.

Nandini looped the tow rope around Norma Jean's neck and said something to her, and she lowered her trunk. Nandini placed her bare foot on the center of the trunk and took hold of Norma Jean's ears, and Norma Jean hoisted her up and over her head and Nandini swung one leg over the elephant's back.

"You see how I am doing this, Mr. Rudy?"

"It happened too fast."

"Maybe we try something simpler the first time."

"That's a good idea."

"*Utha, utha,*" she said, and Norma Jean raised her front leg. "Take hold of her ear and step up on her leg. It is like an elevator for you."

Rudy grasped Norma Jean's left ear and stepped up on her raised knee, and Norma Jean lifted him up so he could scramble over her head and onto her back.

"Shouldn't you be in front?" he said to Nandini.

"I sit in back seat," she said, "for your first driving lesson."

Rudy touched his bottle of nitroglycerin pills, but he'd already taken one pill that evening.

"Keep your back straight," Nandini said.

It seemed to Rudy that Norma Jean was vibrating with excitement, but it might have been his own nervousness.

"Flick your toes under her ears," Nandini said.

Rudy flicked his toes, but Norma Jean didn't move.

"Harder."

Rudy flicked harder, and this time the elephant started to move forward, out of her stall, like a great ship moving away from the pier. They both had to duck as they left the barn.

"Keep flicking your toes."

"It hurts."

"You'll have to become accustomed to it."

"Her ears are rough."

It was dark, but there was enough moonlight to find their way around Father Russell's Pontiac. Rudy could hear voices laughing on the veranda. Nandini was hanging on to him, holding on to his upper arms with her hands.

"Push with your left foot," she said. "Put your heel right on her head where you feel it is soft. Push hard."

Rudy pushed, and Norma Jean veered slowly to the left, up the tractor path and into the upper grove.

Norma Jean wandered from side to side, picking avocados at random and tossing them into her mouth.

"Dig with your heels again, into her head," Nandini said. "She is loving elephant, but you have to maintain control. Tell her to stop shilly-shallying and move on."

Rudy dug his heels into her head and said firmly, *"Agit, agit."*

Norma Jean started to move and then stopped again.

"Louder." Nandini tightened her grip on Rudy's upper arms. *"AGIT, AGIT."*

"This is better."

By the time they reached the crest of the hill Rudy's legs were cramping and his toes were bleeding, but he was absurdly happy. He'd ridden his grandfather's draft horse; he'd driven one of Harry Becker's semis nonstop from Gainesville, Florida, to Chicago; he'd ridden in a steam locomotive with his uncle, an engineer for the CB&Q, when he was a boy, and as a young man he'd made the game-winning free throw in a championship basketball game. But this was better.

"Tell her to stop," Nandini whispered in his ear. "Tell her *dhuth.*"

"DHUTH," he shouted. *"DHUTH,"* and Norma Jean stopped.

"Good. She can smell the river now. It's good you can make her stop." They were at the spot where they'd seen the javelinas that morning. Now there was only the river and the night sounds — the weird cries of the nightjars and the swish of big brown bats screening the air. Sphinx moths fluttered their wings in the moonlight. A great horned owl hooted in the distance.

"My wife adopted a chicken once," Rudy said, turning to look over his shoulder at Nandini. "She saw it down in one of the neighbors' yard one day, and then a couple of days later it was walking around on top of a car across the street. There were some kids standing around the car and one of them asked, 'Is this your chicken, ma'am?' She brought the chicken home and put it in the side yard, which was fenced in. It must have been somebody's pet, because it was very tame. It was a lovely chicken and my wife liked to hold it in her arms and talk to it, and the chicken would talk back. It liked music too, and would always come to the porch window when I played my guitar."

Nandini laughed till she started to hiccup. "And how are you saying this chicken is like an elephant?" She took one of her hands off his upper arms to strike her chest. "Ha ha ha. Now you tell her to turn around — left, and left again." It was more like turning a boat around in choppy water than like turning a car on firm ground, but Rudy managed to get Norma Jean turned around and they started back toward the barn.

"I'll tell you," he said. "That chicken was no end of trouble. We put ads in the paper to find the owner, and my wife made announcements on the radio. In the winter I had to build a little house for it on the side porch, and I had to put a heating pad under the floor of the house so it wouldn't be too cold, and then I had to build a little door and a little window, and put up a little mirror so she could admire herself; and then I had to build a little perch for her on top of her little house, and we had to put a sheet over her at night and buy straw and then clean out the straw once a week and make sure we found all her eggs. The chicken poop ate through the paint on the floor of the porch. She pecked holes in the screens in the summer, she ate all the grass seed we put out."

"I'm thinking your wife have a very good heart," Nandini said.

"She had a very big heart, Nandini. But if a chicken can be so much trouble, what about an elephant? That's what I'm saying."

"I think maybe you are turning things upside down, Mr. Rudy. You're always thinking about how much you have to do to take care of this elephant, but you are not thinking of all this elephant must do to take care of you, to keep you from being lonely, to keep your spirits up if you are sad. I think she has much work to do in this arena."

Rudy thought he heard in her voice an invitation to join her on a deeper emotional level, but he didn't know what to say, so he didn't say anything.

"Molly is telling me this is a big change in your life, coming here to Texas." She wasn't holding his arms now. He missed her touch. He wanted to turn to face her, but he was afraid he'd fall off if he tried to turn around.

"I made a big change," he said, "that's right. Yes. A very big change. And you? I understand you may be making a change too."

"It's very frightening, but exciting too," she said, her voice in his ear. "I am going to Detroit Auntie, then Ann Arbor, and then to New York City to stay with my brother before he go to Paris. Like you, I am waiting for a sign."

"I don't know how seriously you should take signs."

"But you believed your signs were most serious. Like the special knowledge of migrating birds."

"Do you really think Norma Jean is a good sign?"

"Oh, Mr. Rudy, Norma Jean is not a sign, she is the thing itself."

"I'd like to believe that."

When they got to the barn Nandini said, "Tell Norma Jean to put her leg up." She touched Rudy again and whispered the command in his ear: *"Utha, utha."*

"Utha, utha," Rudy said, and Norma Jean raised her right front leg.

"Now hold her ears and climb onto her elevator leg."

Rudy did as he was told and swung himself onto Norma Jean's knee and then onto the ground. His legs were so cramped he could hardly stand.

Nandini whispered something to Norma Jean, and the elephant raised her trunk and lowered Nandini to the ground so swiftly Rudy couldn't see how it happened. Norma Jean picked up a twig from the floor of her stall and began to draw something in the dirt.

"Look," Nandini said. "Norma Jean is drawing a picture for you."

It was too dark to see if she was actually drawing something.

"This is a sign too," she said. "This is the sign you are looking for. A maximum good sign."

◆

That night, lying on the Russian's cot in the barn, Rudy couldn't sleep. He turned on the Russian's radio and listened to Bob and Helen, never a smart thing to do.

People were calling in with accounts of how God had intervened in their lives to give them a sense of direction, and Bob and Helen were supplying the biblical framework: God has a plan for each and every one of us. We need to *find* the plan. One man, for example, called in to say that he'd been struck by lightning on the golf course, on a Sunday morning. The lightning had knocked a nine-iron right out of his hands on the fifth hole, but it hadn't harmed him. He never took up his clubs again. Didn't even pick up the club that had been knocked out of his hand. Just left it lying on the fairway. He went on to become a successful preacher.

Rudy started to roll his eyes in the dark, but then he realized that he was no different from the man with the golf club.

Everything Means Something

There was lots to be done before Siva and Nandini left to visit Detroit Auntie. Father Russell took Molly and TJ into town to see what could be done about getting a marriage license at short notice and to look at the empty seminary, which the priest had offered to place at their disposal. Most of their friends would be staying there, and a few of the Indian relatives too, and some Harringtons from Michigan. Rudy called María at the *floristería* to see if her art dealer would be interested in looking at Norma Jean's paintings. And Norma Jean, directed by Nandini, nudged the old outhouse at the edge of the lower grove back onto its foundation, and then she cleared some mesquite trees that had sprung up in the open strip that divided the upper and lower groves.

"You can't get rid of them," Rudy explained. "You can't poison them, and if you prune them, they just get thicker; if you cut them down, they grow back as thorn bushes." But Norma Jean wrapped her trunk around the small trees, one after another, and tore them out of the ground.

"You see, Rudy," Nandini said. "Lord Ganesh is removing obstacles, one by one. And now is time for her lunch." A slight smile at the corners of her lips expressed her satisfaction.

Norma Jean lunched in her stall. Rudy and Siva and Nandini went to eat at the Taj Mahal. Nandini and the manager argued back and forth in Hindi while Rudy and Siva drank tea. Rudy was convinced that the matter was hopeless, but in the end everything was settled amicably. The menu had been completely revised. More expensive north-Indian dishes had been substituted for less expensive south-Indian ones, and at the price Rudy and the manager had originally agreed upon.

In the afternoon, Norma Jean took a little nap and then painted six pictures instead of her usual four.

The next day, Rudy and Nandini and Siva met with the pandit to clear up the matter of the inauspicious day. Rudy offered to drive out to the ashram, thinking that on the way back they might stop at the bird sanctuary at Bentsen State Park, but the pandit preferred to meet in town at El Zarate, where he'd met with Rudy before. Siva, steering his rented Mercedes with one hand, dismissed the pandit with the other as a superstitious old fool and ridiculed the idea of an "inauspicious day." Nandini warned her brother to let her do the talking.

Siva parked across the street from the café and they got out of the car. Nandini was wearing her green sari; Siva was dressed in a lightweight shimmering silk suit; Rudy wore jeans and a white shirt with the sleeves rolled up. According to the thermometer on the bank it was ninety-six degrees, but the café was air-conditioned.

"*Namaskaar.*" Nandini and Siva greeted the pandit, who was waiting for them in a booth, dressed in his saffron robe. The pan-

dit nodded at them. He was a tougher customer than the manager of the Taj Mahal. Rudy wanted to leave things to Siva and
Nandini, but the pandit, who was sitting across from him on the
inside of the booth, next to Nandini, spoke directly to him.
There was no escape from his piercing gaze.

"Do you believe in chance, Mr. Harrington?"

Rudy hesitated.

"This is not a trick question, Mr. Harrington. What I'm asking
is this: do you think it is an accident that the four of us are sitting here in this café, drinking tea?"

"No, I don't think it's an accident," Rudy said. "I called you up
and we agreed to meet here."

"And before that?"

"Before that . . . Before that I called you up and we met here in
June."

"And before that?"

"Before that . . . I don't know. I went to the Taj Mahal, the
manager gave me your card . . . How far back do you want me
to go?"

"As far as you wish, but however far back you go you will find
all experiences linked by slender threads. I don't believe in
chance, Mr. Harrington. In India we have a clearer understanding of these things."

Siva was getting impatient. "The question is," he said, "whether
you're going to perform the ceremony or not. If you're not, then
I'm sure we can find another pandit, even if we have to go to
Houston or San Antonio. I'm not sure we need a pandit anyway."
Nandini, who was sitting next to Rudy, reached across the table
and put her hand on her brother's arm.

"Permit me," the pandit said, looking at each of them in turn
and then focusing his gaze on Rudy. "You seldom see radiance in
the face of a middle-aged man. But that is what I saw in your

face, Mr. Harrington, when you first consulted me in this very café. Radiance. I'm not sure you were even aware of it, but it is what attracted me to you. You were radiant that your daughter was marrying; you were radiant that she was coming to your home here in Texas; you wanted to express your conviction that the coming together of these two young people was not simply a matter of observing certain social proprieties but something holy, something grounded in the fundamental nature of things, in the *Sivaloka,* even though I cautioned you against a love match. Am I right?"

"Yes," Rudy said.

"And you wished me to arrange matters so that they would unfold not just in a psychological mode but also in harmony with this fundamental nature? Is that correct?"

"Right," Rudy said, "but you have to see that it's impossible to change the date of the wedding now. I sent out the invitations six weeks ago. People have made travel plans, plane reservations, hotel reservations, my son-in-law's got to get back to Ann Arbor for the beginning of the semester."

The pandit sighed. "You mean inconvenient, not impossible."

"All right, then, inconvenient."

"Exactly. You understand then that fundamental reality is not always convenient. I want to make sure there is no misunderstanding on this point."

"I understand," Rudy said.

"Very well, then," the pandit said, "as long as you understand. I will perform the ceremony, a ceremony, but I cannot take responsibility for an inauspicious outcome. You can only hope that Lord Ganesh will take that responsibility upon himself."

Nandini, Siva, and the pandit began to discuss the details of the ceremony, first in English, then in Hindi. Rudy drank his tea. He didn't understand everything, but what he did understand was this: for the pandit, everything meant something; for Siva, nothing meant anything. He and Nandini, he thought, were somewhere in between. He said as much on the way home.

Siva was driving; Rudy was riding shotgun; Nandini was sitting between them and Rudy was very conscious of the points at which their bodies touched.

Siva laughed. "But don't you see, Rudy?" he said. "At the end of the day it all comes down to the same thing."

On Thursday morning, Siva and Nandini flew to Detroit. Rudy drove them to the airport in McAllen.

"You may have a rival in Detroit," Siva told Rudy, lighting a cigar despite the NO SMOKING signs. He held the cigar out at arm's length and looked at it. Nandini was in the restroom.

"Why are you telling me this?" Rudy asked. "It's none of my business anyway."

"No, of course not, but I thought you ought to know."

"It's none of my business," Rudy said, repeating himself.

"Yes, I understand, but you should not give up hope. I thought you ought to know that too."

"Please," Rudy said. "What you're saying doesn't concern me in the least. There's no need to talk about it."

But by the time he sat down to dinner that night with Molly and TJ, he knew he was in love. He knew it the way he knew when he was coming down with the flu. He hoped that maybe if he just kept moving and drank plenty of liquids, the symptoms, which weren't really bad yet, would disappear. But at the same time he knew they wouldn't. He knew that he'd known her for less than a week, but now that she was gone he was continually probing his feelings for her, the way he might probe a sore tooth with his tongue, engaging her in imaginary conversations, imagining her saying such delightful things. He was perfectly aware of the difference between these fantasies and an encounter with a real person, whose words would be dictated by her own interests, not by his — perfectly well aware that the woman in his imagination probably bore only the slightest relationship to the real woman, who had landed in Detroit at 1:24 that afternoon and was now no doubt sitting down to an Indian dinner at her aunt's house in Royal Oak. She wasn't beautiful, but she was full of life and high spirits, and in her presence he too felt this way: full of life and high spirits. She had taken him by surprise, ambushed him from inside the walls, and he found himself replaying in his mind Uncle Siva's remarks about her position: a widow whose life in a remote part of India was troubled by dacoits and by unrest among the native tribes. He was powerless to resist the fantasies that came crowding in, fantasies in which he saved her from being carried away by the current, in which he carried her in his arms up through the little cove to firm ground, even though she was a strong swimmer.

What was Rudy to do? How was he to understand this inner turmoil? Was he like the old house next door to them in Chicago after the crazy contractor'd gotten through with it? Had too many load-bearing walls been knocked down? Or was the damage only superficial, a necessary prelude to reconstruction? Was Rudy as crazy as the contractor? Or was he an architect with a dream? Should he call in the wrecking crew or the carpenters? He wanted to ask TJ about what exactly Detroit Auntie was arranging for his mother, but he didn't because he didn't want to reveal his feelings. But out in the barn, after supper, he opened his heart to Norma Jean, who took his wrist in the tip of her trunk and put his hand in her mouth so that he could massage her tongue.

When Rudy went back up to the house, Molly and TJ were sitting on the veranda. TJ, who'd caught several mice out in the barn, was practicing making them disappear with a vanishing tube from Rudy's dad's collection of magic tricks. There was a hinged door in the front of the tube, which resembled the cardboard tube in a roll of toilet paper, only smaller. The back of the tube was attached to an elastic cord that TJ had pinned to the inside of his coat. He'd stuff a mouse into his right hand, which concealed the tube, and then release the tube, which would disappear under the flap of his coat. Rudy understood this part of the trick, but he didn't understand how TJ got the mice to reappear in his coat pocket or in his sleeve. "Look," TJ'd say, and Rudy and Molly would look at his outstretched hand, and a mouse would run out of his sleeve, and TJ would catch it and put it back in a cardboard box and repeat the trick, with variations, with another mouse. Molly made him keep the box of mice out on the veranda that night.

Rudy and Molly opened the late responses that had been accumulating and went over the guest list one last time. One of the responses was from Rudy's cousin, or grandniece, or great-niece — Gary and Vivian's daughter, Christine. Rudy hadn't heard from Gary since the letter from Africa that he'd read on the plane, the one suggesting that the Second Coming was at hand. He tried to remember Gary's dad, his own older brother, Alfred, but he could barely picture his face. What he remembered was that Al's widow, Francine, had been living with them, and that after Al was killed at Verdun she always insisted on setting an extra place for him at the table. She did that for the three years that she lived with them on the farm, and as far as he knew, she kept on doing it. He couldn't remember his brother, but he could remember the extra place at the table — the empty chair, the clean plate with the fork on the left and the knife and spoon on the right.

The total came to eighty-seven out-of-town guests, mostly Indian relatives and TJ and Molly's friends from Ann Arbor.

When he was satisfied with his ability to make the mice disappear and reappear smoothly, TJ set out to solve the geometry problem that Rudy had set him — Rudy's old favorite: if the bisectors of two angles of a triangle are equal in length, prove the triangle is isosceles. "It's not so simple," Rudy said, standing behind TJ and peering over his shoulder. "You can *see* it's true, but you can't *prove* it's true. My math teacher gave this problem to me when I was in seventh grade, and I worked on it for a year because I loved geometry. She couldn't figure it out either."

"I'm not a geometer," TJ said, "but this doesn't look too difficult. If you'll give me a few minutes . . ."

The thing that bothered Rudy about TJ was this: he, Rudy, knew that he could explain everything he knew about avocados to TJ. After a couple of hours, TJ would be able to grasp it all — the physiology of the plant, the different varieties, the growing cycle, the advantages and disadvantages of different grafting methods and different cultivars, grove maintenance, marketing strategies. But TJ might spend weeks or months or even years explaining what he knew about parallel universes to Rudy, and Rudy would never understand it, because to understand parallel universes he'd have to understand abstract mathematics and quantum mechanics, and he couldn't even prove that if the bisectors of two angles of a triangle are equal in length, the triangle is isosceles.

Rudy tried not to bother TJ, but he couldn't stop himself from watching his son-in-law-to-be try first this and then that. "You can *see* it's true," Rudy kept saying, "but you can't *prove* that it's true. I've never gotten over it. Maybe all the important truths are like that," he said. TJ just shook his head and drew another triangle.

The Veil of Maya

Meg had just argued her first case before the Seventh Circuit Court of Appeals and had won. She walked up and down the veranda replaying some of her arguments, as if she were addressing a black-robed judge, but Rudy — the judge — wasn't listening to her words. He was listening to the sound of her voice, and he knew that her *aventura* was over and that she hadn't told Dan, who'd taken the boys to the grocery store. *Well,* he thought, *the story won't be over till he finds out, and then we'll see.*

And Margot. Margot had been arrested at the airport in Rome for trying to take an antiquity out of the country, an Etruscan statue that she'd bought in London. She'd had all the necessary papers, but she was detained anyway and had to take a later flight.

"Italy's been good for you," Rudy told her on the way home from the airport. "Maybe I should send your sisters!"

She laughed. "Maybe you should come yourself, Papa."

"I've got an avocado harvest to deal with," he said.

"After the harvest," she said, so he knew she wasn't planning to come home soon.

"Maybe I'll do that," he said. "Maybe in April?"

Rudy slowed down as they drove by Medardo's trailer park so that Margot could admire the yard ornaments. "So," he said, "you're not mad anymore? About the house?"

She looked at him and smiled. "Florence is beautiful in April," she said. "A little crowded, but that's okay. And no, I'm not mad. But you have to admit it was a bit of a shock."

"And the man you fell in love with?"

"Back to his wife. In Rome."

"I'm sorry," he said. "You seemed so happy . . ."

"I *was* happy," she said, "and I'm happy now," but she told him the story of how they'd fallen in love. It was a long story, and she told it they way she used to tell him about a movie she'd seen, taking almost as long to relate the plot as it would take to see the film, because she didn't want to leave anything out.

She hadn't finished by the time they got back to the grove, so Rudy kept on driving down the farm-to-market road till he came to the mission chapel, La Lomita. He parked the car in the parking lot while she finished her story.

It was a sad story, but it was a wonderful story too. He thought he was a lucky man to hear such a story from his youngest daughter.

The Russian had left almost eight hundred of Norma Jean's paintings behind, two hundred already framed. On Monday morning, Rudy and his three daughters and two sons-in-law turned the barn into a museum while the boys climbed on the walls of Norma Jean's stall. Dan had his hands full trying to keep them from falling in. Rudy gave them each bananas and carrots to feed her, and promised them that they could sleep out in the barn with him one night.

TJ got up on a ladder to pound in the nails and Rudy and Dan and the girls labeled the framed paintings and handed them up to him. The girls used the names of recipes from the Chinese cookbook that Rudy found in the Russian's barn, and when they ran out of recipes they got more names from TJ, starting with the four fundamental constants that hold the universe together: *Strong Nuclear Force, Weak Nuclear Force, Electromagnetic Force, Newton's Law of Universal Gravitation*.

It took them three hours to hang a hundred and fifty paintings. When they were done everyone except Rudy went up to the house to fix sandwiches for lunch. Rudy stayed behind to admire their work. The wall of paintings was so beautiful, even in the dim light of the barn, that he put aside his hope of ecstasy and his fear of loneliness, his anxiety about keeping Norma Jean, his worries about the wedding, put aside everything he knew about the certainty of death and the untrustworthiness of the senses, put aside his failure to validate his earlier visions, and let the bright colors wash over him, let himself be ravished by the bright beauty.

In the afternoon, Rudy set up Norma Jean's paints in the barn. She was anxious to paint and kept shoving Rudy aside with her trunk to get at the brushes, which were laid out in a row on the tray attached to the lower part of the easel. She selected a broad brush with a bent handle that the Russian had made specially for her and set to work. She dipped the brush into a large can of red paint and used her upper trunk muscles to apply bold strokes of color directly to the canvas.

When he heard someone come into the barn he thought it was

Molly, but it was Nandini, bringing him a cup of tea. Norma Jean already had a painting well under way and they both watched her without saying anything.

"Does she ever step back to look at what she's done?" Nandini finally asked.

"You can see for yourself," Rudy said.

When she was satisfied with the design, Norma Jean put the broad brush down and selected a smaller brush, which she held with the handle up inside her trunk. She flicked the canvas with light blue paint till it was speckled like a robin's egg. Rudy and Nandini stepped back to admire the vibrant surface, like the surface of the big Seurat at the top of the fancy staircase in the Art Institute, Rudy thought, that he and Helen used to admire — *A Sunday on La Grande Jatte.*

When she'd finished Rudy attached another canvas to the easel.

"Does she ever make corrections?" Nandini asked.

"She doesn't need to make corrections," Rudy said. "She gets it right the first time."

Using her broad brush, Norma Jean covered the second canvas with warm colors. She struck the canvas; she mashed the brush into the canvas; she swung the brush back and forth, twisting it and turning it, setting it aside whenever she needed the smaller brush — which she manipulated with the wristlike muscles of her lower trunk — for more delicate work.

"Have you read my brother's books?" Nandini asked.

"One of them. *Philosophy Made Simple.* I guess he wrote that when he was a graduate student at Yale. But I haven't finished it. And I haven't read *Schopenhauer and the Upanishads.*"

"But you know about this shadowy reality he is sometimes talking about. The reality behind reality. Shadows. Dark forms. We can never make them out. What is the name for it?"

"The *Ding an sich*. The thing in itself. The pandit calls it the *Sivaloka*. Plato, Kant, Schopenhauer, the Veil of Maya. It's very complicated. For a while I thought I could catch a glimpse of it from time to time. But I could never really focus on it. Just a glimpse, like the glimpse you get of . . ." — he hesitated — "Marilyn Monroe's underpants in *The Seven Year Itch*." He glanced at her to see if he'd gone too far, said something indelicate, made *brutta figura*. But she smiled.

"Yes," she said. "I have seen that film in London with my brother many years ago. You get a glimpse of something like that and you never forget it."

"But it's very complicated," Rudy repeated.

Nandini shook her head, as if to deny the complexity. "May I show you something else, Mr. Rudy, that you will never forget?"

"Of course."

Nandini took Rudy's hand in hers and placed it on Norma Jean's chest, just in front of her left leg, so that he could feel the beating of her heart. Norma Jean continued to paint.

"This elephant, believe me, Mr. Rudy, know more about this *Ding an sich* than my brother."

Rudy kept his hand on the elephant's heart, feeling the slow beat, like a drumbeat in the distance, across the border, on the other side of the river.

"One time I am camping many years ago with my husband, Ashok," Nandini went on — this was the first time Rudy'd heard his name — "in the Kaziranga Park. It is raining a little, but everything is very cozy in our small tent. We are cooking rice and chapati on a little propane stove and we are lying next to each other in the dark. When the wind is picking up, a corner of our tent begin to flap, and Ashok is wanting to stake it down. But I tell him, no, let it flap. I like it, you see, that everything is so cozy and neat, but that one part is flapping free."

She laughed and took his hand, and he thought for a moment that she was going to press it against her own heart.

At that moment, a new life began for Rudy, at least in his imagination. He knew now that she knew that, though nothing had been settled, there was something to *be* settled, something that would be settled before she left. The opportunity would not simply slip past them. Conscious decisions would be made. Nothing would be left to chance. To speak of it at this point would be almost indecent. This was *Molly's* wedding, after all, Molly and TJ's. Let the young people enjoy, let them celebrate. There would be time afterward for the grown-ups to arrange things, to negotiate.

Norma Jean finished her fifth painting of the day. Rudy removed the canvas from the easel and began to put her paints away while Nandini led her back to her stall.

Nirvana

They'd gone out to the barn — Rudy, Uncle Siva, Nandini, María, and the art dealer from San Antonio — to look at the wall of Norma Jeans. It was hot already and they were drinking iced tea. The dealer, a man Rudy's age, had loosened his tie. Norma Jean was eating her favorite meal of smashed oranges mixed with alfalfa. It was three days before the wedding. Rudy had just told the story of the two kids in the pontoon boat, how it had made him think of the *Ding an sich.*

"*Sangam,*" Uncle Siva said, putting his hand on Rudy's shoulder, "the auspicious confluence of two mighty rivers." *Sangam.* It was the same word the pandit had used to describe the coming together of two families. "Two great philosophical traditions come together in the work of Schopenhauer," Siva said. "Plato and Kant flowing from the west, the Upanishads flowing from the east. Schopenhauer used to read the Upanishads every night before going to bed, in a Latin translation of a Persian translation. It was called the *Oupnek'hat,* and he regarded it as the consolation of his life. He seized on the idea of maya, do you see, illusion. The phenomenal realm is the realm of maya, which conceals reality from us like a veil."

"So, there *is* a way to lift this veil?"

"Yes and no," Siva said. "You see, this is where Schopenhauer differs from Kant. The noumenal and the phenomenal are not really two separate realms but two different manifestations of a single, undivided reality. To lift the veil is to become aware of this undivided reality in a different way. Let me put it as simply as possible. When we look inside ourselves — and this is more or less what Kant neglected to do — what do we find? We find the *will,* which is an unfortunate term. It's unfortunate in German too: *der Wille.* The Hindu word *iccha* would be more precise, but it's not likely to gain currency."

"The *will,*" Rudy said.

"Always striving, always demanding, always craving, wanting wanting wanting. It's only in moments of better consciousness, moments in which we circumvent ordinary empirical conscious-ness and cease to will, that we lose the sense of ourselves as sep-arate individuals and can participate in the timeless vision apprehended by saints and artists."

Rudy knew a little bit about the "will," but he was stunned. This was what he'd been looking for all along: "'The timeless vision apprehended by saints and artists,'" he said. "That's it exactly."

"Or Marilyn Monroe's *chaddi,*" Nandini added, smiling.

"Underpants," Siva translated.

Yes, Rudy thought, *the glimpse of Marilyn Monroe's underpants.* He could still see it in his mind's eye, and that was it exactly too. "Well," he said, turning to María's art dealer, "what do you think?"

"The timeless vision apprehended by saints and artists?" The dealer laughed. "I like it. I can see it; I can see what you mean. To tell you the truth, I've been looking for something like this." He waved his arm at the wall of paintings. "Maybe we're onto the next big thing. Norma Jean may be the new Miró or Kandinsky or Arshile Gorky. What do you think? And if worse comes to worst I could always sell this stuff to hotels. They've got all those walls. They've got to put *something* on them. It might as well be elephant art. And she can turn them out in a hurry. No problem there! What'd you say? Five or six a day? People are tired of sunsets on the desert and moonlight on the river and lonely old cacti. *I'm* tired of sunsets on the desert myself. Let 'em look at *Plum Blossom and Snow Competing for Spring* or *Strong Nuclear Force* or *Ants Climbing a Tree.* Where do you get these titles anyway?"

"You want to have a show then?" Rudy asked, without explaining about the titles.

"Absolutely. Maybe get Norma Jean up to San Antonio for the opening. She could stay overnight at the zoo, have a sleepover with some of the old jungle crowd."

"What are you thinking?" Rudy asked.

"What am I thinking? I just told you what I'm thinking."

"I mean about price."

"Yeah. Well, I was thinking five hundred, but you don't want to go too low. Maybe start at a thousand, fifteen hundred. Maybe get a tie-in with the save-the-elephants crowd. Give a percentage, one percent, two percent. People like that. Of course, you gotta get them out of those cheap frames first."

Rudy thought the dealer was crazy, but he liked him anyway and invited him to the wedding.

During the three days that remained, there was a great deal of coming and going, as there always is before a wedding. This had been the case at Meg's wedding, and it had been the case at

Rudy's own wedding, though Helen and Rudy had had a reception in the church basement, with cake and punch and little silver trays of mints and chocolates, not a dinner with poppadoms and samosas and curries and spicy grilled fish and cucumbers in yogurt.

Norma Jean's pleasant disposition and satisfying barrel shape acted like a magnet, drawing everyone toward the barn, which reminded Rudy of the big museum in Florence, not the most famous one, but the one across the river that had three or four rows of paintings on each wall. And María had brought dried wildflowers. Bouquets of shooting stars, tansy, yarrow, sage, and Indian paintbrush hung from the rafters and over the windows. The girls had moved the card table holding Molly's jigsaw puzzle — with a picture of the Kalighat, the most important temple in Calcutta, which Molly had visited with TJ — to the barn, where, in the afternoons after Norma Jean's bath, they listened to the radio and drank tea as they worked on it while Norma Jean poked around in her stall, making a little pile of grain for the mice, until it was time to paint.

Meg and Margot were going to wear identical simple long dresses for the wedding ceremony, but Molly was going to wear a red sari trimmed with gold. The groom's party — TJ and Uncle Siva and a friend of TJ's from the University of Michigan — would gather in front of the barn, where the guests would be greeted by Norma Jean. Once the guests were assembled, TJ and the groom's party would fetch Molly from the house, and Nandini would lead Norma Jean to the *mandap,* where she would lend an auspicious presence.

Fortunately no one had an idée fixe about exactly how things ought to be and must be and therefore had to be. Even the pandit, Sathyasiva Bhagvanulu, and the priest, Father Russell, who — by taking care of the marriage license and by putting the seminary at the disposal of the wedding guests — had earned the right to act as an unofficial consultant, were flexible and didn't insist that every detail had to be precisely this way or that. So during the remaining days, Molly was content to leave the details up to Nandini, and Rudy was content to cook for everyone and to do as he was told. The result of all this activity was a sense of well-being, like the pleasant hum of a beehive, rather than anxiety.

On Tuesday morning, Siva and TJ drove over to Pharr to look for the cotton plantation where William Burroughs had lived in the forties. Rudy went into town to buy red and purple sheets to drape over Norma Jean, and then he made a second trip for a spool of a certain kind of thread; and then he made a third trip for turmeric to smear on the bride and groom just before the ceremony. When he returned, Father Russell's battered old Pontiac with white sidewall tires was parked in front of the barn next to the pandit's forest green Cadillac Seville. In the barn, Meg and Margot were working on the jigsaw puzzle while the priest and the pandit conferred with Nandini and Molly about the final details. A friendly rivalry had developed between the two priests. Father Russell had brought a big sack of sweet corn from his garden at the seminary and the pandit had brought a clay idol of Lord Ganesh.

Uncle Siva and TJ had returned from Pharr without having located the plantation. "The locals don't want to talk about Burroughs," Siva said. "Or Kerouac. Kerouac describes the house in *On the Road,* you know."

"I don't know about that," Rudy said, "but there are pictures of those two guys at Joe's Place in Reynosa. One of Burroughs's friends was killed by a lion at Joe's, but there aren't any lions there now."

"Good lord," Siva said. "We'll have to visit. My treat."

"Not this afternoon," Rudy said.

They were standing in the barn doorway. Uncle Siva was smoking one of the large cigars that he carried in a special case. The smell, sweet and pungent, filled the barn. TJ was sitting at the card table with Meg and Margot, drinking tea and drawing triangles on a piece of paper. Rudy looked over his shoulder before sitting down on a bale of alfalfa next to Nandini, who was sewing a final bit of gold trim onto Molly's wedding sari. Nandini was wearing a pair of jeans like Molly's and a white blouse, and she had three spools of special thread in her lap. An elephant-shaped raffia sewing basket — a prewedding present — sat at her feet.

Molly couldn't sit still. The Russian's radio was on, and she got up and stood for a minute or so in the middle of the floor with her arms hanging at her sides and then began to dance to the music. When Percy Sledge started to sing "When a Man Loves a Woman," she asked TJ to dance with her, and then she made all the men dance with her, even Uncle Siva and Medardo, who had stopped by to see how things were going. She and Rudy danced to "Monday, Monday." The songs were punctuated with news about a tropical storm that was developing in the Caribbean, but everyone was glad that the weather had turned cooler.

"I'm unforgivably happy," Molly said. "I don't care if it rains. I can't help it. Will you forgive me?" She'd just finished dancing with Uncle Siva, who was an excellent dancer.

"What do you think?" TJ asked, looking up from the bisectors problem. "Shall we forgive her?"

"Oh, I think we are forgiving her," Nandini said.

"What was the happiest moment in your life?" Molly asked Uncle Siva.

"I suppose it depends on what you mean by happiness. Can you give me a definition?"

"How about the first time you fell in love?"

Siva laughed. "That was probably the *un*happiest day of my life."

Molly looked around for help. Father Russell came to her aid: "I believe that our natural hunger for joy and beauty and ecstasy gives us a glimpse of the happiness we shall experience in heaven," he said, "and that the joy and beauty and ecstasy and love that we experience imperfectly here on earth represent heaven the way the pencil marks that an artist makes on a piece of paper represent the three-dimensional world, or the way the notes that a composer makes on a piece of staff paper represent a symphony."

The pandit was quick to disagree: "Trying to reach happiness by fulfilling your desires is like trying to reach the horizon by running toward it. True happiness is to be found not in the fulfillment of desire but *escape* from desire, *escape* from the wheel of karma, the cycle of death and rebirth, in nirvana or *moksha.* Deep emotional attachment, or *moha,* is always infected. It is the root cause of the problems of the world. Siva Singh is right to regard the first time he fell in love as the *un*happiest day of his life, but I speak not only of greed and appetite and craving but also of *moha* toward blood relations. Very few can escape its clutches."

"I'm glad to hear that," Rudy said.

"No, Mr. Harrington, excessive *moha* will destroy you. Detachment is what is called for if you wish to maintain a proper balance between the physical and the spiritual, the mundanity of outer existence and the atman within. Ganesh, you know, in his aspect as the Big-Bellied One, Mahodara, is the dispeller of *moha,* infatuation or delusion."

"I think people are happiest," Rudy said, "when they're standing on the threshold of a new life: about to get married, or crossing the international bridge with an elephant, like the Russian, or getting ordained into the priesthood. I remember when Helen and I decided to buy the house on Chambers Street — Helen was my wife. When we walked into our house for the first time — before we bought it, it wasn't ours yet — it was full of antique furniture, including an invalid's chair that General Lafayette had brought to America during the Revolutionary War. Even the defects were charming. The parquet floors were almost black; the kitchen was a mess; the soil pipe was cracked; the knob-and-tube wiring wasn't up to code; there was no shower. The next time we saw it, it was empty, but we filled it with love and imagination," he said, and then stopped. He didn't want to say any more. In the master bedroom upstairs he'd kissed Helen. They'd thought the real estate agent was downstairs. He really kissed her, lifting her skirt, just as he'd done in the Drake Hotel on their wedding night, sliding his hands down inside her panties. But the funny thing was that when the real estate agent walked in on them, she didn't say excuse me and back out of the room; she wasn't embarrassed at all. She understood and shared their happiness and excitement. The three of them stepped out onto the little balcony at the front of the house. The roof came down over the door, so you couldn't open the door all the way.

"It's like the lover on Keats's urn," Margot said. "My mother's favorite poem. 'Bold lover, never never canst thou kiss, though winning near the goal.' It's not the kiss but the moment just before the kiss that's the moment of real happiness."

"That's because the kiss," Siva said, "entails disappointment. Always. Inevitably. Without exception. Life is a painful process. Youth grows old, love grows cold. The journey is never as liberating as we anticipate. We shuffle back and forth between boredom and anxiety."

Rudy started to object, but Uncle Siva went on, following the current of his own thought: "Sathyasiva Bhagvanulu is right," he said, nodding at the pandit. "In a way. What most people really do want is relief — not the fulfillment of desire, not even the re-nunciation of desire, but the eradication of desire. True happi-ness is impossible. The little bits of happiness that we do experience only make us more miserable by contrast."

"Most people," Rudy said, starting to protest, but suddenly his whole mental being was jolted, the way his body was occasion-ally jolted when he was descending a stairway and miscalculated the number of steps. He slipped, or fell, or stumbled, into Uncle Siva's point of view, a kind of Schopenhauerian pessimism. He suddenly understood why, on Sunday morning, a man in Wes-laco had shot and killed his wife and three children and then himself, why a woman in Pharr had sealed up the house, turned on the gas, and lain down with her sleeping children in their bedroom. It wasn't insanity or hatred that drove them, it was that *moha* had become too great a burden. They wanted relief, eradi-cation of love and desire, freedom from deep emotional attach-ments, from love and heartache. He saw now in his own failure to validate the visions that had brought him to Texas the first step away from wanting and toward salvation, away from *moha* and toward *moksha*. At that particular moment he could imagine no happiness greater than the sudden destruction of the world — not the Second Coming, with its attendant complications, but complete annihilation.

"What I think," Siva said, tipping back in his chair, as if he wanted to relish the moment, "what I think is that trying to get the answers you want to life's questions directly from someone else is like trying to cheat on an examination. You have to create your own answers. And when you have your own answers, then you'll find that you can't communicate them directly to other people. You can only point and say *tat tvam asi*. That thou art."

Rudy took a step backward, as if stepping back from the edge of a cliff. He imagined himself standing in his driveway, looking at his old house and saying *tat tvam asi. Helen and I were never dis-illusioned with our life on Chambers Street. Our marriage ended in death, not disillusionment. Even Helen's affair with Bruni has become part of the pattern, a bright thread in the weave, a thread that I would not remove now even if it were in my power to do so. Life is good. I've got to get a grip on myself and not be disoriented by every twist and turn in the argument.* This meditation, which couldn't have lasted more than a second, was interrupted by piercing screams.

TJ had lifted his empty mug, which he had placed upside down on his saucer, and a mouse had run out, leaping off the saucer onto the table. Molly and Margot jumped up and screamed, putting their hands over their hearts. The mouse ran back and forth over the jigsaw puzzle, which was almost completed. The mouse looked this way and that, and then charged down the table toward the pandit, who pulled his long beard back out of harm's way, spilling his tea in the process. At first he was angry, but then he began to laugh and to speak to TJ in Hindi. TJ answered, evidently explaining the friendship between this particular mouse, which he'd caught in Norma Jean's stall, and this partic-ular elephant, because the pandit got up to have a look at the little pile of grain Norma Jean had left by the mouse hole at the back of the stall.

"I thought elephants were afraid of mice," Margot said.

"Lord Ganesh descends to earth on a mouse, you know," the pandit said. "Symbolically, the mouse will carry God's grace to every corner of the mind."

"The pope had an elephant," the priest said, not wanting to be outdone by the pandit. "Pope Leo. The Tenth."

"That's the guy," Margot added, "who said, 'God has given us the papacy, let us enjoy it.' Mama always liked that story."

"I don't know about that," Father Russell said, "but he had an elephant named Annone, a present from the king of Portugal.

Annone would dance before the pope and genuflect to him. The pope loved him and he loved the pope. Aretino refers to Annone in *La Cortigiana,* and Giulio Romano —"

But Father Russell was interrupted by the pandit. "What nonsense," the pandit said, "the pope doesn't know a thing about elephants," and then he said something in Hindi, and then he said, "Be good, see good, do good," and sitting down, he began to sing: *"Om Sivaiah, Om Sivaiah, Shambo Shankara Om Sivaiah."* He continued to sing the same words over and over for several minutes, his face becoming more and more swollen until he started to choke. He leaned forward over the table, and Siva pounded his back. When the pandit covered his mouth with his hands, Rudy thought he was going to throw up, but then he pulled a large egg-shaped crystal, covered with blood, from his mouth. He wiped it on his napkin and placed it on the table, and Rudy saw that it was not an egg, but a bright blue lingam.

So, Rudy thought, the pandit has a few tricks of his own. This was even better than the mouse. He knew that TJ had caught the mouse earlier and kept it in his pocket, but he had no idea how the pandit had produced the lingam. Everyone was staring at the pandit and the lingam.

"What was that all about?" Rudy asked the pandit.

"The *pativrata* does not reveal the secrets of her connubial experiences," the pandit said. "Nor does the good *sadhak* reveal the secrets of his spiritual experiences." He put the lingam in his briefcase and left them with a blessing: *Om suklambaradharam vishnum.*

> *Om, attired in white and all-pervading,*
> *O moon-hued, four-shouldered One*
> *with smiling face so pleasing,*
> *upon You we meditate*
> *for removing all obstacles.*

TJ caught the mouse, which was still running around on the jig-saw puzzle as if it were searching for the entrance to the Kalighat, and shoved it into his cupped right hand. When he opened his hand, the mouse was gone.

"When Annone got sick," the priest said, determined to have the last word, "the pope stayed with him night and day, and when Annone died he commissioned Raphael to do a memorial fresco, only it was probably Giulio Romano who actually painted it, right at the entrance of the basilica of St. Peter. But it's gone now."

Rudy smoked cigars and discussed Schopenhauer and Nietzsche with Uncle Siva; he discussed the upcoming harvest with Medardo and elephant art on the phone with the dealer in San Antonio, who was going to send a photographer, after the wedding, to get some shots of Norma Jean painting. He danced and talked with his daughters in the barn. They'd become, all three of them, the women Helen would have wanted them to be: open-hearted, confident, spirited, and even wise.

He was happy, but not in any of the ways he'd been happy before. He could say to himself, not this, not that, but he couldn't explain to himself what *it* was. He could only look around him and point and say: *Tat tvam asi,* that thou art.

The Gift of a Virgin

It was Norma Jean, not Molly, who was the center of attention. The days revolved around her, as if she were the one getting married: her morning bath in the river; her painting session in the afternoon; her pedicure after she was done painting; her breakfast, lunch, and dinner. And on Thursday afternoon after her bath she herself became a work of art, as Nandini decorated her with her own tempura paints, blue and red and purple. The Indian relatives took hundreds of flash photos, and even Detroit Auntie, a formidable old woman who dressed in beautiful yellow saris embroidered with animals and flowers and birds, and who had grown up in Assam before marrying a Bengali trader, insisted on taking her tea out in the barn.

By this time everything was beginning to happen of its own accord. The wedding was out of Rudy's hands. No one individual was in charge — not Detroit Auntie, who agreed with the pandit that the wedding should be postponed till the following Monday, a more auspicious day; not Molly or TJ, who would have been greatly inconvenienced by any postponement; not

Uncle Siva, not Nandini, not the pandit, who appeared from time to time in his saffron robe to perform various ceremonies or pujas. And yet, at the same time, Rudy couldn't help but feel that everything that was happening was happening because he was willing it to happen, that the world was flowing through him, like water through the gate of the lateral canal.

On Thursday evening delicious curries and breads and platters of aromatic rice arrived, as if by magic, from the Taj Mahal in McAllen, and after dinner all the guests gathered in the barn to dance and talk. Late in the evening, when everyone was tired of dancing, Rudy got out his guitar and played quietly while the others talked.

The Indian contingent from Detroit — children, grandchildren, and great-grandchildren of Detroit Auntie, Nandini's mother's sister — was settled in comfortable motel rooms along Highway 83. Philip and Daniel, as they had been promised, slept out in the barn with their grandfather and Norma Jean. TJ and Molly's friends from Ann Arbor were looked after at the seminary by Father Russell, along with a few scattered Harrington relatives.

On Friday morning, the day before the wedding, the temperature dropped into the lower sixties. Rudy built a fire in the woodstove, and the Indian women gathered in the kitchen, instead of on the veranda or out in the barn, to drink their milky tea. Their husbands stood outside the barn with Uncle Siva, smoking cigars, while inside the children watched Nandini touch up Norma Jean with another coat of paint. Norma Jean fidgeted so much that Rudy had to hold her tail as Nandini walked round her, daubing here and there, painting earrings on her ears and yellow diamonds and red rubies on her forehead, a fretwork of colored flowers on her trunk, till Norma Jean was herself transformed into a bride. "I am not expert," Nandini said, hitching up her jeans, but when she stepped back to survey her work Rudy could see that she was pleased.

Nandini and the girls spent the rest of the day closeted in the girls' bedrooms upstairs. By late afternoon huge gray clouds had massed in the sky, like a herd of elephants about to charge, and the weather reports were not encouraging. They were forced to rethink some things. Dinner would have to be held in the house, and if it rained on Saturday, it would be impossible to proceed from the house to the *mandap,* which had been erected at a point equidistant from barn, house, and garage. The wedding would have to be held in the barn. The pandit would have to build the sacred fire in Rudy's Weber grill. In the evening, the caterer's men from the Taj Mahal — a Bengali Indian and three Mexicans — set up their own grills on the veranda.

About six o'clock it began to rain. Rudy put on a slicker and went back and forth between the house and the barn, where Nandini, who'd darkened her eyes with kohl and put on a light blue sari for the party, was trying to calm Norma Jean, whose trumpeting heralded the storm, and who was rumbling too, deep in her chest. She had not had a bath today, and she was restless because she had not been allowed to paint. Nandini talked to her in Assamese, in a kind of gentle singsong. A horse-fly that had been bothering Norma Jean earlier had disappeared.

"We can use the rain," Rudy said, putting a good face on things. "A nice shower. It'll blow over. Nice to have it cooler."

Nandini's blue sari, which had little mirrors embroidered in it, didn't look warm enough. Rudy went up to the house to get her a sweater. When he got back he closed the shutters in the barn on the ground floor and then those in the loft, so it was dark in the barn. The electric lightbulbs at the front and back were not powerful enough to illuminate this darkness. From the loft he could look down on Norma Jean, who was drinking from her big water tank, which was almost empty. Nandini had moved to the door to watch the storm. He could see her in silhouette, like a figure cut out of black paper, as she adjusted the sweater over her sari and smoothed her hair. She turned to look up at him, and though he couldn't see her face, he thought that the fact of her looking meant that she wanted to confirm their earlier unspoken understanding that there *was* something to be settled. The electricity went off and then came back on. Rudy wanted to tell her about Helen's death. He wanted to tell her about a storm that had hit Chicago right after he'd gone to work for Becker, a storm that had knocked down one of the big awnings at the market. He wanted to tell her everything.

A bird flew in the open door. A sparrow. Out of the impending storm. It ducked under the eave, circled around, fluttered its wings, and perched on Norma Jean's head. Norma Jean reached up with her trunk as if to greet it.

Rudy climbed down from the loft and turned on the hose to fill the water tank. "I have to change my clothes," he said, leaving the water running and opening a bale of alfalfa. He cut the twine with a knife so that the bale unfolded, spreading itself open, like a poker hand. Rudy knew it was dangerous to wish too hard for something. All the philosophers were agreed on that. Moderate your desires. Be satisfied with what you have. Stop wanting, craving, yearning.

A bolt of lightning lit up the entrance to the barn. Rudy heard the thunder at the count of two. Close. *How Helen had loved storms,* he thought. She'd sit with the girls in the bay window behind the piano, sit on the piano bench and watch the rain bounce off the brick street. Or she'd sit out on the little balcony over the bay window. The roof covered only half the balcony, so she'd get soaked anyway. Sometimes Rudy would join her.

He asked Nandini about the monsoons in Assam, and she told him about the tremendous noise the monsoon rains made on the metal roof of the old tea-garden house, which had belonged to a British planter and which was not a proper Indian house at all. Her father had always meant to build a proper house, but had never gotten around to it.

What would a proper Indian house be like, he wanted to know. She started to explain, but the wind picked up and tore one of the shutters loose. The banging upset Norma Jean, and Rudy drove a nail into the shutter to hold it closed.

Norma Jean was becoming increasingly agitated, and Nandini decided to chain her to one of the heavy eyebolts on the wall at the back of her stall. Norma Jean trumpeted loudly and bumped Nandini's chest with her trunk, but she lifted her leg and allowed Nandini to fasten Rudy's tow chain to her metal anklet. The sparrow, which was still perched on Norma Jean's head, seemed unconcerned. It walked around and disappeared behind one ear.

Rudy went up to the house to put on clean clothes. The house, which María had filled with green and yellow asters, was full of people. Uncle Siva was acting as host, ordering around the caterer's men who were preparing spicy fish and kebabs on the long grills on the veranda, sampling the soups and the chutneys and the different breads. The pandit had arrived, wearing his flowing robe. Father Russell was there too, in his priest's collar.

The rain stopped as suddenly as it had started, but the wind had increased. One side of the *mandap* had come loose and Rudy thought they ought to take it down while they had a chance, before the wind blew it away. Four of them went out — Rudy and Medardo and of two of the men from the Taj Mahal. The poles that supported the ends of the tent had collapsed and were thrashing about, but the three ridgepoles were still in place. All they could do was knock down the ridgepoles so that the tent lay flat on the ground.

When Rudy got back to the barn, another shutter had come loose. He nailed it shut. The rain started again, and it began to thunder. A tremendous blast of lightning lit up the doorway. Norma Jean let out a high-pitched scream and pulled against her chain. Nandini stood in front of her, stroking her trunk, trying to soothe her, but the elephant pushed Nandini to one side with her trunk and strained forward. The heavy eyebolt in the wall of the barn might have restrained an unruly stallion, but Norma Jean, who weighed three tons, tore it out of the old wood with a great wrench of a noise and smashed through the stall door, dragging her chain and part of the wall itself behind her. Rudy and Nandini both yelled and waved their arms: *dhuth, dhuth, dhuth.* The sparrow was still perched on Norma Jean's head as she disappeared through the door into the storm. There was another crack of lightning, another scream. When they reached the door they could see that Norma Jean was down on her left side on the gravel, about thirty feet from the barn, her two right legs bobbing up and down as if they were made of rubber. They ran to her. Her eyes were closed, her moving legs slowed, then stopped. Nandini felt for her pulse, her heart. She yelled something. Rudy could see her lips move but he couldn't hear her. Rudy threw himself on Norma Jean's neck and kissed her face, and then they went back to the barn.

"Lightning struck her leg chain," Nandini said; "we have to get the anklet off."

They went back out into the pouring rain. Rudy managed to get the chain itself loose, but the leg was burned and swollen around the metal anklet. There was no way to release it.

They were joined by Medardo, and the three of them managed

to untangle the tent and drag it so that it covered Norma Jean. Medardo went up to the loft, pried open the shutter that Rudy had nailed down, and let down a rope from the window, and Rudy attached the end of the rope to the trailer hitch on the pickup. He eased the pickup forward till the rope was taut. They managed to slide the tent up the rope and then stake the outer edges to provide a sort of shelter for the elephant.

Experience had outdistanced Rudy's systems of explanation. He had no words to name what had happened. An accident? *Accident* was inadequate. Tragedy? Disaster? Omen? Rudy went from the jury-rigged tent up to the kitchen, where Meg and Margot and TJ were comforting Molly, who sat at the kitchen table and wept, and then he followed Nandini, still in her blue sari with the little mirrors in it, back out to the barn. Nandini picked up a pail and the shovel that Rudy used for Norma Jean's *leed* and motioned Rudy to follow her. He followed her up the tractor path into the upper grove and then down to the river. She was after river mud and sawgrass to make a poultice for Norma Jean's leg.

The river was flowing faster, but Rudy didn't think there was any danger of flooding. The excess water would drain into the floodway, and the house was on the only hill in the county. Rudy sank his shovel into the mud and grass by the cove, near the opening he'd cut in the chaparral.

They made two trips, and under the makeshift shelter their hands touched repeatedly as they packed the mud-and-grass poultice around Norma Jean's injured leg. TJ and Molly brought down dry sweaters and blankets and a half bottle of white wine, which they drank out of paper cups. Molly's eyes were red.

"The pandit's saying it's not an accident," she said; "he says it's a *baadha,* a bad omen, an obstacle."

Molly was in the kitchen when Rudy came downstairs in the morning after a short rest. He'd been up most of the night with Norma Jean. She'd told TJ everything, she said. Last night, after everyone had left. She'd "confessed." She wanted TJ to know who she was.

"Everything?" Rudy asked. "The trips to California? The baseball player? The men at the dance studio?"

"Just about."

"That probably wasn't a good idea."

"Don't scold me, Papa."

"How did he take it?"

"I think he's in shock. He went back to the motel."

"You were upset," Rudy said. "Who wouldn't be?"

She nodded.

"What do you want to happen now?"

"I want to get married."

"So *you* don't think it was an evil omen? A *baadha?*"

"I don't know what to think, Papa. You can't say it was a *good* omen, but the pandit didn't have to upset everyone like that. It was terrible. He kept talking about the gift of a virgin, said we were trampling on the ancient ceremonies. What business is it of his whether I'm a virgin or not?"

"That's true," Rudy said. "The pandit behaved badly. And Father Russell wasn't much better. The accident upset everyone. What about TJ? What does he think?"

"I don't know."

"Because of the *baadha,* or because of what you told him?"

"Either one. It doesn't matter. I just didn't want to get married under false pretenses."

The pandit had announced on Friday night that because of the *baadha,* or evil omen, he was no longer willing to perform the ceremony on Saturday. He had warned Rudy, he said in front of all the guests, against scheduling the wedding on an inauspicious day, but Rudy had refused to listen to him. And now look what had happened. Everyone, including Father Russell, had agreed with the pandit that under the circumstances it would be impossible to proceed, that at best the wedding would have to be postponed.

The Starlight Motel was located on Highway 83 — the "longest main street in the USA" — on the dividing line between Mission and McAllen. Rudy, who'd stayed at the Starlight on his first trip to Texas, located TJ's rental car in front of unit 12 and parked next to it, but he didn't get out of the cab of the pickup for a few minutes because he didn't want to confront the possibility that TJ no longer loved his daughter. What could he say to TJ? If he could ask one philosopher to go into the motel room with him, who would it be? Plato? Aristotle? Epicurus? Descartes? Berkeley? Hume? Kant? Schopenhauer? Nietzsche? He ran through the list, but in the end he knew he had to go alone.

He knocked on the door. TJ seemed stunned. His eyes, large and deep brown, were unfocused; his mouth was pursed, thin lips taut. His face showed that he did not understand what had to be done.

"Did I wake you up?" Rudy asked, though he could see that he hadn't. TJ was in his pajamas, but the TV on the dresser was on.

A notebook was open on a small desk in front of the window. TJ had been writing something. Nervous, Rudy jangled his keys instead of putting them in his pocket.

"Can I do something for you?" TJ asked.

"Yes, you can get dressed and get in the truck. Everyone's waiting for something to happen."

TJ stepped back into the semidarkness of the room.

"I think you know how much I love my daughter," Rudy said, "how very pleased I was when she told me about your engagement, and how happy I've been imagining you as my son-in-law."

"Mr. Harrington, I think we've found ourselves in a very bad situation."

"I wanted . . . I thought we ought to talk about Molly, about this situation."

"I have just written a letter to her, in fact. Perhaps you would be kind enough to take it to her." TJ handed him the letter he'd been working on at the little motel desk and sat down on the bed.

"I'd rather not look at it right now," Rudy said, though he glanced at it and saw the words *important* and *necessary* and *impossible* before putting it back down on the desk. "What I don't know," he said, "is how much love you have in your heart for Molly."

"I love her enormously, Mr. Harrington, but I don't understand how she could . . ." He waved his hand. "In India . . ."

"Stop," Rudy said. "Please don't say anything else. But let me tell you something."

"What is it?"

"My daughter is not a *pativrata*. She will not worship you as a god."

"No, of course not. But she's, how shall I say — damaged goods."

Rudy felt light-headed, as if he were going to faint. "My wife was not a *pativrata* either. She fell in love with another man, in Italy. This was after we were married, TJ, not before. We had three children. Molly was seventeen years old, sixteen or seventeen."

"But how does this apply to me?"

"That's what I'm trying to understand," Rudy said. "Parallel universes. Now I want you to tell me something, TJ. What do you think people are doing in your parallel universes? They're acting out their fantasies, don't you think? And in this universe people are acting out the fantasies they have in some other universe."

"Mr. Harrington, the concept of parallel universes is a bit more complicated than that, or maybe less complicated. I never meant to suggest . . ."

But Rudy interrupted him. "Then let's just stick to this universe."

"Mr. Harrington, I don't want to blame everything on her, but after a certain point it becomes impossible to forgive."

Rudy started to say that Molly was truly sorry and that it was never impossible to forgive; but he knew that Molly was not sorry, and that Helen had not been sorry either, and instead he said, "TJ, there's nothing to forgive. Do you see what I mean?" He sat down beside TJ on the bed. "You said 'damaged goods' a little while ago. That was the expression you used. Do you know that that's what your uncle said about your mother? Your mother, TJ. 'Damaged goods.' But I think your uncle was mistaken, and I think you are mistaken too. I think what you meant to say was 'warm and open-hearted and generous.' I think you meant to say 'loving and kind and giving.' Because those are Molly's fundamental constants, TJ. Those are what you get when you lift the Veil of Molly and look beyond the world of appearances." Rudy shook his head. "At Christmas, do you think I didn't hear you two? The pans were rattling in the kitchen. And I was sad because I missed my wife, but I was happy for you too. I was more than happy — I was full of joy."

TJ said nothing and the moment stretched out into a long silence. Rudy studied the faded flowers in the wallpaper, irises, like the ones María had brought on the night Uncle Siva arrived. The chatter on the TV was interrupted by the loud bray of a commercial. TJ let out a sharp, high-pitched laugh. He got up and turned off the TV and went into the bathroom. Rudy could hear him blowing his nose. When he came out he had a wad of toilet paper in his hand. "Nothing seems interesting or important," he said, sitting back down on the bed next to Rudy.

"Everything depends on metaphor, you know," Rudy said. "That's what Aristotle says. The greatest thing is to be a master of metaphor. Damaged goods? That's the wrong metaphor."

"But what is the right metaphor?"

They sat there like a couple of philosophers looking into the heart of the mystery, as if they were looking for pictures to form in the flames of a fire or from the stains on a garden wall.

"I have the *mangalashtak*," Rudy said finally, "that I picked for the wedding. The pandit thought I should compose one myself, but I didn't think I'd do a very good job. This is a poem that my wife sent to me before we got married." He took out his billfold to show TJ Helen's letter, but at first he couldn't find it and he started to panic, the way he always did when he lost things. He remembered folding the letter and putting it in his billfold. He took everything out of his billfold and spread it out on the desk, shoving TJ's papers aside. Several crumpled bills. Scraps of paper with addresses and notes and phone numbers. An old shopping list. A bit of dental floss wrapped in a piece of pink paper, for emergencies. Credit cards, driver's license, social security card, a deposit slip from the bank, receipts. He closed his eyes for a moment. "I wish my wife was here. She could recite it for you. She'd know it by heart."

"It is not necessary. Maybe you could just tell me the idea."

"It's not so simple," Rudy said. "You need the words." Finally he found it in one of those slots behind the hinges of the billfold, along with his emergency hundred-dollar bill.

He unfolded the poem, the *mangalashtak,* and handed it to TJ, who read it silently.

"I didn't really understand it either," Rudy said, "till Helen explained it to me. These first four lines are called a quatrain. See how it rhymes: *blue* and *you, pearls* and *girls.* The speaker's a young woman. She's telling her lover that she's not going to love him like other girls, she's not going to lock up her love up in a secret compartment — that's the silver casket. She's not going to attach all kinds of conditions to her love. She's not going to give him all the traditional love gadgets listed in the second four lines: the lovers' knot is a kind of ring with two pieces of metal that fit together with a secret spring for a perfume compartment. I think that kind of ring was originally used for poison.

"Then there's a change, you see. It's called a *volta.* That means 'a turn.' Now she tells him what she's going to give him: *love in the open hand, cowslips in a hat, apples in her skirt.* Everything's natural, you see what I mean? And then the ending is a couplet: *calling out as children do: 'Look what I have! — And these are all for you.'*

"Molly's not a child, TJ. Love in the open hand is what she'll bring you, apples in her skirt. That's the metaphor you want."

Rudy got up and went into the bathroom and ran cold water over his face. TJ's leather dopp kit was next to the sink, zipped shut. There was nothing out on the counter. No shaving lotion, no razor, no deodorant. The towels, hanging neatly on a rack over the toilet, had not been used. Rudy took one down and dried his face.

"How's Norma Jean?" TJ asked.

Rudy looked at himself in the mirror and smiled. "Still out cold," he called, putting the towel down and then picking it up again. "I don't think there's much of a chance. The vet from the Brownsville Zoo's coming this morning." Rudy stayed in the bathroom, but they began to talk about the elephant, and the re- markable paintings she'd done, and the sweetness of her dispo- sition, and how she'd set aside the little pile of grain for the mice, and how tragic her death would be.

"But who would marry us now?" TJ asked. "The pandit and the priest both said —"

"Don't worry about those old goats," Rudy interrupted, com- ing out of the bathroom, holding the towel against his face so TJ couldn't see his expression. "You give Molly a call. I'll round up a justice of the peace and meet you back at the house."

"By the way, Rudy," TJ said, "I have your proof." He shuffled through the papers on the desk. "Here it is. In $\triangle ABC$, let $\angle ABC = 2\alpha$, and $\angle ACB = 2\beta$. Okay? And let BE and CF be the internal bisectors of the angles ABC and ACB respectively. Now, sup- pose . . ."

Rudy listened to TJ's solution to the two-bisectors problem. TJ had not proved that it was true, but he'd proved that everything else is false, a proof he called reductio ad absurdum. The proof required only a few simple steps, and Rudy was able to follow it without difficulty. The only problem, TJ said, was that some mathematicians didn't accept reductio ad absurdum as a valid principle. But Rudy accepted it, so it didn't matter.

The house was full of people when Rudy arrived with a justice of the peace — Medardo's cousin from Hidalgo, the one who'd nota- rized his will. Uncle Siva, assuming the duties of the generous

host, had already opened several bottles of Pol Roger and un-
molded several of the *Saint-Cyrs*. No one knew what to expect,
but the mood was festive. Molly's eyes were red, but she was
smiling. TJ, sitting next to her, had shaved and was wearing his
wedding suit. Nandini was still outside with Norma Jean.

There was one more delay, however. Just as they'd gotten
everyone arranged and the justice of the peace, standing on the
third step, looking down at the wedding party, was opening his
book, the vet from the Brownsville Zoo arrived — a big burly
man who looked as if he was used to doctoring lions and tigers
and elephants.

Siva handed him a glass of champagne and Rudy went with him
to have a look at Norma Jean. Nandini, who'd put on one of Rudy's
jackets over her sari, was resting her hand on Norma Jean's head.

The vet had never seen anything like it and wanted to put her
down. Rudy agreed that this was probably the best thing, but
Nandini begged them to wait. He couldn't come again till Monday, the vet said, and warned them that by Monday Norma Jean
would be suffering from muscular necrosis and would not be
able to stand up even if she regained consciousness. He cut away
enough dead flesh around the metal anklet on her leg so that he
was able to unfasten it; he rubbed the wound with an antibiotic
lotion and gave Norma Jean a shot. He left another hypodermic
needle and more antibiotics with Nandini, who had had some
experience with sick or injured elephants, and he volunteered to
stay with Norma Jean during the ceremony.

"*Estamos aquí presentes . . . ,*" the justice of the peace began, without looking up, reading from a small three-ring binder that he
held open in both hands. Standing on the third step, he lowered
the binder and looked down on Molly and her sisters, and on TJ

and Uncle Siva, who was standing up with him. And then he turned some pages and began again in English: "We are gathered here in the sight of God, and in the face of this company, to join together this man and this woman in holy matrimony."

Molly, wearing a white dress trimmed with yellow and blue lace, took TJ to be her lawfully wedded husband, and TJ, in a pale blue suit, took Molly to be his lawfully wedded wife. Ninety people filled the large living room and the broad hallway that led to the kitchen. María was there, in a low-cut dress, and the art dealer, who had his arm around her waist, and Uncle Siva, in his Italian silk suit, which did not seem to have been damaged by the storm. Standing next to his nephew, he was so resplendent he might have been mistaken for the groom. Rudy's heart seized up, the way it sometimes did when he was overexcited. He was standing next to Nandini, who was wearing one of her aunt's yellow saris. The fire in the woodstove was not the sacred fire they'd planned on, but it kept the house warm. It was all over by eleven o'clock. The catering truck from the Taj Mahal had already arrived, and the Indian chef and his Mexican sous-chefs began to prepare the wedding banquet on the veranda. Rudy put a bottle of the Pol Roger in a paper bag and hid it in the cabinet under the sink in the kitchen, and he camouflaged a *Saint-Cyr* in the back of the freezer by wrapping it in a sheet of newspaper, and then he took a plate of poppadoms and samosas out to Nandini, who'd gone out to check on Norma Jean. They ate the poppadoms and samosas with their fingers. They were hot and spicy.

A beautiful woman with long black hair approached Rudy as he was opening a bottle of champagne. She held out her glass and he filled it. She was about Molly's age and looked familiar, like someone he'd known a long time ago.

"Christine Harrington," she said. "Gary and Vivian's daughter. Your brother was my grandfather."

"Oh, for heaven's sake," Rudy said. "I saw your name on the list, but I haven't seen you since . . ."

"Since I was in high school," she said, finishing the sentence for him.

"And look at you now."

"The invitation came to my grandmother's," she said. "It didn't have my name on it, but I thought I'd come anyway. Maybe reconnect."

"Are you staying in the seminary?" he asked.

"Yes," she said, "but I'm catching a ride to the airport this afternoon with one of Molly's friends."

"How is it?"

"The seminary? Oh, it's very nice. Kind of spooky, though, all those crucifixes on the wall and pictures of bleeding hearts wrapped in thorns. My grandmother would have a fit."

"How is your grandmother these days? I've always been sorry we lost touch."

"She's in a nursing home now, on old US 12, just north of the old drive-in theater."

"Still setting an extra place for your grandfather?"

"She is, in fact. She didn't do it for years, but when she moved into the nursing home she started up again. I thought they were going to kick her out. We finally got something worked out. They give her an extra salad plate at dinner and an extra knife and fork."

"Whatever works."

"She just can't let go," Christine said, shaking her head. "Eighty years old and she can't let go."

Rudy filled their glasses with more Pol Roger. "Here's to letting go," he said, raising his glass. Christine raised her glass and touched the edge to Rudy's.

"To letting go."

"Letting go is good," Rudy said. "It's very good. But holding on is good too."

The photographer Rudy'd hired failed to show up, so during the festivities Meg took pictures with a new Instamatic camera: Molly and TJ cutting into a *Saint-Cyr;* Uncle Siva proposing a toast; the vet giving last-minute instructions to Nandini; Medardo in sandals and linen trousers and a salmon-colored shirt, open at the collar, talking to his cousin; Dan and Meg with their arms around the bride; Philip and Daniel clowning on the stairs; the justice of the peace palming the hundred-dollar bill Rudy'd just extracted from his wallet; Margot admiring her sister; María and the art dealer chatting with Siva; Nandini and Rudy standing with Molly and TJ as they prepared to leave for the airport in McAllen. TJ was leaving for Ann Arbor the following morning for the beginning of the semester. Molly would be spending the night with him at a motel near the airport and coming back to Rudy's in the morning. She was leaving for India on Monday.

As they said their good-byes, Rudy dug down as deep as he could for some final words of advice, but he couldn't come up with anything. She wasn't a virgin, and she wasn't a gift. She was just Molly.

Nandini began to cry, and Rudy felt himself on the verge of tears too as he handed Molly into the rental car and kissed her good-bye. But these were pleasant tears, appropriate to the occasion, and when he and Nandini looked at each other, they both smiled.

"I would like to have a puja," Nandini said as the car disappeared down the long drive. "We must call the pandit in the morning."

"The pandit hasn't been very agreeable," Rudy said.

"Nevertheless," said Nandini, "he is the only one who can help us now."

Will the Circle Be Unbroken?

Though Narmada-Jai was in a coma — Nandini had begun to call her by her Indian name — they were aware of her at all times and spoke to each other in hushed tones, as if they were in the hospital room of a patient in critical condition. In the evening, Medardo came to stay with her so that Rudy and Nandini could go up to the house for a while to rest and clean up and have a bite to eat. Dan and the boys had gone back to Milwaukee on their scheduled flight, but Meg had stayed behind to be with her sisters. Meg and Margot persuaded Nandini, who was completely exhausted, to take a whirlpool bath while they went to the motel to get her things.

Rudy made up a bed for Nandini upstairs. When he was finished he sat in the kitchen and listened to the hum of the whirlpool bath while he waited for Meg and Margot to return. His happiness at being near Nandini seemed to him to be inappropriate, under the circumstances, but he couldn't help himself. In his imagination he could see her coming out of the grove in her sari, could see her knees moving under the deep green cloth and her neck bones peeking out beneath her dark hair, could hear her scolding Narmada-Jai in her soft voice, telling the elephant to raise her leg so he and Molly could use it as a step. He could hear her questions about the grove — hectares, acres, kilograms, pounds.

That night he sat up with Narmada-Jai for a long time. He played his guitar for an hour but didn't sing, and then he lay down on the Russian's cot, which he'd moved to Narmada-Jai's makeshift tent. He did not know what Siva had said to his sister, and now Siva had gone to New York. He would have to speak for himself. He had not said anything to the girls, but he sensed that they sensed. He knew that they loved him and wanted him to be happy, and he could see that they themselves were doing everything possible to make Nandini feel a part of the family.

Rudy tried to push her away from the center of his thoughts, but it was impossible. He thought of the Russian crossing the international bridge with Narmada-Jai in tow, of Molly's happiness, of the priest's expectation of heaven, of Margot calling from Italy to say she was in love, of Meg acting out her first victory before the appellate court, and of Medardo's face as he left for Reynosa on Friday evenings. He and Nandini were also standing at a threshold. Was this simple foolishness? Ignorance? *Moha?* Maya? Did he know the real woman at all, or only a puppet in his imagination — a fantasy woman who offered no more resistance to his desires than the clay idol of Lord Ganesh that the pandit had brought for the wedding? But he couldn't help himself. This was, he realized, his last chance to experience if not beauty, then joy, even ecstasy.

He had never expected to be in love again. He had come to associate all the symptoms of love with adolescence. They got you started down the road, but then you discovered that there's more than bed to marriage — one of life's great truths — and had to move on to the next, more mature, phase. But his heart was open wide now. He had to acknowledge that he was no longer the same man he'd been at the beginning of his philosophical quest. He felt that he could see what no one else could see, not only his own inner turmoil, but the inner feelings of others, as if he were observing them from an invisible vantage point in one of TJ's parallel universes. *What if?* he asked himself. And at every *what if?* the universe split apart, and it would split apart again depending on what Nandini decided. In one universe Rudy and Nandini would manage the grove together. In another Nandini would go back to her tea garden in Assam. In one universe they would step into their new lives; in another, they would step back into their old ones.

The next morning Nandini spent an hour on the phone talking to the pandit, arranging a puja — some kind of ceremony for Narmada-Jai. If the puja didn't work, they were going to call the vet and ask him to put the elephant down, but Nandini was hopeful, more than hopeful. She'd seen miracles, she said. She'd fed the statue of Ganesh in Guwahati a little spoonful of milk. All over India it had happened, she said, and in other countries too. Even in Los Angeles. The statues had drunk milk.

Medardo, who'd dropped by to see what needed to be done, was also optimistic. "Like the Virgin Mary shedding tears," he said. "I saw that too in Monterrey, two times."

So they were in good spirits when Molly came back from McAllen, and no longer spoke in hushed hospital tones. TJ had almost missed his flight, Molly said, smiling. They were still sitting at the breakfast table, their dirty dishes in front of them. They'd eaten eggs scrambled with the two avocados that had been sitting on the counter, which had finally begun to soften.

Medardo had gone out to sit with Narmada-Jai. Nandini had both elbows on the table and was supporting her chin on her interlocked fingers.

"What are you staring at?" Molly asked.

Everyone laughed. Molly blushed. "We just wanted to see what you looked like married," Margot said.

"How do I look?"

"Radiant."

"Are you sure you're actually married?" Margot asked.

Molly laughed. "There was a certain amount of confusion."

"That pandit was a piece of work," Margot said. "You're lucky he *didn't* perform the ceremony."

"The priest wasn't any better," Molly said, "but at least the justice of the peace seemed to know what he was doing. And anyway, don't you really marry yourselves? Legally, I mean. Even in Christianity I think that you marry yourselves. The church just sort of presides over it. At least that's what somebody told us when we went for premarital counseling."

"*You* went for premarital counseling?" Meg asked.

"Yes, *we* went for premarital counseling."

"Don't you have the license? That's what makes it legal — a marriage license from the state of Texas, the thing you got when you went into town with Father Russell?"

Molly put her hand over her mouth. "I don't remember."

"Didn't the JP ask about it? What kind of a JP was he anyway? Do you *have* it, even if it isn't signed?"

Molly looked around. "He *said* we were married. He pronounced us man and wife."

"Jesus Christ," Meg said.

"Well, you didn't think of it either."

"I wasn't the one getting married."

"I *feel* married."

"How does it *feel?*"

"Kind of tingly."

Nandini put her hands over her eyes. Rudy was afraid she was crying, but she was laughing. "You're married," he said. "The JP took the certificate into town, to the courthouse."

"Why didn't you say so?" Molly asked.

"I wanted to see if you could remember signing it," Rudy said, looking at the second hand on the old kitchen clock he'd brought from the house in Chicago. The transparent front cover was missing, and part of the white plastic frame at the back had broken off. Helen had taped it together. If it had been in his power he would have stopped time at that moment, would have placed his finger on the clock face to block the second hand. He thought of the old hymn, "Will the Circle Be Unbroken?" They were together again as a family. Meg and Molly and Margot. And in a parallel universe it might have been, might be, Helen laughing and covering her face with her hands instead of Nandini.

Rudy had read about Zeno's paradox in *Philosophy Made Simple,* and so he knew that the second hand, which was now at the six, could never reach the twelve, because first it would have to reach the halfway point, the nine, and then, having reached the nine, it would have to reach another halfway point, between the ten and the eleven. And then it would have to reach still another halfway point. No matter how close it got to the twelve, there would always be another halfway point. But the second hand did not slow down as it approached the twelve. In fact, as it swept past the twelve, through an infinite number of halfway points, it seemed to be accelerating, carrying with it what was left of the morning.

"You ever see Sandro again?" Molly asked.

Margot shook her head. "He's moved to Rome. But I'm still living in his apartment! It belongs to his wife. She's cut the phone off, but it'll be forever before she can get me out of there."

"Why don't we have lobster tonight?" Meg said.

"All you can get here," Rudy said, "are those frozen rock lobster tails."

"But they're good," Molly said. "Have you ever had lobster, Amma?"

Nandini smiled. "Of course, but I'm sure that anything your father prepares will be very fine," she said, putting on a jacket. "But what is 'a piece of work'? You are saying that the pandit is 'a piece of work.'" She was in jeans and a sweatshirt. The temperature was still in the low sixties.

"She meant," Rudy said, and then he paused, not sure how to explain. "She meant that if anyone can work a miracle for Narmada-Jai, the pandit can."

The wedding presents were piled up in the living room — on the leather couch, on the two Windsor chairs, on the coffee table. Molly opened them one by one: toasters, blenders, knives, a copper pot from American friends; saris, jewelry, an Indian cookbook, another raffia elephant sewing basket. And even a tiny illustrated copy of the Kama Sutra from one of TJ's cousins! There was a present for Rudy too. Margot had bought it for Molly, but she gave it to Rudy instead. It was an Etruscan statue. A young girl, naked, left leg stretched out in front of her, right leg curled underneath her, the way Margot used to sit — all the girls, actually. She held a bird in one hand, a sparrow or a meadowlark. She was about nine inches high and was the most beautiful thing Rudy'd ever seen. When he looked at her he was stunned. He looked away and then back. He looked away again, and then back.

"Is this the antiquity you bought at Sotheby's?"

Margot nodded. "It was very exciting."

"How much?"

She shook her head. "You know better than to ask, Papa."

He handed it to Nandini.

"Maximum beauty," she said. "Absolute maximum."

"I want *you* to have it," he said, looking around him to see what he'd done, and for a moment, time — silent, invisible, odorless, tasteless, untouchable, neither river nor harvester but a thing in itself — stood still, stopped as surely as the second hand on the kitchen clock would have stopped if he'd blocked it with his finger.

But time was invented to keep everything from happening all at once. You can't get on without it. Rudy was the only one who noticed a slight tremor, no more than a dog's tail brushing against his leg. The others kept right on talking and admiring the statue, and then the girls went upstairs to bed, and Rudy and Nandini went out to relieve Medardo, so he could go home to get some sleep. Narmada-Jai was still unconscious, but her sides rose and fell. Rudy put his hand under her leg till he could feel the beating of her great heart, which continued to measure out the seconds and the minutes and the hours.

God Is Dead

The weather was cool and cloudy after the storm. Nandini, who'd spent most of the night out with Narmada-Jai, was now asleep upstairs. Meg and Molly had gone outside to stay with the elephant. Rudy started to empty the dishwasher, but the dishes made too much clatter and he decided to wait. He boiled water for tea. When Nandini came down, half an hour later, she was holding the Etruscan statue.

"Maximum beauty," Rudy said.

"Absolute maximum."

They sat at the kitchen table drinking Assam tea with milk and sugar and chatting about this and that, like two young lovers too shy to say what's in their hearts, till Medardo came to spell the girls at around seven o'clock. There were clothes to be washed and dried, suitcases to be packed and repacked, blouses to be ironed, reservations to be confirmed. Rudy boiled a dozen eggs, and he and Nandini drank more tea. When the eggs had cooled they took two of them out to Medardo.

Rudy thought they should call the vet, even though the pandit was due later in the day. When an elephant's been down two or three days, the vet had said on Saturday, it can't get up again, but Rudy couldn't bring himself to say this to Nandini, at least not in words. He put his arm around her, however — the first time he'd touched her, except to shake her hand, or to sit next to her in the car — and he thought she knew what he was thinking, because she leaned her head against his chest and let him hold her in his arms.

Rudy took Margot to the airport in McAllen. She said she was happy for him, but without explaining what she meant. He remembered how frightened she'd been when he'd put her on the plane at O'Hare, when she'd left for Italy on her own, last November, spending her own money because he hadn't wanted her to go and wouldn't pay for her ticket. She'd been twenty-nine years old. Now she was thirty. "Italy's been good for you," he said, for the fourth or fifth time.

At the gate he asked her again: "How much did you say you spent for that little Etruscan girl?"

She shook her head and laughed.

"So Nandini better keep it in a safe place?"

She laughed again. "I think it will be safe with her."

When he got back to the house, Meg and Molly were preparing to leave for Houston. Meg would fly to Milwaukee, Molly to New York, and from New York to Calcutta. From Calcutta she'd go by train to Guwahati, where someone from the tea garden would meet her. Rudy and Nandini, who was staying for the puja, watched them pack the car. Nandini had some last-minute advice for Molly.

"When you get to the end of the driveway," Rudy said to Molly as she closed the trunk of the car, "the wedding will be over. That will be it."

"Don't, Papa," she said, and he knew he could still make her cry.

They drove off, and Rudy waved and kept on waving, remembering his own parents, long dead, standing on the porch of the small farmhouse outside St. Joe, waving to him and Helen and the girls as they pulled out of the driveway. Now he understood how they'd felt. He didn't think of them very often now. They had faded away in his memory, like travelers disappearing into a dark wood, or ships disappearing over the horizon.

Rudy drove into town to pick up some things for the puja: fresh fruit and a basket of flowers and more turmeric. The pandit, who arrived at three o'clock, brought lamps and bells, incense and holy ashes and sandalwood paste, a red powder called *kunkuma,* an alcohol burner for the sacred flame, various small pots, colorful clothes to dress up the image of Lord Ganesh, and a small cassette player. The temperature was still in the sixties and Rudy, Medardo, and Father Russell — who didn't want to miss anything — all wore jackets. The pandit, in his saffron robe, seemed to be indifferent to the chill.

"It is not good for a non-Hindu to try to worship Shiva or Murugan," the pandit said as he was arranging all these things, "but all devotions are acceptable to Lord Ganesh. But you haven't eaten, have you? For three hours, I mean. You should not have eaten for three hours. And you haven't cut yourself? That is not acceptable. Nor should you perform the ceremony after deep anger or emotional upset."

Rudy hadn't eaten since breakfast, and he hadn't cut himself, but his emotions had been racing. He answered no, however, and so did the others, and the pandit made a little altar of empty avocado flats, low to the ground, and placed on it the clay idol that he had brought earlier. While Nandini chanted the one hundred and eight names of Lord Ganesh, Rudy went up to the house to boil a cup of rice and to get a bowl to catch the water that the pandit would use to bathe the image. The pandit wanted all the things necessary to the puja to be prepared in advance so he wouldn't have to interrupt the ceremony to look for something.

When Rudy returned with the cooked rice and the bowl, a kite was circling overhead, flapping its wings and then gliding, and Rudy had the uneasy feeling that he was being watched. Nandini saw it too, and recognized it: *"Cheel,"* she said, and the pandit looked up in the sky. The kite flapped its wings and glided unsteadily down into the dense mesquite trees on the far side of the little hill. *Another omen?* Rudy wondered; *another baadha?*

The pandit prostrated himself before the altar and knocked on his temples three times with his knuckles. He crossed his arms and, with his arms still crossed, pulled his ears. Nandini sat cross-legged, but Rudy and Medardo and Father Russell kept shifting position, despite disapproving looks from the pandit, who had put a tape of chants of the Vedas on the little cassette player and was making food offerings — the fruit Rudy had brought, some cooked rice, still warm, and various sweets. The pandit passed the food to everyone to eat after it had been offered to Lord Ganesh — the idol, not Narmada-Jai.

The ceremony itself, which involved a lot of bell ringing and prayers, which the pandit offered in Sanskrit, made no more sense to Rudy than the Greek Orthodox Easter service they'd attended one year with one of Helen's friends, but he followed along as best he could, holding up his spoonful of water for the idol to sip, bathing the idol's feet several times, tossing raw rice and flowers. At the end the pandit offered the tray of food to Lord Ganesh a second time, in sincerity and love, and then he invited the others to pick up a pinch of rice with the fingertips of their right hand. As he finished the last chant they released the pinch of rice, and then closed their eyes and imagined Lord Ganesh accepting and enjoying this meal. But when Rudy closed his eyes it wasn't Lord Ganesh he imagined. It was Norma Jean — Narmada-Jai. Their fellow creature. Could she understand what had happened to her? Did she understand more or less than the humans? More or less than Brownie and Saskia, who were still up in Milwaukee with Meg and Dan and the boys?

Rudy wanted Narmada-Jai to live, to remove one more obstacle. When he opened his eyes he saw that Nandini was offering the elephant a sip of the water that had been used to bathe the idol, holding the little spoon at the tip of Narmada-Jai's trunk, and then at her triangular mouth, which hung halfway open. Rudy thought of Helen, at the end, how buoyed up with hope they'd be if she asked for a soft-boiled egg. But Narmada-Jai showed no interest in the water.

After the puja they gave Narmada-Jai a sponge bath. Rudy went to get two buckets of water. By the time he got back from the barn, the pandit had packed up his things. Nandini was arranging more fruit on a tray. When she gave it to the pandit Rudy noticed an envelope sticking up between a bunch of grapes and a green peach. His *dakshina,* she explained later. "You wouldn't expect a lawyer or a doctor to come for nothing."

"No," Rudy said. "Of course not."

The vet was going to come from Brownsville as soon as he got off work at the zoo, but the waiting was hard. Rudy'd always had dogs when he was a boy, and when they got so old they couldn't get up and walk around, his dad had taken them out in the woods and shot them. The hardest thing, he thought, was that he hadn't been able to talk to them — to Buster or Jack or Buckle — hadn't been able to explain. And now he wanted to explain to Narmada-Jai, to explain what had happened and what was going to happen, but he couldn't explain to himself what had happened. The Russian was right: *You can't understand it without vodka.*

Late in the afternoon Medardo brought his five-man crew around and they introduced themselves and looked at the prostrate elephant and then carried the ladders into the lower grove. They were going to pick as many avocados as possible in the lower grove before the next storm hit. This one, malingering out in the Caribbean, had been officially declared a hurricane — Hurricane Beulah. Mission was on the fringe of most hurricanes, but they were expecting some severe weather in the lower Valley.

Rudy and Nandini ate sandwiches in their little camp next to Narmada-Jai. Rudy took the dirty dishes up to the house. The vet still hadn't come. Just as the kitchen door closed behind him he heard a shout from Nandini. He couldn't see what was happening because of the canvas from the *mandap,* but he could hear Narmada-Jai making noises. By the time he got to her she was rocking back and forth, one front leg caught under her stomach, another kicking helplessly in the air as she struggled to roll over. There was no way to help her, but Nandini was encouraging her, repeating a command he hadn't heard before. Narmada-Jai rolled one way and then the other, finally managing to get over onto her knees. She rested for a few minutes and then struggled to her feet. Rudy poured some vodka over a fistful of alfalfa and gave it to her. She chewed the alfalfa and then she put her trunk up in the air and sniffed. Nandini and Rudy walked beside her as she limped toward the grove.

"She is wanting to go to the river," Nandini said. "Like elephants in Assam are going to Brahmaputra to die." She started, a second time, to sing the one hundred and eight names of Lord Ganesh.

Narmada-Jai stopped from time to time to pluck an avocado and flip it into her mouth. Her last meal. Rudy thought of the Texas convict. He'd sent half a dozen immature avocados, hard as rocks, to the assistant warden in Huntsville. What else could he have done? Narmada-Jai was walking pretty fast, swinging her trunk from side to side and sometimes thrusting it up into the air, like a trombone player in a jazz band.

When they came out of the grove and Narmada-Jai caught sight of the river — more with her trunk than with her eyes — she held herself back, for a moment, and then plunged ahead, down to the spot where she was accustomed to bathe, through the opening in the chaparral into the shallow water of the little cove. She stopped briefly to drink and to splash herself before stepping softly out into the current. They watched her disappear around the bend.

"The Russian said she's a good swimmer," Rudy said.

"All elephants are very expert swimmers," Nandini said. "But she won't swim long. She will take in water so that she not float longer."

"What are we going to do?"

"Nothing. There's nothing more to be done."

They walked back to the barn and sat together in silence for a few minutes before going up to the house. In the kitchen Rudy made another pot of Assam tea. They were drinking tea when the vet arrived.

Rudy explained what had happened, and they walked out to the place where Narmada-Jai had been lying.

"I called the zoo," Rudy said, "but you'd already left. I'm sorry."

"It's all right," the vet said. "At least you won't have to dig a pit to bury her."

"I hadn't thought of that," Rudy said.

"I'm just amazed," the vet said, "that she was able to get up again after being down so long. There's your miracle."

After the vet left Rudy built a small fire in the woodstove, to take off the chill. "Maybe we could talk now," he said to Nandini, kneeling in front of the open door of the stove. "Because this is our last chance."

"Yes. I understand."

"Have you decided anything?"

They went into the kitchen, where Nandini poured the last of the tea. Rudy added a little vodka to his cup.

"Decided?"

"About immigrating to the United States?"

She nodded.

"Ann Arbor? Detroit? New York?"

She shook her head.

"Texas?"

"Rudy, my brother is speaking to me about . . ."

"Siva?"

"Yes, of course. He is a very strong advocate for you. He holds you in very high regards." She took Rudy's hand. "At first I'm thinking, maximum good idea. Even before I have met you I am hearing about you from my son, who is enjoying your hospitality in the month of December. And of course from your daughter, Molly. You must be very proud of such fine daughters. It is probably not so unusual in the United States as in my country, where daughters are beheld differently. But my father is always very loving to me, equally with my brother in every way, and when I am not allowed to assist at the English school in Guwa-hati, he is sending me to learn some English language from our neighbors, the Johnsons, who are staying behind after independence. Every day I am riding my grandfather's elephant, Ramu. Mrs. Johnson is glad to have company. They have a very big garden. Five thousand coolies. The Johnsons are dead now, but this is where they are making Molly's movie —"

Rudy interrupted her: "Your brother spoke to you . . ."

"Maybe you think it is strange for women, this way, I know it is not American . . ."

"I did," he said, "till I saw you coming to rescue us. In your beautiful green sari."

"It was a very happy moment, don't you think so? Even though Molly is telling me about Narmada-Jai, I am never expecting to be seeing an elephant in your garden. Maybe you are hiding a one-horn rhinoceros too. Then I would feel just at home."

"I wish you would feel at home. After such a short time."

"Excellent tea. Your daughter has learned this very well, has imparted her skills to you. I promise you that in India I will look after her as if she is my own daughter. And of course she is."

"You were saying you spoke to your brother, Nandini. And your brother spoke to me. He led me to believe that you were thinking seriously of coming to live in the United States, that you had even filled out the forms for an H1 visa. He mentioned that there are problems with bandits."

"Dacoits," she said. She tried to say something but stumbled. She started to cry and then checked her tears. Rudy already knew what she was going to say, but he didn't know how to stop her.

"Mr. Rudy," she said, "after what has happened, what my brother is hoping cannot be possible."

"Nandini. I'm sixty years old. I never expected to fall in love again. But I've fallen in love with you. It's that simple. *Prem*. I know it's been only a short time . . ."

"That is how I am marrying the first time. *Prem*. A love match."

"And now?"

"I am having this dream a little bit too, dreaming of leaving everything behind, my old life, my tea garden, with all its problems, even Champaa, to come to make a new life, but then I receive a sign that I must turn back. Lord Ganesh has placed an obstacle in my path. A *baadha*."

"You mean Narmada-Jai? I thought Lord Ganesh was supposed to remove obstacles, not put them in your way."

"We pray to him to remove obstacles, but when he does not, then we must turn back, not try to go around the obstacle. The obstacle is there for a reason. The lightning is striking her, Mr. Rudy. I am trying to interpret it in every which way, but finally I am accepting the truth that the pandit is right. It was a *baadha*."

"But Narmada-Jai came to a good end, wouldn't you say? I mean, the Rio Grande's not the Brahmaputra, but it's a good river. She died a good death. The vet said it was a miracle that she was able to stand up again."

"Yes, but afterward, Mr. Rudy, and that too is a sign."

"After what?"

"It is after I have made my decision to go home."

"You're not even going to go to New York?"

She shook her head. "No. I am already telephoning to the airport."

Rudy started to argue: "Your brother said you'd never be able to remarry in India . . ." He thought she almost faltered at this point. She began to cry again. He put his arm around her to comfort her. "God is dead, Nandini," he said. "We can do whatever we want to do. We *should* do whatever we want to do."

But after a while she stopped him. "No, Mr. Rudy, you mustn't say that."

"It's not just me, Nandini," he said. "My daughters love you too. Don't you see that?"

"Yes, I can see that too. It is maximum good family my son is coming into."

"How can I explain love itself, Nandini? — not mutual convenience, but the thing itself. For which we risk everything. I am a young man again. I'm afraid to touch you. Afraid to take your hand. To kiss you." He took her hand, even though he was afraid. "I'm thinking about the tent," he went on. "About the one corner flapping in the night. You told Ashok not to stake it down. Don't stake it down now, Nandini."

"The pandit was right, Rudy. What happen to Narmada-Jai is a *baadha*, a very bad sign. I hope Molly and TJ will overcome it."

"But don't you think it was a good sign, for us and for them? In the end? The way she got up and went down to the river?" But he realized that he was repeating himself. "There are so many good signs, Nandini: love, reason, self-interest, desire, TJ and Molly, how my daughters love you, *prem*."

But opposing these arguments was a powerful counterforce, deeper than reason, more primitive than love. Rudy didn't know what to call it: Superstition? Religion? Spirituality? Tao? Karma? Dharma? It was like encountering some force of nature, like Hurricane Beulah, or one of the fundamental constants, like the strong nuclear force, or the weak nuclear force, like gravity or electromagnetism. Rudy couldn't understand it any more than he could understand how these constants held the universe together.

◆

That night Nandini took another whirlpool bath. Rudy lay down on his bed. He was very tired, but he didn't sleep. He listened to the hum of the whirlpool in the bathroom downstairs. After her bath Nandini came into his room. She sat on the edge of the bed and he pretended to be asleep for a while, waiting to see what she would do. He thought he might be in a parallel universe.

"Don't be angry with me, Rudy," she said. "And don't be sad." She walked her fingers up his back from his waist to his neck. He reached around and put his hand on her thigh. He turned over and looked at her. She was wearing a special sari, lacy, like a negligee.

"You don't have to do this," he said.

"This is what I want to do. Is it okay?"

He nodded.

After a few minutes she raised her arms up and unfastened the lovely bird-shaped clip that held her hair back. He could hear her put it down on the little table next to the bed. He touched her, tentatively, the way he'd touched Narmada-Jai the first time, not knowing what to expect. He was always surprised by the Pendleton-blanket feel of Narmada-Jai, and now he was surprised by the feel of Nandini, like a smooth peach. He kept his hand on her back while she unwrapped her sari. He rubbed the back of her knee a little with his fingers, as if he were searching for something.

"A little bit higher up," she said, putting her hand over his eyes.

He raised his hand as far as he could without shifting position. He could feel the pull of the silk sari sliding under his hand, and then the smooth skin of her thigh.

"You wouldn't let Molly and TJ sleep together in Assam," he said.

She laughed. "Maximum restraint yield maximum pleasure, don't you think?"

He was naked under a flannel sheet and a light blanket, but he'd left a couple of sticks of ironwood on the fire in the wood-stove, so the house was not too cold.

She stretched out beside him. He moistened his finger with his tongue and touched her nipples, which contracted and then hardened, and then he traced her milk line down to her crotch, her sacred yoni. The insides of her thighs burned his hand, and his heart started to beat faster. He reached for the little bottle of nitroglycerin tablets next to the bed, and then decided to let whatever was going to happen happen.

Had she changed her mind? Was it possible after all to imagine a future together? He cupped her head in his hands and kissed the creases on her forehead. Her sari and his flannel sheet had become tangled. He kicked the sheet aside. The sari fell to the floor with a whisper, and he could feel her breathing in his ear. How did she know what to whisper to create such intense sweetness, such promises of bliss? How did she know so exactly to whisper what he wished to hear? And how did he understand the words she murmured in song, even though they were in Hindi? *Come to me, my darling, my breasts are young and firm, my thighs are soft as satin, my crop green and young, ready to be irrigated.* Her breath in his ear was warm as a breeze in early spring. What philosopher could explain such warmth, such sweetness, like fresh herbs crushed in a mortar? What philosopher could give an account of the deep infrasonic rumbling that came from the most intimate part of her self, like the sounds he'd sensed coming from Narmada-Jai out in the barn? *God is dead,* he thought, but he fitted himself into her as if he were pressing the last piece into a puzzle.

Just Another Day

Socrates was a stonecutter, a blue-collar worker; but did Plato ever hold down a real job? Aristotle? Epicurus? George Berkeley became a bishop, but how hard could that be? David Hume? Immanuel Kant? Arthur Schopenhauer? Friedrich Nietzsche? Were they all academics? Rudy was thinking about manual labor now. He'd already sold half his crop to Becker in Chicago and half to Nick Regiacorte in Houston, and so — once he'd finished his morning phone calls — he'd go out in the field and work with the picking crew.

There was nothing about manual labor in *Philosophy Made Simple,* but Rudy'd been asking himself, how would the course of philosophy have been different if these philosophers had had to pick a thousand pounds of avocados a day? And sometimes he even imagined that the men on the tall wooden ladders to his left and his right — Medardo's picking crew from his hometown, Montemorelos, who bunked in a double-wide at the back of the trailer park — were not Rinaldo and Felipe and Carlos and Antonio and Hilario, but Socrates and Plato and Aristotle and Immanuel and Arthur. *Would they be good workers? Do a day's work for a day's pay? Would Medardo scold them, as he scolded Rudy, if they failed to press the knobs on the end of their blades up against the stems just so, to preserve the button? Would they look forward, as Rudy did, to gathering around the glass-topped table on the veranda at the end of a long day to drink a bottle or two of* cerveza fría? *What would they talk about? The good life? The One and the Many? The* Ding an sich? *The Veil of Maya? Free will? The mind-body problem?*

And while they were talking would they be thinking about the last woman they'd gone to bed with? The last woman they'd loved? Or maybe the first? Would Rudy be able to follow their conversations, or would it be like trying to follow the conversations in Spanish on the veranda, which started out slowly and calmly enough, as they discussed the approaching hurricane or the new clutch that Rudy and Medardo had installed in the tractor, but which soon accelerated as they took up the problem of Rinaldo's oldest boy, who was already giving the girls a hard time, or of Carlos's mother-in-law, or of Hilario's wife's sister, who'd taken up with a married man?

It was a question for Uncle Siva, who'd sent a copy of *Schopenhauer and the Upanishads* and a note thanking Rudy for his hospitality and suggesting that he might enjoy Leibniz's critique of Locke's empiricism. *I'll see if I can find a decent translation,* he wrote, *and send it to you.*

They enjoyed reasonably good weather after the storm that had killed Norma Jean, but Hurricane Beulah was on the news every night as it moved across the Caribbean into the Gulf. They worked in the lower grove every day, picking as many avocados as they could in the week before the hurricane was expected to make landfall, filling the field bins, which Medardo carted away

with a hydraulic lift. They worked right through Saturday —
Diez y Seis, Mexican Independence Day — and Sunday, but on
Monday, after taking two loads of avocados to the packing house
in Hidalgo, they called it quits. Medardo went to batten down
whatever could be battened down at the trailer park; Rudy went
into town to stock up on pasta and canned goods and candles
and flashlight batteries. He bought four sheets of three-quarter-
inch plywood to board up the windows, he filled water jugs and
the big bathtub, and he nailed down the shutters in the barn that
he'd opened up again after the wedding.

Beulah entered the Texas coast at the mouth of the Rio Grande
on the morning of September 20. By the time Rudy got around to
boarding up the windows, it was too late. He couldn't hold on
to the sheets of plywood in the wind. Gusts of 135 miles per hour
were reported at Brownsville, and of 86 miles per hour as far inland
as Corpus Christi. Beulah spun off eighty-five tornadoes, and
damage in the lower Valley was estimated at half a billion dollars.
Medardo's trailer park escaped damage, but the packing house in
Hidalgo was destroyed by a tornado. The forty thousand pounds
of avocados they'd picked the week before disappeared. Neither
Mission nor McAllen was hit by a tornado, but the Rio Grande
spilled out of its banks and out of the floodway, and the military
launched Operation Bravo, sending out amphibious and high-
wheeled vehicles to rescue people who were stranded. Blankets
and medicine and food and snakebite kits were airlifted into
flooded areas. The airport in McAllen was flooded. Light planes
had been towed to the McAllen Country Club. A herd of cattle
was driven down Highway 83 to get them out of the floodplain.
Reynosa was flooded from the international bridge to Joe's Place.

The farm-to-market roads were all closed. Rudy couldn't get
out for several days. He could have asked to be evacuated, but he

had plenty of food and water, so he decided to stay. The phone lines were down, and there was no electricity.

It was during Hurricane Beulah — at the peak of the storm — that Rudy finished *Philosophy Made Simple,* read the last chapters by the light of a paraffin lamp, reached the end of the story. He couldn't work up much interest in logical positivism, which seemed to him to reduce the fundamental questions to the level of grammatical mistakes, or in pragmatism, which was a kind of surrender. But existentialism was another matter. Helen had considered herself an existentialist. "Existence precedes essence," she liked to say. Maybe so. Rudy'd never given it much thought, but now he saw it as the tail end of something that had started with Nietzsche or maybe even earlier, with Kant and Schopenhauer, though according to Uncle Siva, Kant had been a religious man himself. Think of Jean-Paul Sartre's paper cutter. This paper cutter, according to Sartre, had a purpose in life because someone had designed it. Someone had had a plan. Someone had wanted to cut some paper and had designed a paper cutter to do the job. But a human being doesn't have a purpose in life because no one designed a human being. No one had a plan. Human beings are just here. That's existentialism in a nutshell: a paper cutter. Or the opposite of a paper cutter.

Oh, there was more, of course. At the kitchen table, Rudy turned the pages of the last chapter. What he concluded was that we're all heading into an unknowable future; there's no way to chart a course with any certainty; we face death troubled by angst and *nausée* and ennui; we search for ways to set the world on a firm metaphysical foundation, but we have no reason to believe that such a metaphysical foundation exists. The only meaning our lives have is the meaning we give them.

Outside, the storm raged, frightening but exhilarating. Through the kitchen window, when he raised his eyes from his book, Rudy could see nothing, and when he turned his eyes inward, the darkness was equally profound, the storm equally frightening and equally exhilarating. He closed the book around his thumb, thankful for these moments, thankful for *moha,* for passion, for all the threads that attached him to this world, this life.

He thought about Narmada-Jai plunging into the river. God is dead, but this death hadn't been so bad. Not as bad as being crucified or burned at the stake. More like the death of Socrates. She'd just disappeared into the river. And he thought of Nandini unfastening her lacy sari and of the sound the sari had made as it rustled to the floor. He'd thought that night, when he heard the sari whispering to the floor, that she must have changed her mind, decided to stay. He thought that in the morning they could visit the pump house in Hidalgo and then walk over the bridge to Reynosa for lunch at Casa Viejo. But in the morning she packed her things and he took her to the airport in McAllen. From McAllen she'd flown to Houston, and from Houston she'd followed the same route that Molly had taken: from New York to Calcutta, and from Calcutta by train to Guwahati. She hadn't stopped to see anyone. She'd gone home.

"The ancient Vedas," the pandit said, "elaborate the social doctrine of the four *ashramas,* or stages of life. You have already passed through the first two stages: the *brahmachari,* or chaste student; the *grihastha,* or married householder, begetting sons — or daughters, in your case — and sacrificing to the gods. Now you have entered the third stage. You have retired to the forest as a *vanaprastha,* to devote yourself to spiritual contemplation."

They were sitting in a booth at El Zarate, where they'd met quite by chance. At least Rudy thought it was quite by chance.

"Well," Rudy said, "an avocado grove is not exactly a forest, and *Philosophy Made Simple* is not exactly the Upanishads. Even so . . . What will become of me now?"

"That's a good question," the pandit said. "Will you move on to the fourth stage and become a homeless wandering ascetic, or *sannyasin?* The concept has always been problematic." The pandit paused to blow on his tea. "A man may become a *sannyasin* on a mythological level," he went on, "without literally becoming a homeless wanderer."

The pandit picked up the check that was on the table and said something in rapid Spanish to the waitress. "Everything is flux," he said, producing a twenty-dollar bill from under his saffron robe and turning to Rudy. "To meditate is to become aware of this flux as it happens moment by moment." The waitress took the check and the twenty.

"I'm aware," Rudy said.

"To meditate," the pandit said, as the two men stood up, "is also to become aware of the continuum of consciousness that lies behind that awareness."

"The *Ding an sich?*" Rudy asked.

The pandit shook his head. "Not exactly," he said. "More like *ananda,* God-consciousness — individuality being literally destroyed as the world expands and takes on splendor. It cannot be explained, only experienced."

The waitress brought the pandit's change, and the pandit gave her a generous tip. He invited Rudy to visit the ashram. Rudy didn't say yes, but he didn't say no.

It was Helen's birthday, October 6, and he'd taken the day off. He was going to stop at the public library in McAllen and then at the Lebanese place on the way home for some fresh pasta. He was planning to listen to Helen's favorite opera, *Il saraceno,* in the afternoon, and then fix Helen's favorite supper: *spaghetti alle vongole,* followed by a little fillet and a nice avocado salad. He wanted to have some flowers too, and to say good-bye to María, who'd sold her *floristería* and was moving to San Antonio to marry her art dealer and help manage his two galleries. He left his car in Hidalgo, in the lot by the river market, and walked across the international bridge. A sign on the bridge warned him not to pee: FAVOR DE NO ESPERAR AQUÍ. — POLICÍA. Or was it warning him not to loiter? He'd have to look it up.

He had a future to look forward to: María's wedding to the art dealer at the end of the month, and the Norma Jean opening, both in San Antonio. The dealer had already sold three Norma Jeans for a total of six thousand dollars. Rudy got 50 percent, after the cost of framing. He was going to Milwaukee for Christmas and to Italy at the beginning of April, after the harvest, to visit Margot.

The future wasn't the problem. The problem was the past. What to do with the past? There was so much of it.

On the Mexican side of the bridge he walked to the *floristería,* which was located just beyond the Plaza Morelos, sandwiched between a *dentista* and a *relojería.* María's name on the side of her van had already been painted over — Alejandro Torres — but it was still there on the window in the front of the shop: MARÍA GRACIA, FLORISTA. ARREGLOS PARA BODAS, QUINCEAÑERAS, Y MÁS.

María was behind the counter, examining a vase of brightly colored flowers. Rudy knew she needed glasses, but he'd never seen her wearing them before. Behind her was a handsome new refrigerated case with sparkling glass windows.

"You look good," Rudy said. "Happy, relaxed, prosperous, ready for the next thing."

When she looked up at him her face broke into a broad smile. "Rudy," she said, removing her glasses and setting them on the counter. "It's been forever. Come and kiss me. This is my last day. The new owner takes over tomorrow."

"I'm happy for you."

"Thank you, Rudy. I know you are."

"I need some flowers," he said. "Maybe some wildflowers."

"Fresh wildflowers I can't do," she said, leaning over the counter. "You should know that. Tell me what you need them for, and I'll come up with something better."

"I just felt like some fresh flowers," Rudy said.

"Have you heard from Nandini yet?"

Rudy shook his head. "No, but her brother sent me a copy of his book, *Schopenhauer and the Upanishads*. I haven't looked at it yet."

"I'm sorry, Rudy," she said. "She was a lovely woman." She removed one of the flowers from the vase and pinned it to his lapel. "Paphiopedilum," she said. "Named after the island of Paphos, where Aphrodite, the goddess of love, was worshipped. The *pedilum* part means 'shoe.'"

"In Greek?" Rudy asked. He looked at the beautiful flowers in the vase: white calla lilies and purple irises and multicolored orchids.

She nodded. "These come from near Mexico City," she said, touching the long stem of one of the calla lilies. "You can buy them for nothing in the markets there. This white sheath isn't really a petal at all; it's a leaf. The real flowers are inside. See these little flowers?" she said, pulling the sheath back.

Rudy looked. Dozens of tiny flowers were clustered around a yellow spike. He shook his head. "Amazing. I'll take these too," he said.

She looked at her watch. "Alejandro — the new owner — will be here any minute," she said. "Want to stay and have lunch with us?"

"Thanks," he said, "but I've got to be getting home."

Rudy took out his wallet while she wrapped the flowers carefully in newspaper. He had a twenty and two tens and a couple of hundred-peso notes. "On the house," she said, waving his money away. "You can get me something extra special for the wedding." Rudy thanked her, turning for one last look as he went out the door.

❖

Late in the afternoon Medardo stopped by with the entire picking crew. They were on their way to Reynosa for a cultural Friday. They'd stopped by as a *cortesía* to see if Rudy wanted to go along. There were six of them in the car, but there was always room for one more. All six were smoking, and the smoke puffed out the open windows of the Buick Riviera. Through the smoke Rudy could see their eager faces as they leaned forward in the soft leather seats. They were just boys, but they had wives back home in Montemorelos. Rinaldo and Carlos had children. Medardo would give them each a hundred pesos — Rudy's pesos — which they'd spend at the Lipstick or the Tropicana while Medardo enjoyed himself at Estrella Princesa.

Rudy shook his head. "Not today," he said. "I'm going to listen to some music and fix a little supper and take it easy."

"Just another day, huh?"

"I guess so," Rudy said, but as they drove off he thought: *Just another day.* For them it's just another day. And for me and for the pandit too, and for María. Just another day, and something that had been about to sink in for a long time finally sank. He was overwhelmed. God really *is* dead. It hadn't seemed to make that much difference at first, no more difference than the death of a distant, elderly relative. What he hadn't realized before now was that even the smaller meanings had to go too, like lifeboats that are pulled down into the vortex when the big liner sinks. He hadn't counted on that, hadn't thought it through. He no longer cared about the big meanings. Let them go. But to think that there was nothing out there *at all*. All the holidays that mark the progress of the year, all the rites, rituals, ceremonies designed to ground human experience in some larger reality . . . smoke and mirrors. Nothing but human creations. *Christmas is just another day, a human invention, like Easter, like Thanksgiving, like Ganesh Chaturthi, the birth anniversary of Ganesh, the son of Shiva and Parvathi, like every birthday, every baptism, every commencement, every funeral, every inauguration, every wedding. All that effort to convince ourselves that the desire of two people to fuck is grounded in some larger, ultimate reality, or that a man's life or a woman's love really matters in the larger scheme of things, or that endings are really new beginnings. There are no signs, no omens, not even little ones. There's only what we choose to do. The triptych I saw on Christmas Eve, the vision of the river — even these small signs have to be discounted completely. Nothing out there was calling to me. Nothing. The lightning that struck Norma Jean was a natural electrical discharge, nothing more. In every case we just did what we wanted to do, and then we attributed it to signs and omens and callings. I sold the house in Chicago and came to Texas because that's what I wanted to do. Nandini went back to Assam because that's what she wanted to do. It's as simple as that.*

But it wasn't as simple as that. It was still Helen's birthday.

Rudy sat down in his study and glanced at the copy of *Schopenhauer and the Upanishads*, which was sitting on top of *Philosophy Made Simple*. It was an imposing book, almost three inches thick. He hadn't opened it yet, except to look at the inscription:

> *For Rudy,*
> "The Idea of the elephant is imperishable."
> —ARTHUR SCHOPENHAUER
> With warmest wishes,
> Siva Singh

It was hard to believe there'd be so much to say about Schopenhauer and the Upanishads.

Rudy put the books aside and took out the file folder containing Helen's papers. He hadn't looked at the letter from Bruni in three or four years, and he wanted to see if he could read it, now that he had a pretty good command of Spanish. He could. Not all of it, but most. There wasn't much to it. Instructions about what to do with a special bottle of vinegar he'd brought back from Modena. A few drops on fresh strawberries, or on a *bistecca,* or on thin slices of Parmesan cheese.

Maybe, he thought, he'd look up Bruni when he went to visit Margot in April, challenge the man to a duel, like one of the characters in *Il saraceno.* Or maybe buy him a drink. He laughed. What he remembered most about his trip to Italy, back in March 1953, when Helen was having the affair, was that they'd gone to Venice and Bruni was supposed to be going along, but of course he hadn't gone, and in Venice . . . Helen had everything pretty well organized, and when they got on the water bus in Venice she gave each student a map with all the information about where to get off and the hotel where they were staying and how to get there, and the telephone number. Everybody had this information except Margot, who was fifteen and who wasn't supposed to go off on her own anyway, but when they came to the first stop, just as they were pulling away from the dock, one of the students said to Rudy, "Isn't that your daughter getting off the boat?" and Rudy looked up and there she was, going up the ramp from the dock up to the street, looking straight ahead, carried along by the crowd. Rudy shouted at her, but she couldn't hear him, and by the time he found Helen, who was up in the front of the boat talking to a group of students, they were already pulling over to the next stop, so he could either chew Helen out or he could get off the boat and go back to find Margot, which is what he did, except that on the way back they met the next boat coming from the station, and there was Margot on it, leaning over the railing, but she couldn't hear Rudy yelling, so he got off the boat again and start running to San Zaccaria, which he could see on the map, figuring he could get there before the boat did, because the boat had to make a big loop. But two boats stopped and he didn't see her, so he got on the next boat and just kept looking at every stop, but he still didn't see her and pretty soon they were heading out to open sea, right off the edge of the map. But when they finally got to the end of the line, the Lido, there she was, sitting on a bench, like a regular park bench, waiting for him.

On the way back to San Zaccaria, she told him all about her school. It had been hard at first. Her teachers had known she was coming, she said, but they hadn't known she didn't speak Italian, so they made her read out loud on the first day. She just said the words the way you'd say them in English, and everybody laughed. The math was harder than it was at home, and she had to read Homer and Dante, and her teachers interrogated her in front of the class, just like the other students. She cried herself to sleep every night. It was a real horror story. But when Rudy asked her if she wanted to come home with him, she said no.

The hotel wasn't marked very well on Rudy's map and they had to ask directions. They walked up to a policeman, and Rudy said something in English and showed him the map, but the policeman couldn't understand what Rudy wanted, so Margot had to do the talking. They chatted away for a while and Rudy couldn't understand a word, and then she took his hand and said, "It's okay, Papa, I know the way," and Rudy was thinking: *She's reading books I'll never read, talking a language I'll never understand. She's being carried away from me, just like she was on the water bus, only to a place where I'll never be able to go.*

And he'd felt the same way about Helen. She was being carried away from him to a place where he could never go. He knew he couldn't follow her.

That night the three of them ate in a nice restaurant down by the big lagoon. There were waiters in white coats all over the place, and the food was good, not cheap, but Helen had an expense account — the program paid for everything. There was a big family at a table not too far from theirs, and Helen kept saying that a couple of the women were giving her dirty looks, but whenever Rudy looked over, they were just laughing and having a good time. "Helen," he said, "why on earth would they be giving you dirty looks? That's crazy. Look, they're just having a good time." But in a few minutes she'd start again. He couldn't talk her out of it, and then he figured her conscience must be bothering her, so he left it at that.

And then, at the end of May, she called to say that she had cancer and was coming home.

He looked through Helen's record albums for *Il saraceno*. He didn't really care much for opera, but this was Helen's favorite and they'd listened to it together several times when she was sick. In the last act, the Count and Il saraceno encounter each other outside Isabella's window and, as they're waiting, each one for the other to leave, they sing a duet: "O happy men, if love, which rules the stars, rule your hearts." Of course they sing it in

Italian, but Helen had translated it for him. Isabella appears and the two men kill each other, and then Isabella, after singing her lungs out, kills herself too. It's very sad.

He put on the record and arranged María's flowers in a vase while he listened to the overture and to Isabella's first aria, but the music wasn't what he wanted. What he wanted was to listen to Helen's tapes, which were on the shelf over his desk. He knew they were blank, but somehow he thought that he might hear *something* if he played them one more time. He turned off the record player and put the record back in its sleeve. His old Ampex 960, top-of-the-line in its day, expensive, one of the very first two-track recorders on the market, was in one of the storage cabinets in the tack room. He had no idea what was available now. The little cassette players, which were everywhere, were so much more convenient. He lugged the heavy tape recorder in from the barn, cleaned the tape heads with a Q-tip dipped in alcohol, and put on one of his old tapes as a test. For several years, when the girls were young, he'd made a tape every Christmas: talking, telling stories, playing his guitar, singing — blues and hymns. He advanced the tape for a minute or so, to make sure the fast-forward was working properly, and then stopped it and pressed the play button. He heard himself, his best song:

. . . murder in the first degree,
The judge's wife cried out, You got to let that man go free,
'Cause he's a jelly roll baker, bake the best jelly roll in town,
Why he's the only man around, bake good jelly roll with his damper down.

He moved the recorder to the coffee table in front of the living room sofa, rewound the tape, put another stick of ironwood in the stove and closed the top vents partway.

He threaded the first of Helen's tapes and hit the play button.

He'd recorded Helen on both channels at slow speed, 3.25 feet per second. One hour per tape. He could remember arranging the two mikes over the bed. And he remembered hooking up the defective punch-in/out switch, which he'd bought at a place on Wabash, not far from the dance place where Molly was giving lessons. He never bothered to take it back.

She'd made the tapes right after she came home from the hospital the last time. She wanted to die at home. The girls were all living at home, so they could help take care of their mother. Meg had her law degree from Northwestern. She didn't have a job yet, but she'd already met Dan, and she was taking the Howard Street El up to Evanston two or three times a week. Molly had dropped out of Edgar Lee Masters and was giving dancing lessons down in the South Loop. Margot had apprenticed herself to a bookbinder in Hyde Park. She took the El downtown every morning and then the Jeffrey Express to the South Side.

When he leaned back, the couch creaked. He put his knees up and covered himself with a light quilt. He tried not to move around a lot. He tried to open himself to the silence, but it was hard to stay focused. He remembered embracing María on the couch one night when she'd come to see about the flowers for the wedding, her head propped up on the arm where his head was propped up now. Afterward she'd asked him about his childhood, and he'd told her, and she'd told him about her childhood in Matamoros. He remembered the sound of Nandini's sari sliding to the floor on the day after Narmada-Jai went for her last swim. He remembered the first time he'd lifted Helen's skirts, on their wedding night, in the Drake Hotel in Chicago, standing behind her as they looked out at the lights at the end of the breakwater. He was twenty-three years old, she was twenty-four, and Schopenhauer's life force was flowing through them. And the last time too — in the hospital bed in their bedroom, right after she'd finished making her tapes — as if something inside her had refused to grow old, had refused to become ill. Had this been the life force too? Afterward she broke down and cried for the first and only time during her illness, and there was nothing Rudy could do except hold her in his arms.

He tried to bring his mind back to the silence. "Like a long-legged fly upon the stream," Helen used to say, "her mind moves upon silence." From one of her favorite poems. Keats? Yeats? Rudy couldn't remember, but he could almost hear her voice:

> *She thinks, part woman, three parts a child,*
> *That nobody looks; her feet*
> *Practise a tinker shuffle*
> *Picked up on a street.*
> *Like a long-legged fly upon the stream*
> *Her mind moves upon silence.*

◊

He didn't rewind the tape, because he didn't think he'd ever listen to it again. He just put it back in its box.

He threaded the second tape and waited for it to start. But of course there was nothing to wait for, no sound, not even tape hiss. Just the slight rustle of the reels, turning. Chakras. Wheels. The wheel of karma. Had Helen escaped, gotten off the wheel? And if she had escaped, where had she escaped *to*? Nirvana? *Moksha?* He wanted to walk around, wanted to pee. But he held it in till the tape came to an end. His body wanted a beer but settled for a small glass of water.

◊

His body was fighting hard now. Twitching. Straining. Telling him to turn this way and then that, the way it sometimes did when he couldn't get to sleep at night. And his imagination was acting up, filling the room with fantasies about lives he might have lived. But these fantasies were crowded out by memories of this life, the one he was living now, in *this* universe — snapshots of his life's journey. *Am I at the beginning of this chapter? Near the middle? Approaching the end?*

Time slowed down. It was agonizingly slow. He looked at his watch. 7:48. He listened to the silence. He waited. He looked again: still 7:48.

He leaned back into the silence, tried to shut down his imagination. And just when he was about to give up, he succeeded for a few minutes, and there was nothing at all. This encouraged him to go on. He wasn't changing position so often. He hardly noticed when the tape came to an end. Just a slight change in the quality of the silence. He stretched his legs. He was getting hungry, but he was anxious to get back into the silence.

His own breathing filled the room. Everything had become brownish gray, metallic, the color of the magnetic tape, the color of Narmada-Jai. How desperate he'd been when he played those tapes the first time. Desperate to hear Helen's voice. Now she'd been dead seven years, almost eight, but it seemed to him like seven weeks, seven days, seven minutes. Her death was still as fresh as a tomato from the garden.

Now he was getting discouraged. His body was fighting him again. Hunger too. Imagination and fantasy were his enemies. Even reason was his enemy, telling him it was silly to go on. Stupid. Irrational.

He was thinking about supper now. The littleneck clams called to him from the refrigerator. The unopened package of fresh spaghetti from the Lebanese place in McAllen sat impatient on the kitchen table, next to the bouquet of María's flowers. The fillet, wrapped in butcher's paper, hid in the back of the refrigerator, behind the bottle of pinot grigio, which reclined on its side. The Nero Wolfe novel — his safety net, someone in charge who would unravel everything in the end — bided its time on Helen's desk in the study.

The house was getting chilly, but he didn't want to put any more wood in the stove, didn't want to disturb the silence, which was reaching a critical mass. He could feel his heart slowing down, his breathing too. The sun set. And then he could do it. It was as easy as shipping your paddle in a canoe and letting the current carry you downstream. He didn't have to do anything more. The light was gone, out there. He could feel the sound of the river, like the thrum of the elephant's song.

The tape ended. His hunger was gone. He couldn't feel the cold.

He put the tape back in its box and threaded a new one. It was the next-to-last tape. Now he was floating downstream again — encountering a few small rapids at first, the canoe turning this way and then that, and then it was perfectly calm. The silence encompassed everything, spreading out, like the river spilling out of the floodway, covering everything in the valley, the delta, everything but his little hill, his *lomita*.

Time sped up. The new tape seemed to be over as soon as it began. And when it ended, time slowed down again, and he was overcome with sadness and loss, and then a sense of joy when he remembered that there was still one more tape.

There's something different about the silence now, this silence. This silence is charged, like the air before a storm. Rudy pictures Narmada-Jai plunging into the river. The image fades and he's back in the canoe, lying back, not thinking. And then he hears it, perfectly clear: Helen's laughter. He hears her laughter everywhere, sees her craning her neck to look for him as she and Margot come down the gangway of the SS *Rotterdam* and then disappear into the crowd and then reappear in the customs house. He's come out to New York to meet them. They'll spend the night at the Waldorf-Astoria and take the Twilight Limited back to Chicago. Rudy arranges with a porter to have their luggage sent directly to the hotel. The customs officer looks them over and chalks their suitcases without opening them. Helen's sick now, and they probably don't know the worst yet, but it doesn't matter. She's coming toward him, suitcase in her hand, and she's calling to him, "Rudy, old pal, I'm home."

It's Helen's voice all right, and now she's mad. They're in the kitchen. They've made love and Rudy's sitting at the kitchen table, drinking coffee, looking through the Sunday *Trib*. The girls have been rampaging through the house. Now they're at the toaster for the fourth or fifth time. Every time, the same drama plays itself out: three girls fighting over two pieces of toast. Meg holds one slice high over her head. Margot and Molly pull at her arms and simultaneously struggle with each other over the second slice. Helen is on the phone, talking to someone in Italian. Finally she loses patience, clamps her hand over the mouthpiece: "No more toast for the rest of the day," she shouts.

Rudy puts the paper down and looks up. The girls are momentarily stunned. Their mouths open wide. There's a moment of silence. Helen starts to laugh. Meg puts her fists on her skinny hips: "Mother," she says, "you're a woman of empty threats."

Now Helen is laughing and trying to explain to the person on the other end of the phone what has just happened, and why it's so funny, but she can't remember the word for toast in Italian. "What's the word for toast in Italian?" she asks. "I can't remember." But nobody knows.

And now the girls have gathered around her as she holds her adopted chicken in her arms. He hears her cluck and chortle to the chicken, hears the chicken cluck and chortle back, and then she's turning to him, in a room on the eighth floor of the Drake Hotel. Helen turning to him. "I've never done this before," she says. "You'll have to show me the way." And now they've undressed each other and she says, "How like you this? And this?" And she takes his erection in her hand and says: "O Rudy, this is going to be such a great adventure. Not just *this*" — squeezing him — "but *this.*" She lets go and holds out her arms. *"This life, this everything."*

The noise of the crowd is deafening. He's shooting two free throws with twenty seconds left on the clock, the last game of the season. The game will decide the league championship. Not the NBA, of course — only the old Midwest Industrial League. There's a center jump after every basket; all the players shoot two-handed set shots because the jump shot hasn't been invented yet; and at 6' 2" Rudy is the tallest man on his team, the South Water Bluestreaks, which is down by one point — 38–39. He shoots his two free throws underhanded, lifts the ball up toward the basket like a shaman releasing a bird into the air. He sinks both shots, and after the game, savoring the moment of victory, wanting it to last forever, he walks across the crowded floor of the gymnasium to speak to one of the refs, who's talking to a beautiful girl in a chartreuse dress. "Rudy," the ref says, "let me introduce you to my niece, Helen." And Rudy says, "How do you do?" and holds out his hand. Helen shakes her long red hair and takes his hand in hers and smiles. Her voice is rich and deep. "Pleased to meet you," she says. "You must be very happy."

The tape has come to an end long ago, the light has faded, the silence has thickened. If he doesn't do something now, the silence will carry him down, just as the river carried Norma Jean down, down past Pepe's, down past the international bridge at Hidalgo, on past Brownsville and out into the Gulf. But the phone rings. For a minute he thinks it might be Helen, calling to say she's coming home, but then he clears his head. He loses count of the rings. The phone rings and rings, but he doesn't answer it. Just as a passenger in an airplane that follows a certain parabolic arc will experience a brief period of weightlessness at the pinnacle of the arc, so at the pinnacle of his own parabolic arc Rudy experiences the cessation of willing, and for a brief moment he sees things as they really are.

ACKNOWLEDGMENTS

For their hard work and good advice: my agent, Henry Dunow, and my editor, Pat Strachan.

For his hospitality in Mission, Texas, and for sharing his knowledge of the region: Noe Torres.

For sharing his knowledge of Texas avocados and the Texas avocado industry: Medardo Riojas.

For their help with Hindu customs and words: Shalini Lulla, Shalini Krishan, Nandini Singh, Rachana Umashankar.

For their help with Spanish: Tim Foster, Jorge Prats, Robin Regan, Xavier Romano.

For his help with parallel universes: Chuck Schulz.

For his advice on Rudy's heart condition: Dr. Robert Currie.

For his advice on flowers: David Graflund.

For their fund of general knowledge: Bill and Syd Brady.

For reading an early version of *Philosophy Made Simple:* Monica Berlin.

For proofreading the manuscript: Terry Jackson.

The *Philosophy Made Simple* that Rudy studies was written by TJ's uncle Siva and bears little resemblance to the *Philosophy Made Simple* written by Richard H. Popkin and Avrum Stroll.